Vauxhall

Gabriel Gbadamosi

TELEGRAM

For my children

First published 2013 by Telegram

1

Copyright © Gabriel Gbadamosi 2013

ISBN 978 1 84659 146 4
eISBN 978 1 84659 147 1

A full CIP record for this book is available
from the British Library.

Printed and bound by Bookwell, Finland

TELEGRAM
26 Westbourne Grove, London W2 5RH
www.telegrambooks.com

Gabriel Gbadamosi is an Irish-Nigerian poet, playwright and essayist born in London. He was AHRC Creative and Performing Arts Fellow at the Pinter Centre, Goldsmiths, and a Judith E. Wilson Fellow for creative writing at Cambridge University. His plays include *Shango*, *Hotel Orpheu* and for radio *The Long, Hot Summer of '76* (BBC Radio 3), which won the Richard Imison Award. He has presented Night Waves on BBC Radio 3 and Art Beat on the World Service. *Vauxhall* is his first novel.

www.gabrielgbadamosi.com

'Only a poet could have written *Vauxhall*. I can hear Yeats and Joyce in it ... Gbadamosi paints a vivid portrait of 1970s multi-cultural London, giving that time in our recent history its own music, voice and clear light. *Vauxhall* is written in the way that English should be written – clean, swift and with flashes of lightning.'
Bonnie Greer, author of *Hanging by her Teeth*

'A tenderly observed, fascinating portrait of a childhood in South London, as it moves from post-war darkness into an uncertain new era.'
Blake Morrison, author of *South of the River*

'Immediately appealing, this is a quite an odyssey through the maelstrom that London was in the 1970s. A remarkable achievement.'
Brian Chikwava, author of *Harare North*

'An impressive feat of memory and skill ... the streets, the fraught encounters, the sense of family and growing understandings of youth are winningly brought to life in a series of deft, artful vignettes.'
Diran Adebayo, author of *Some Kind of Black*

Ninu ilé Baba mi, ọpọlọpọ ibùgbé ni o wà

John 14.2

Part One

The Sari

Her forehead was crumpled on the pavement.

'She made a grab for the wire as she fell,' someone said.

I looked up at the telegraph pole, its wires reaching out in a spiral overhead to all the houses in the street.

Her mother stood crying into a fold of the sari she held across her mouth, to stop the truth leaking out. She was talking in another language. It was grief. She wanted the girl to get up out the puddle of blood. She wanted her to fly up to the hand-hold of the wire. To fly backwards in time, up to the windowsill on the top floor, and press her hands and face against the coldness of the glass. But she wouldn't. She was out of reach – the girl whose name I didn't know, who never went to school and never waved back.

The window was open and the curtain was hanging out, like she'd held on to it. I could feel her slipping. I grabbed hold of Manus's sleeve, but he shook me off. I had to stand on my own. There was the feeling of when the ice-cream van came and I couldn't walk away, when I'd stood there listening to the hum of the engine take over from the blare of the loudspeaker, and she'd thrown me down a sixpence – out of the blue, a flash of money, an arc of silver rolling in the gutter, just missing the drain. I looked up and caught a glimpse of her through the net curtain, closing in sunlight.

I liked it she'd seen me. She was like me, trying to be invisible and pretending not to look because I didn't have the money to buy ice cream.

Now she was at my feet. She'd fallen through the air, and the sticky blood had footprints in it running madly around in the street.

'Get an ambulance.'

'Call the police.'

'Get these children away.'

'She made a grab.'

'She changed her mind.'

We'd been playing in the street, building the wicket for tin-can-tacky and organising ourselves into runners and finders. Some of the girls were playing feet off London and sitting on Sky's wall while we sorted it out. I ran inside to get more tin cans out the bins to build up and knock down for the start. Manus and Connor were squabbling over who should get the stone to fling at it and Danny over the road knocked it down with his own stone but everyone shouted they weren't ready. I was building it up again with Yakubu and Thaddeus, with Paul Mersey standing over it, when someone said, '*She's fallen.*'

I looked up and couldn't see what they were talking about. Busola was biting her thumb, all the girls along the wall were looking up the street. No one had fallen – Theresa was *it* and still trying to get up. I couldn't see why everyone had stopped, but there was a rush up to that end of the street and I had to stop people kicking over the wicket as they ran.

We were the first ones there, but everyone made a big circle to keep away. I pushed in past Paul Waller and Marcia's little brother to get next to Manus but had to step back because the pool of blood was still spreading. The edge of it was curved and thick and shiny. It was moving out from her head and underneath her in a splash from her feet towards the kerb. We all watched it happening.

The door burst open and her mum came out. A man was behind her shouting and dragging her back. She was fighting him off, and screaming. A boy with a round face who we didn't know was behind them. All the grown-ups started looking out their windows, opening doors and running out. Some of them were pulling children away. We hadn't seen anyone dead before.

'She jumped,' Mandy said as her mum picked her up.

Soap suds spilled on to the pavement and ran along the gutter on our way to school. On the way back, the sky was brownish purple as the storm broke. The brick fronts and the windows of the houses shone in the rain. A car went past, lifting a skirt of brown water on to the pavement, rippling all the way along the street. I saw a lady get completely splashed under her umbrella and stop, speechless, as if she'd been crying and there was no way any more to get dry.

'Clean clothes, everyone! School clothes off.' My mum looked serious as she dried my hair in the towel, so I knew what was coming.

'Michael? How was your teacher?'

'Fine,' I said. 'She was sad, she said a man was killed today. She wrote his name out and told us to remember. What happened, Mum?'

'*Sh.*'

Our dad called us all into the living room. He was back from

Liverpool. 'Who saw that girl fall?'

No one spoke.

'Who was there yesterday?'

'I wasn't,' I said.

'... Anyone else?'

Everyone looked at me. Manus rolled his tongue up under his teeth. Busola pulled at her bottom lip. Connor pressed his lips together into a crooked line. They were all telling me the same thing, '*Your big mouth.*'

It was too late to go back.

'I didn't see her fall,' I said.

A bang of thunder rumbled on the windowpanes. The sky looked bruised and dark over the rooftops. Rain came down again, like an open tap that couldn't stop flooding.

'I don't want to see any of you leaning out of the window,' he said.

After supper, we all rushed to look out at the storm, pressing our faces to the glass and leaving mist patches. The street was empty – a brown wash, the colour of clothes in the bathtub, the colour of mud. The terrace of houses opposite became a wall of water and brick. All the windows and curtains were closed.

'Daddy's going to sleep. Let's be quiet,' my mum said.

We switched off the light and sat up on chairs at the window with blankets over our knees, watching the storm change and the streetlights go orange. Gusts were whipping along the street, spreading in ripples where rain was flooding over on to the pavement. There were dark surges of water rushing into the drains. My mum told us a story about all the people who didn't have a roof over their heads, who were lost and had to be out there in the rain, turning cold.

Manus was yawning and Busola was leaning back on my mum's lap, her thumb in her mouth and her eyes closing.

'How could anyone be out in that and not drown?' Connor said.

My mum was rocking Busola to sleep. 'Just spare a thought,' she said. 'Every one of them had a mother.'

I looked back at the water and imagined the people floating face up along the gutter and folding, like pieces of soggy paper, down into the drains.

The family were loading their things on to a lorry. We could see the women had these dresses Marie said were saris. She said her mum had some because her dad, Jimmy Singh, was West Indian.

'They float, don't they?' Sandra said.

'Maybe she thought it would work like a parachute,' Danny said.

'It didn't though, did it?' Connor didn't even look up, and we all went quiet thinking about it. We were sitting on Sky's wall after school because the streets felt different after all the rain and our dad was gone again to Liverpool so we could stay out.

Sky's mum called her in, but she said her name in Portuguese so it sounded like *Say Who!* We all laughed and pointed at Sky, saying '*Who? You!*' Her mum was nice and didn't tell us to get off the wall, but she kept Sky away from us most of the time. '*Boa noite,*' she said firmly, and shut the door.

The only thing we had left to look at was the people moving out. 'Look, there he is,' Julie said. The boy with the round face came out with a bird cage and was getting into a car.

'Why wasn't he in school?' Sandra said. We didn't know. They hadn't been there very long. Some people moved in and then didn't feel they were in the right place and moved out again. But there were lots of people living in the houses and even more in the flats around the school, so it was just interesting to watch people come and go and not join in. Only this was different.

The boy turned round and looked up at the house. He saw us looking. For some reason we all waved. There was something wrong in the way he looked back. It was like we weren't there, or if we were, why hadn't the rain come and washed us away? He was bossing his mum into the back seat of the car and giving her the cage to hold. Another older woman got in beside her and he slammed the door. It caught on her dress blowing out, so he opened it and slammed it again. He looked up at us like we shouldn't be watching, and got in the front seat beside a man with a beard we hadn't seen before. The car started and drove off with his mum putting the bird cage up at the back window.

'She's looking at us,' Danny said.

We watched them go.

'He's stuck up,' said Julie.

Overcrowding

'You're in trouble,' Manus said, 'Daddy's looking for you. Don't say you've seen me.' And off he went, round the bend, wherever he was going.

I was crouched down by the bonnet of a car up the top of the street, watching people coming and going, trying to get my nerve back to go home. Everyone had been sent out to look for me, and at first I thought it was because our dad was home from Liverpool and I was late coming back.

Busola found me in the playground and said, 'I haven't seen you. Dad wants you home.' I didn't believe her, because what was she still doing out? But she came up to me again on the swings, 'You better go.'

'I'm waiting for you,' I said. 'Why ain't you going?'

'He ain't looking for me,' she said, and laughed and ran off.

I did a few more kicks to get my swing up so it joggled on the chain, so I could look down at the ground, and up at the sky. She was on the roundabout. She looked round and round, and tilted her head. She looked puzzled.

'You're adopted, you are!' she shouted when she saw me looking. She always said that.

'No,' I said, and gripped the chain tight to fling it back, '*you are!*'

I wasn't going home because of her. Why should I listen to her? What did she know? Why was she so horrible to me? I kept my arms back behind me on the chain and swooped down. I kicked my legs up and swung in the air. It was getting late. As I came down she was showing me getting my throat cut with the side of her hand. And then she ignored me, going round and round, with her blank face on.

So I left her there.

On the way I saw Connor playing out with his mates. Everyone was out late. They were kicking a football up at the chain-link fence over the sloping roofs of the sheds by the flats.

'What've you done? Everyone's looking for ya!' He wasn't looking at me and went on keeping the ball up off the ground every time it fell back off the roof which was the game he was good at so it was always his turn.

'Nothing!' I said, trying to choke back all the feelings with my fists clenched, but I could feel myself crying.

'Then keep your mouth shut,' he said, and went on counting, '*fifty-six ... fifty-seven ... fifty-eight ...*'

I got as far as the lamp post and saw some people in suits coming out the house. They turned down the street towards the main road and the door slammed shut after them. I lost my nerve and ran back and ducked down behind the bonnet of the car to get it back.

I couldn't think what I'd done wrong. That's when Manus looked over the top of the bonnet at me.

'You're ridiculous, and you're dirty,' he said. 'Look at you!'

I had some of the grease and the dirt off the tyre on my hands where I'd been leaning to peer over. I didn't know what to do so I wiped my hands on my shirt, and used the back of my hand to wipe the tears off my face, and I wiped that on my shirt too.

Manus sighed, like he was gonna have to be clearing up after me again and he didn't want to. So he told me to stand up, wipe off the snot and go home because I was in trouble, and off he went.

I could see what he was thinking. When I started school I had to put my hand up to go to the toilet. The teacher said I could go but I didn't know where it was and I couldn't get out the gate to go home because it was locked, so I went round behind the outside stairs to the sheds where there was a puddle of rain and tried to wash the poo off as it was coming down the backs of my legs into my socks. The bell rang and the juniors came out to the playground and saw me crouching in the puddle. I told them to go away but they got Manus because they knew he was my brother. He looked at me and didn't say anything, he just yanked me up out the water by the arm and told the playground lady he was taking me home to clean up. I followed him all the way with my socks squelching and my pants sticky.

'Don't you ever learn?' he said, and I knew it was my fault he was missing school.

This time I didn't know what I'd done. Why would my dad be angry with me just because I wasn't in when he got back from Liverpool? I leaned my back against the car and dug in the cracks between the paving stones with a pebble. Some ants came out and scurried off. I knew my dad wouldn't just get angry at me for something I hadn't done. It wasn't like that, there was always a reason. It was just making it worse not going home, and everyone out looking for me, and wanting to blame me for playing out late.

I got up and felt calm. I could hear the brakes of lorries slowing on the main road before they turned the corner. There was the rattle of shutters closing down on the shops. It was all right, I hadn't done anything. The light was going. I got to the front door and knocked.

My mum opened it. She frowned and shook her head at me. 'You're more trouble than you're worth!' she said.

'*No I'm not.*' I only muttered under my breath, but I wasn't gonna be nice to her, because whatever it was she should have been looking after me.

'Go on, go up!'

I gave her a look. I was angry, but mostly I was going to cry.

She bit her lip. 'Ah, no,' she said, 'Don't. Go on, your daddy's waiting.'

'Where have you been?' He was lying propped up on his arm on one of the empty beds in the front room. He put his glasses on and I had the feeling he could see where I'd been hiding. All the beds had been made, but no one else was home.

'Playing out,' I said.

'At what time do you call this?' He looked at his watch and looked back at me. My mum came in and stood by the window. It was her fault, she was the one who should have been watching me. I looked across at her and burst into tears, the ones that flood you and can't stop, and you struggle to get your breath back.

My mum threw her hands up and shook her head.

'Come and sit down,' my dad said, more softly than I could make sense of.

I sat on the edge of the bed, trying to stop sobbing. I was crying because I was confused. Because my dad was after the truth and I didn't know what it was, my mum wasn't telling me. And I was crying because I wasn't in the wrong, and because I was stubborn. And because it was late.

'This is serious,' he said. And, after a pause, 'What happened this morning?' I looked at him, and up at my mum. 'What did you tell those people?'

I told them there were eighteen of us living in the house.

They knocked and wanted to come in, but my mum leaned out and said she was busy. I was sitting behind her at the bottom of the stairs as she talked on the doorstep with one leg crossed behind the other, keeping the door with her shoulder.

'How many people are living in the house?' asked the woman who looked and spoke like a teacher. The man was wearing a suit and was asking for people's names for the register.

I counted up the people on my fingers – us in the front room and my mum and dad in the bedroom on that middle floor, six. The three Carthys at the top, and Mr Babalola and Florence up there in the back room, that's nine ... eleven. Nana who was staying with us in the front room, twelve, and Mr and Mrs Singh and Marie in the front room on the ground floor, fifteen ... then the two Nigerian students sharing the room towards the backyard with Mr Ajani.

'Eighteen!' I shouted, and put my hand up.

'I was going to say we'd some guests staying from Nigeria,' my mum was saying, 'short-term, like, and family had come over from Ireland until they found a place, but he didn't let me get a word out. I said, *Ah, he's only a child*, but you should have seen them scribbling. I didn't know where to put my face.'

My dad was shaking his head as she spoke. And then she laughed and they both looked at me.

'He'll be the death of me!' she said. 'So I told them to come back when you were in.'

They were looking at me, and I still didn't know the answer. I counted up again in my head because sometimes I had the feeling there was one of us missing – it still came out wrong. *Eighteen?* But I knew that was the wrong answer, so I kept my mouth shut.

'Do you know how serious this is?' my dad said. I could feel it was but I couldn't work it out, so I frowned. 'Overcrowding? I could go to prison.'

I felt I was falling. Those people could put my dad in prison and I'd been showing off that I could count.

They moved out to the kitchen to let me get ready for bed. I heard them talking about the Carthys moving out as I put on my pyjamas, and stop when I went in to wash and brush my teeth in the sink. My mum came to fold me in to the sheets and give me a kiss on the cheek, and tell me not to worry.

But I wasn't sleeping. I was lying there on my own, listening. I could hear doors opening and closing, the sound of footsteps on the stairs as people came and went, the rattling of pots in the downstairs kitchen, running water, voices. There was the traffic on the main road, cars going past in the street, my dad being angry at the council and my mum whispering. Outside, someone went whistling by on the pavement, clicking their heels. He could have gone to prison. I turned over in the warm sheets, trying to stay awake to hear what happened when the others came in, and wondering where Nana was because she was staying to be close to everyone. Instead, what I heard as I fell asleep was my dad saying those people were from the council, Big Ben was just there and they wanted the land, they wanted to clear us out, they wanted to knock the house down and get rid of us.

Blue Rose Orange

I tumbled out of bed, tripped and caught myself on the banister. It felt light on my feet jumping down the stairs, two, three, four at a time. Again on the next flight, I missed my footing and had to stop from falling too far by putting my hands out in front and waiting for my legs to catch up.

It was strange because they were my stairs, I knew every creak. There was the feeling of being alone and upside down, and the strangeness of the smoke swirling everywhere. Through the door of the front room I saw a thin column of flame spurting up to the ceiling from the dome of the paraffin heater and spreading outwards. It had so many colours in it – blue, rose, orange, red, black – it was only as I burst out into the night air in my pyjamas I could grasp the reason I woke up was the house was on fire.

I didn't know I could fall out the bed like that, and there'd be nothing to stop me as everything flashed past. It was like it was happening to someone else – only my mum's face in the hospital made me realise it was us. Fire engines came and ambulances, hose pipes, helmets and flames leaping up out the windows. I saw a man drop Busola from the top window where we slept now the Carthys were gone and lots of people rushing to catch her. Later, they said it was Mrs Ralf's son who'd gone in to find her before the firemen came, which was odd because his mum hadn't liked us making noise and we avoided her.

My dad said if ever he came home again to see the house on fire and his children being thrown out the windows and crawling around in the street, he'd turn on his heels and never come back.

'This has set me back,' he said, pointing to the damage done by the firemen's axes. They hacked away at all the wood of the door frames and the wooden mantelpieces over the boarded-up fireplaces. There was black smoke damage on the walls and ceilings and it smelt horrible.

'Never, ever let me see you playing with matches.'

It was one of lots of fires – the frying pan fire, the spilt paraffin fire, the playing with matches fire – the choking fire that landed us all in hospital when we thought there was nothing wrong with us. But the fire we always came home to was that mess of tar and soot and pools of water before our dad put it all back together.

'You get back on your feet, you think you've recovered, and look what happens.' There was a look in his face at seeing the blackened walls, gutted rooms and smashed-up doorways that was like he'd been killed but kept coming back.

'We're all safe, thank God, we have our lives,' my mum said. And I saw him crying as he walked out the room.

He gave up what he was studying in Liverpool and came home. 'I have no choice,' he said, because he couldn't sleep any more worrying what could happen. He was going to live with us all the time and not go back to Liverpool or Nigeria. 'From now on, we are all under the same roof. I am making sacrifices and all of you will have to buckle down and work hard. If we have to stay here, so we have to make it work.'

'Bedtime,' my mum said.

We weren't allowed out so much any more. We had to be home by the time he got in from looking for a job and go to bed when the news came on. You heard the bong of Big Ben as you climbed the stairs, and got a glimpse of the clock on television looking like the moon, then you heard it coming again faintly over the river. My mum wasn't saying anything, but she was cooking for him and it was what she wanted. 'Go to sleep,' she said, and I drifted off in the bunk bed beside Busola while my mum went back to talking with my dad.

I got caught in the sheets and woke in the middle of the night. Busola was bunched up asleep beside me and I was sweating. There was no noise anywhere in the house. I heard a lorry going past on the main road, and then the sound of a train echoing along the embankment.

I lay back and thought about what woke me up. The man who was killed, Martin Luther King. But I couldn't see his face, only his name in chalk on the blackboard. I blinked, and saw the girl falling slowly in her sari, floating down through the air, with me watching from the ground, only it was snowing and she was shaking her head. I wanted to lift my arms to catch her, but she saw me sweating from the burning cold of the snow, and turned away and vanished on the pavement.

Frost

The school bell rang out over the roofs and into the streets as my mum was holding me back at the door, buttoning up my duffel coat because it had turned cold. I could feel the sharpness of the air in my nose and my breath was smoking, but I wanted to catch up with Manus and Connor who were joining the other children coming out the houses on to the street and running to school. Busola was staying home because she had a temperature and wasn't well. It meant she had to stay in bed all day, but I wanted to get out even though I had a runny nose. My mum put her hand on my forehead but I shook it off because she felt cold.

'Come straight home from school,' she said, and I ran off up the road after everyone because the bell had stopped ringing. I looked back and she was still at the door watching me, so I ran on until I turned the corner. I was feeling hot and dizzy and sticky, so I slowed down and watched some of the other people who were late run on ahead of me. I walked slowly, round past the London City Mission, and saw the two trees by the side of the flats had dropped their leaves on the ground. I didn't know why I hadn't seen it before. There was white frost on the fallen leaves. I wasn't sure from the way I was feeling I could go all day at school, so I slowed right down as I came up to the wide black iron doors to the playground that were kept locked. The entrance gate further along the wall was still open because a mum was coming out of it, and it didn't click as it closed. I thought I shouldn't go in, I should go home. But there was a mystery story on the school television in the afternoon and I didn't want to miss the episode. I saw one of the playground ladies coming to the gate as I looked in through the gap by the hinge. I wasn't sure what to do so I ran across the road and ducked down out of sight behind a car. I put my head up and peered through the wet, misted windows. She leaned out to see if anyone was coming, then went in and shut the gate. I heard the lock click and then I knew I wasn't going in.

'*Oi! You! Get into school!*' An old lady was standing outside her door on the ground floor of the flats behind me. She had on lots of coats over a big apron and was watching me. She waved her arm up at the school like she was pointing at the roof, '*Go on! What you hiding for? Get in there!*' I looked up where she pointed and felt sick as some pigeons flew over the top, my neck was stiff. When I looked back, her arms hung down with her elbows pointing out and her shoulders hunched round like that was how she had to stand being old. I couldn't look at her face. Her apron was grey and her coats were dirty. I hung my head down. She didn't know I wanted to go in, I didn't know how to tell her I didn't feel well. She was still shouting, '*You naughty boy!*' as I got round the corner by the railings to go home, saying she was going to tell my mum and I should be ashamed.

I turned off down Auckland Street towards the railway arches and thought about what I should do. I didn't want to have to stay in bed all day. I wanted to go to school. But I couldn't think properly.

'I don't know what's wrong with me,' I said, and then got worried someone could hear me, but I passed by the shops and by the corrugated iron of the bombsite and no one stopped me. There was frost on the doorsteps. People had gone to school and the street was empty. I kept on going with the long sun behind me and my shadow out front. The old lady was telling me go to school. I couldn't see her face, only my long legs and the shadow of my duffel coat. I didn't know why I was running away. It was my fault for not going in, and it was me who wanted to go in the first place.

'Can I go?' I said.

It was back when Busola first started going to school, and I was leaning out the window with my mum. The bell was ringing and I could see the pointed roofs of the school over the houses at the top of the street. Manus was holding Busola's hand to look after her, and Connor turned on the pavement to wave up at us. Everyone was going except me.

'Can I?'

'Yes,' my mum said, 'as soon as the school says you can.'

I got as far as the school gate and lost my nerve. They were all inside, the playground was empty and I could hear singing. The school keeper with keys came to the gate and I got frightened. I got in under a car in case he came out to look for me. I stayed really quiet and was scraping some tar off my hand when two women going past with a pram shouted there was a child under the car, so I scrambled out and ran. It was winter because the pink tree and the white tree by the flats didn't have any leaves or blossom on as I looked back to see if anyone was following me.

'Where have you been?' my mum said.

'Just out.'

My dad was there, getting ready to go back to Liverpool,

shaving in the round mirror over a bowl, flicking the razor and scratching his chin with it. He laughed at the way I was breathing, 'Have you been running?' He was looking at me through the tilted-up mirror that made his nostrils look bigger than his eyes. But I could see his eyes were steady, looking down over the bristles on his chin. He was my dad and school couldn't be more scary than that. He dipped the razor in water and flicked it, watching me. I took a deep breath and tried to slow everything down.

'Come and have breakfast,' my mum said, and we went through the steps of bashing the egg on its head and cutting its throat so we could bloody the bread soldiers in the yolk.

My dad was getting his shirt ready to put on over his vest and saying he'd be back in a fortnight.

'What's a fortnight?' I said.

He shrugged the shirt on to his shoulders and said, 'Not long.'

'Two weeks,' my mum said, snapping the eggshells with her thumb and putting them in the bin. She picked me up off the chair and held me up to my dad for him to have a look at me. 'Did you go by the school?' she said.

'No,' I said, 'I just went for a run.'

'He'll be starting school soon.'

He nodded, taking hold of my hand, and said, 'Soon.' I felt him open my fingers up with his thumb and feel the oily smear on my palm, 'What's that?'

I looked at them, but they let me go and didn't say anything.

There were no more questions so I waited until the teachers came out of school.

'Who's that one?' I asked Connor. He was kicking a tin can down the street with his mates.

'That's the deputy head, Mrs Bridewell,' Danny said, because Connor was ignoring me.

I followed her down Auckland Street towards the main road and the train station. It didn't work because she was going too fast and I couldn't catch up. She had black hair and yellow skin with dark blotches on her legs under her stockings. She was holding a brown bag close under her arm and walked in a tight way like someone was after her, so I backed off.

The next day I was waiting for her. She walked in the same way but I crossed in front of her so she could see me.

'Hello, Mrs Bridewell.'

She looked at me and frowned but kept on walking, then looked back over her shoulder, 'Are you at the school?'

I leapt up to her and walked along, looking up and trying to keep in step. 'No, but can I go soon? I'm big enough.'

'Yes, you are a big boy. We'll be looking forward to having you in the school.'

I was breathless. She said *yes*! I peeled off and let her go, turned back and ran home.

'Mrs Bridewell says I can go to school!'

My mum looked at me. 'She said that?'

I suddenly wasn't sure, but I nodded my head because it was what I wanted, and said, 'I'm big enough.'

They let me go to school. But then they folded out these beds and told me to go to sleep. It was the middle of the day. I told the teacher I was too old for that, I'd come to school to play. She told me I wasn't in school, I was in the nursery and I had to go to sleep. I got in under the blanket but I felt cheated. As soon as she left the room, I got up and went out the glass doors into the nursery playground and climbed over the fence into the main playground. The black iron doors were wide open and a van was coming in. No one was watching so I went to the side gate – it was open – and let it clang shut behind me. I ran home thinking I was going to complain to my mum, but on the way I decided I wasn't going to make a fuss because I liked being out and able to run.

I knocked on the front door and my mum looked out the window and shook her head at me, 'What are you doing?'

'I've come home to watch with you,' I said.

The door knocked and Mrs Bridewell was standing there. Her and my mum had a chat. I heard them say it was a bit early and to leave things as they stand. I pushed my head out past my mum's skirt and looked at them.

'Hello, young man,' she said.

'I don't want to go to sleep, I want to play,' I told her.

She laughed, but I tried again.

'When can I go to school?'

She looked at my mum then looked back at me. 'Look at the trees,' she said, but there weren't any trees on our street so I thought that was a bit strange. 'When they start to go brown and lose their leaves you can come to school.'

I was back in Auckland Street and I wasn't in school, I was running away. The leaves were brown on the trees by the flats and on the ground, there was frost in the air and white patches in the shadows. This time it was because I wasn't feeling well, but I still wasn't in school. You had to be in school to be safe. I turned away from the main road in case my dad came back from night work and saw me. Going round by the Vauxhall Tavern, I followed the wall of arches under the railway. They echoed when you walked into them, long brick tunnels that felt cold and dark so I only went in when there were lots of us. An ambulance was parked up by the entrance to the second one, with its back doors open and no one there. Its lights were on and I could see the long bed inside, but it wasn't making a sound, just flashing. As I got nearer, there was a man sitting on the ground under the arch with his back to the wall, groaning in slow bursts that stopped but then went on echoing in the tunnel. The ambulance men were there leaning over a jumble of bags and blankets. I couldn't see the man because he had his hands over his face. They were black with dirt. A police car was parked inside the tunnel on the other side of the road, but no one was getting out because it was cold and the smoke from the exhaust pipe was misting up in the dark. I watched as one of the men from the ambulance cut up the blankets with some scissors.

At first I thought that's why the man on the ground was crying, they were cutting up his things. But there was somebody there under the blankets, because the ambulance man was cutting away hair from where it was stuck to the pavement and lifting the head up which flopped back when he let it go. The other ambulance man helped him lift the person up and I saw it was a woman – her head fell back and her long hair came away, leaving a shadow stuck to the ground. She was stiff with cold as they brought her out the tunnel to the ambulance and that's when two policemen came out their car and walked over to the man who was groaning. There was an icy drip seeping down the brick wall on to the pavement where he was sitting. He was getting wet. The police were helping the man pick up his things and stand, but he groaned and fell over sideways on to the ground, and the policemen were wondering what to do. That's when they saw me and one of them came over and grabbed me by the arm of my duffel coat.

'Gotcha!' he said.

Underneath the Arches

The ambulance men looked round at me as they were struggling to lift the woman into the back of the ambulance. She looked yellow and her eyes were open, an arm fell out the blanket and they turned back to what they were doing.

I looked up at the policeman's face, he didn't have his helmet on, he had a rough neck that was creased, with patches of dried blood under his chin, and he had red and white skin in blotches up over his cheeks. He gave me a shake because I was just looking at him. I didn't know what he wanted.

'What school you in?'

I started to panic, and tried to pull away but he held on to me. I shrank my arm upward into my sleeve to get away but he kept hold and watched me pull, then gave me a sharp tug that made me fall over on my knee and scrape it on the ground. I put my hand up on his sleeve to get my balance and try to get him off me. I could feel the tears coming up in my eyes.

'What's going on?' the other policeman said.

'We got a runner,' he said.

'Hurry up.'

The other policeman turned away and started talking to the ambulance men. I looked up at the one who was holding me. I was on my own with him. I could see he hadn't decided what he was gonna do, but he liked me struggling, so I stopped.

'Where d'you live?'

I thought quickly about what I could tell him, but got distracted by one of the ambulance men going back and scraping up the hair that was stuck to the pavement to put in a plastic bag.

'Or am I gonna put you in the car?'

If I told him I lived with the old lady, I wouldn't know the address but I could tell him it was the ground floor across from the school and she was out. If he took me to school, it would get back to my mum. I tried to stand up but he shook me again and grabbed the back of my collar so it was up against my throat. I reached back to get his hand off and scratched it.

'Cheeky monkey?' He let go my arm but kept hold of my collar and slapped me in the face. I didn't feel it, it was a fight, but I gave him an angry look.

'That's enough, get him in the car,' the other policeman said.

He dragged me swinging by the collar, not letting my feet touch the ground, and bundled me in the back seat, slamming the door and saying, 'Mind your fingers!'

I hadn't been in a police car before. I didn't know what was going to happen. I didn't know how to stop my dad finding out. I could feel my sweat turn cold even though it was warm in the car. I was going to open the door and run for it, but when I looked out the back window to see where they were, the policemen were opening the boot and putting bags and blankets into the back.

The side door opened and the groaning man got pushed in beside me, his face red and covered in dirt. He had tears streaked down it, and looked at me with swollen eyes, dark and glassy like marbles. I looked back but he didn't say anything and put his head down.

The doors slammed shut as the two policemen got in, and the one I didn't know turned round in the driver's seat.

'Right, where we going?'

I looked at the man beside me who gave off a smell that made me feel sick, like mouldy dustbins. He shifted in his seat and I saw he only had one leg. His nose was broken and squashed up against his face with dried blood across it, making it look even more red. He was quiet and shuddering, like his sobs were stifled and couldn't open in the warm.

'I'm talking to *you!*'

The policeman was looking at me, but he wasn't as rough as the other one and looked older and in charge, like he might be going to let me go. 'We're not gonna arrest you this time,' he said. 'Where do you live?'

I told him because it was just around the corner and he could let me walk. He laughed and started the car up, 'What number?'

The man beside me let out a moan and the blotchy policeman who hit me reached back and punched him on the shoulder, 'Fucking crab!' – and punched again – 'Back in your shell!'

'*Language,*' the older one said, moving off out the tunnel. The man bent even more into himself, shaking and dribbling on to his lap. The flap of his trouser leg dangled off the seat beside him, twisted and muddy.

'What a fucking morning, what a fucking shit-hole!' The flushed red blotchy policeman leaned back heavily in his seat, 'They stink!'

The driver was going the long way round the tunnels, back by the crossroads. He shrugged, 'You gotta have the stomach for it.'

The one with blotches turned and slapped me on the leg, 'Get your feet off!' I hadn't realised I'd pulled my legs up on the seat to stop him crushing them when he leaned back. We turned in to the traffic under the railway bridge. 'Look at that,' he was saying – but it was dark and noisy, I wasn't sure what he was going to do, I couldn't hear – '... *monkey and a crab ... you told me* ... this patch was full of villains.'

'Graveyard shift,' the older one said, looking in his mirrors as we came out from under the bridge and I could hear. 'They're still in bed.'

The blotchy one laughed and the car slowed down to turn into my street. 'Don't worry about it,' the one driving said, turning the wheel again, 'they're gonna clear all this out soon. It's just filth.'

There were spots in my eyes and everything was going fast when my mum opened the door. I could feel the policeman's hand on my jaw from when he slapped me and now it felt hot. He was holding me by the hood of my duffel coat and the other one was round on the road opening all the doors to get rid of the smell.

'We're looking for his mum,' the policeman said.

'I'm his mother,' she said.

I looked down because I couldn't look at her, and threw up over my shoes and the front of my duffel coat. The policeman stepped back from the splash and looked at her and looked at me.

'You?'

'Yes,' she said, and looked at me. 'What's happened?'

'You're his mother?'

She crouched down and got a handkerchief out her sleeve and wiped my mouth and my chin, feeling the side of my face with the cold of her hand. She asked me questions quickly with her eyes and my tears started to come down on to my cheeks.

She glanced across at the police car and up at the policeman, and stood up. 'He's sick,' she said. 'Do you want to let go of his hood?'

'He's black,' the policeman said, sounding stupid and wrong, and looking like he wasn't sure what was going to come out his mouth.

'I'm his mother,' my mum said. 'What's that to do with why you're holding him?'

The policeman loosened his grip but didn't let go, his mouth was open and his eyes went sideways over the back of his shoulder to the one standing in the road. 'That's her,' he said.

'Who?' said the older one, slamming the doors and coming round on to the pavement – my mum ignored the one standing over me and spoke to him.

'I'm this boy's mother. Can you tell me what's going on? Why are you here? Who's that in the car with you?'

'That's a separate matter, miss –' but she cut him off.

'Mrs.'

'We found him on the street. He should be in school. Why wasn't he?'

My mum looked down at his feet as he came up to us. He stopped and had to step back away from the sick, wiping his shoes on the pavement.

'That might explain it,' she said.

He looked up at her from under his helmet, wiping his feet, and thought about it. 'OK, let him go,' he said, and nodded the younger one back to the car.

I looked up over my hood and saw the red angry blotches climb up over the policeman's jaw and I felt his fist clench the hood tighter. He gave me a shove towards my mum, but by that time some of the neighbours were leaning out the windows and doors to see what was going on.

'*Ye're* nothing but a bully!' Mrs Keogh shouted from her window over the road. 'Leave the poor boy alone!' She had a booming voice, and leaned up out the window on her arms with her sleeves rolled up.

The policemen looked at her and each other as she stared down at them and more people came out on to the street. I looked up at my mum but she was shaking her head quietly and looking away from my dad who was hurrying up the street in his work clothes, carrying his night lamp. He slowed down to watch what was going on.

'Get in the car,' the older one said, and when the blotchy one didn't move he said it again, 'Get in the car.'

My mum put her arms around me and watched them.

'I have to warn you,' he said, 'it could be serious next time.'

The younger one stopped to take his helmet off and look at us as he got into the car. He was remembering my face because he was gonna get me. The man in the back was looking at me too, because they'd already got him and there was nothing he could do. He looked away as they drove off. I lifted my hand out towards him but it was too late, and my mum said, 'Put your hand down.'

I told my mum and dad I'd got ill and got lost coming home, and they nodded. My dad said I wasn't to bring police to his door because they'd know who you were, and you'd never see the end of it. I didn't tell them the policeman hit me, I just said they'd brought me home. My mum asked who the man was in the back of the police car, and I told her he was a tramp they found sleeping under the arches.

Busola watched as I got into my pyjamas and said there was blood on my leg and I had a bruise, but I didn't answer and got my trousers on quickly.

'You can't hide it,' she said, 'the side of your face is red. Don't be sick over me.'

I just wanted to go to sleep and woke up in the evening with my top soaking and Manus and Connor wanting to go to bed. 'Get out my bed,' Connor said, and I had to take my top off and get back in with Busola, but I was shivering.

'What have you got?' Manus said.

I didn't answer him, but Busola said, 'He got arrested by the police.'

'No, I didn't.'

'They beat him up,' she said, 'look at his bruise on his leg.'

I pulled the blankets tight up under my chin and shook.

The Taste of Black Jack

'Where is it?' said Manus.

It was there, but it was gone. It was a patch of dirt on the pavement with strands of hair in it.

'There,' I said.

Everyone looked. The stain was wet where water dripped down the wall of the tunnel. A train went over and made us get out, rumbling over the walls and shaking the ground under our feet. Only Connor stayed behind, looking down at the pavement where the woman froze, ignoring us and the weight of the train passing. He looked up at me and put out his chin, 'That's where the woman fell asleep? On the ground?'

I shrugged, because maybe she was on blankets.

'Let's go home,' Busola said.

'Don't tell Mummy you saw it,' said Manus, looking at her.

'I didn't see anything,' she said, and looked at me. 'How do I know you're not lying?'

'Why would he?' Connor said, coming up. 'Anyway, you can see the hair on the pavement.'

'He's not good enough to lie like that,' Manus said as well.

Busola poked me with her finger, 'You said they were gonna clear it all out, but they didn't, did they?'

'You said you didn't see,' Manus said, 'but you did.'

'I don't want to see dead tramps,' she said.

'But you did,' Manus said. 'What you gonna do about it?'

We went quiet for a bit, looking back into the tunnel. It felt cold and empty. A train was going over the other way, like you couldn't sleep under there even to be out the rain it was so loud. There was a patch of sky through to the buildings on the other side. You could see traffic passing along the embankment.

'What if one of us dies,' Manus said.

'Why would we?' said Busola.

We looked at Manus. He was screwing up his eyes into the tunnel like he was seeing it mist up in a fog and dead people come out and get him. He was shivering.

'What's wrong?' Connor said.

'I don't want to die with everyone looking,' and a look came over Manus's face that was disgusted.

Busola looked at me again, 'I think it's you're the one playing with matches.'

'It wasn't me,' I said.

'Was it nice?' She was being horrible. 'Or was it an accident?'

'Let's go home,' Manus said. 'Before Daddy gets back.'

I walked behind everyone. Busola was trying to blame me. My face was hot and I felt upset. I shouldn't have told her. Manus was saying Mummy would tell Daddy and he'd smack us for looking at dead people, so she shouldn't tell anyone. I only told Busola because I couldn't hold it on my own. And it wasn't me playing with matches, it was Manus, but he told me not to say anything.

'What did the policeman say?' Connor said again.

'That I couldn't be Mummy's because I was black,' I said.

'Because you're adopted,' Busola said.

'No, I'm not.'

'And what did Danny's mum say?' Manus asked.

'She said he was a bully, and he pushed me.'

'Where did you get all those bruises from?' I looked at Busola and didn't answer. 'You're just trying to get attention,' she said.

'Go inside if you're gonna cry about it.' Connor slipped his bum off the windowsill and spat in the road. We were locked out, it was getting dark and no one was home. We couldn't go anywhere. Busola ignored him and looked off up the road with her thumb in her mouth. Only Manus and Connor could get up on the ledge of the windowsill, me and Busola had to lean back against it to get out the way of people going past in the street.

'Where's Mummy?' she said.

'You're gonna tell her,' said Manus, 'and get us all in trouble.'

She looked up at Connor, 'I don't have to do what you say.'

He jeered at her and climbed back on the windowsill, 'You've got nowhere to go,' he said. 'I can go tomorrow.'

My back jerked up sharp against the ledge. It hurt and there were blind spots in front of my eyes again. It got in the way of faces when I tried to look at them. I stared down until it went away.

'What's wrong with you?' Manus said.

I shook my head, and looked up at Connor. He was looking down the street at the lights and the cars on the main road. The back of my shoulder was stinging from the scrape and there was a tingle down my back where it felt wet. Our mum should have come back from the shops by now, we didn't know where our dad was and none of the lodgers were in. Manus should have had his key but he kept losing it. We weren't supposed to be out so late. He said it was in the pocket of his other trousers, and Busola said he had holes in them.

'Where you gonna go?' I said.

'You can't come,' Connor said, not even looking at me. I followed where he was looking down to the main road. Our dad was coming up the street on the other side from the corner, and he could see us.

'What's going on?'

'We're waiting for Mummy to come home,' Manus said.

'You don't have your key?'

Manus shrugged with his hands in his pockets and looked down. My dad shook his head and opened the door. The house was dark, and the light in the hall wasn't working. The radio was on in Mr Ajani's room at the back on the ground floor and the stairs shook as we stumbled up in the dark.

My dad turned on the light in the front room and lit the paraffin stove, telling us to keep on our coats till it warmed up. He sent Connor to the kitchen to make tea and told Manus to go to the bedroom to look for the key and bring it. 'What are all of you doing outside?' he said to me and Busola.

Busola looked at me. 'Waiting for Mummy,' I said. He looked at me and then at her. 'Down by the railway,' she said.

'All of you?' She nodded. He looked at me. 'So you are feeling better?' I nodded. 'And you want to drag people back to the scene of the crime?'

I was in trouble. Maybe I talked in my sleep. Maybe Busola already told him. Maybe he always knew. He stopped me working it out by telling me to take money off the sideboard and go to the shop to buy my own Lucozade because I was well enough.

I passed the bedroom door, it was open and through the crack I saw Manus standing on his own looking out the window. Connor was in the kitchen as I went down the stairs, trying to get the gas to light with the safety stick. There was the smell of gas as he went on clicking and didn't notice me.

I pulled the front door shut and ran to the shop. It felt like everything was going to explode and I was running away. I could feel the hot shiver down my back and I had an empty feeling in my stomach. The scrape down my back was still stinging. I clenched the money in my hand so it hurt and held on to the hope of Mummy coming back. I slowed down to give her time, and tried to slow down the cars going past on the main road by going as slowly as I could along the kerb. The rush of wind past my shoulder made me jump back on to the pavement as a bus pulled into the stop.

There was no one behind the counter in the shop. I stood with the bottle of Lucozade wrapped up in its orange plastic for as long and as quietly as I could until the lady came out from the back and took the money. I had trouble letting go my fist to give it to her and one of the pennies fell on the floor.

'You all right?' she said.

I nodded and felt myself gulp as I picked it up. My hand was shaking. She took it from me and looked with her head on one side, 'That for you?'

'Yes,' I said.

She picked up a Black Jack, gave it to me and said, 'Look after yourself.'

I was folding the wrapper and sucking the sweet when the drunk man shouldered open the door of the off-licence. He had a bottle in one hand and was leaning over on his crutch. The knot in his trouser leg was swinging under him with the effort of elbowing his way out the door. There were dark rings round his eyes and his broken nose made his face look flat and heavy as he leaned over and saw me. He fumbled with trying to put the bottle into the pocket of his overcoat and stand up straight. I could feel the trickle of liquorice in my throat and I kept moving. He fell over holding the bottle up in the air as the crutch went out from under him. People were coming to the door of the off-licence to help, but he sat up on one arm and watched me walk away. He wanted to talk to me and I wanted to run. His eyes looked black and scared. They followed me like they knew who I was. Someone spoke to him, he looked down at his leg, and I turned and ran.

Everyone was waiting when I got back. Manus hadn't found the key and my dad was telling him off. Busola was sitting up on the sofa not looking at anybody and Connor came in behind me after opening the door with his jaw set for trouble. My dad made us all sit down on the sofa and made Busola move up. He looked at all of us and said, 'Busola, where have you been?'

She didn't look up, but we could see he'd got it out of her. 'Nowhere,' she said.

'Down by the railway. And what were you doing there?'

'Playing,' she said.

'That's a lie,' and no one moved. I was still holding the bottle of Lucozade on my lap and looked at my orange fingers through the cellophane. I thought it might shield me that I'd been ill and he'd sent me out to go and get it. 'I'm talking to all of you,' he said. 'Something has changed. Your mother is in the hospital.

When she comes back, I don't want any of you troubling her.'

I didn't see how it was a lie that we were down by the railway arches, or what it meant that our mum wasn't at the shops but up the hospital. I wanted to know when she was coming back. We hadn't had supper. Manus was scratching at the eczema on his forearm and Busola was holding on to him with her thumb in her mouth.

'What's wrong with her?' Connor said, and my dad looked at him but didn't say anything.

We waited, and I thought my dad was gonna tell him off, but he didn't, he just went on looking at all of us with his eyes shiny under his glasses.

Connor put his head down, the way the man looked down at his leg where he'd fallen, like he didn't know where the ground was – but I pulled away from looking because I was scared if I thought about the man he'd find me. My dad pulled off his glasses, wiped his eyes and put them on again.

'This is serious,' he said. 'I can't stop what's going to happen.' His face wasn't telling us what he meant, everyone was looking at him to see what he'd say. 'From now on she will have to be coming and going to the hospital. But please, don't go under those railway tunnels. It's not safe. I don't want police to bang on the door and tell me something has happened.' None of us said anything, so his voice got harder, 'What do you want down there?' He looked at me. 'Playing what?' I was frightened he was going to tell me I was bad, it was me who took Busola down and showed her the stain on the pavement. But he didn't, he looked at Busola and said, 'You are playing with fire. It's those people – drunk and fighting – out of control – living down there. And you –' He was looking at Manus. 'You don't know any better?'

Manus had nowhere to go. He couldn't hide behind us because he was the eldest, it was his fault. He hung his head down and the tears fell one by one on his lap because you weren't allowed to cry when you were being told off.

'You have to go down there? You don't know police are watching you?'

I thought he was going to be telling him off, but he picked Manus up and walked over to the window, swaying and rocking him like he was little and it was just the two of them holding on to each other, Manus crying and my dad whispering in his ear and lifting open the curtain. It was black outside and they reflected back in the glass, from a time before I was born, when it was just them, holding on, waiting for Mummy to come home.

'What you tell him?' Connor said.

'Nothing.' It was Busola, stung from being told she was lying and all because of us telling her not to say. 'I only told Susan.'

'What did she say?' Connor said, turning over to go to sleep. We were whispering because our mum came back while our dad was making us brush our teeth, and he put us all to bed quickly because it was late. We could hear them moving about upstairs. Manus was awake but he wasn't saying anything.

'She can smell the gas, she says stop playing with matches.'

'Tell her to mind her own business,' Connor said.

I was sharing the bottom bunk with Busola because it was warmer and I didn't want to be on top on my own, but her feet kept digging into me. I tried to kick her off and she said, 'Go up the top if you don't like it.'

'You go,' I said.

'It's all your fault.'

'Shut up, you two,' Manus said. 'Go to sleep.'

Busola lifted her head off the pillow in the dark to look at me from the other end of the bed. '*Your fault*,' she said, just moving her lips.

'*Who says?*' I whispered.

'*Susan.*'

Susan was a girl who lived in the house before us. She only spoke to Busola, so it was just Busola saying worse things than she normally said. I wasn't frightened, but Manus got up on one arm, got out of bed and went over to the window. I knew it was Manus in the dark but I felt there was someone else in the room. I pulled the covers over my head and hid, but Busola farted and I had to come up for air. I couldn't see Manus and the top of my head was cold.

'When you saw that woman dead' – it was Manus in the corner, twisting into the curtains and only his face showing – '*was it like the girl who jumped?*' I shrugged but I don't know if he saw me because he said, 'Was it an accident?'

'She jumped,' Connor said.

'The woman didn't wake up,' said Busola, putting her cold feet on me, 'because she froze to death.'

I was gonna fight her off, but we heard the front door bang open and Marie come in crying downstairs, with her mum and dad arguing.

Manus span out the curtains and giggled. Busola got up and ran over to the door to listen. Connor sat up in bed.

It was too much for me. They argued all the time. I stayed where I was and tried not to listen to Marie's dad shouting about the broken light bulb and the noise of the radio, and her mum telling him to keep his voice down. His voice swayed about anyway like he was at sea, but she told him he was drunk and legless, she was wasting her time. He said he should have been a – it sounded like *honey-man* – what was he doing married? She told him he was a ne'er-do-well, and she'd only herself to blame. He could go back to Guyana, he said, and get twenty of her for nothing. Who had the keys? Marie sobbed, they were waking everybody up, and she wanted to go to sleep. He had them when he opened the front door, her mum said, and if she had her time again she wouldn't go anywhere near a West Indian fella, she shouldn't have listened to him. The arguing moved into the room downstairs, the door closed so you couldn't hear it, and everyone drifted back to bed.

I lay there with my eyes closed trying not to think about being legless, or the man falling over at the off-licence. But what if he couldn't get up? What could he do with only one leg? I tried to keep away from thinking about him and get to sleep. But he knew where I lived. I told myself not to dream and pulled the covers tight. He might get Busola first. If he got in the room there was Manus, Connor was snoring. I hadn't told them about him. I only told them about the ambulance, the woman with yellow eyes, the police car smoking up in the tunnel before they came out and got me. I told them about the policeman in charge saying they were going to clear everything out the tunnel. But I left out about the man sobbing on the back seat beside me, the other policeman punching him and slapping me, the feeling when the red blotches came that he was going to kill me – or that it was the man with the leg missing who stopped it by being there. I cut the man out and kept him to myself. I kept looking at the dark marbles where his eyes should be, the muddy flap of his trouser leg, the way it was too late when I tried to reach him and say sorry. I could see the red of his skin, the black grit inside it, the dirty cracks in his fingernails. There was the mouldy smell, the streaks of tears, the long sobs echoing in the tunnel, all the reasons I should be scared, but instead I was feeling empty. I didn't help him. Then another thing came back to me, the taste in my mouth of liquorice, sticking to my teeth and dribbling on to my tongue as I went past the off-licence and didn't stop. I took a deep breath and shuddered, as though he was inside me and I'd swallowed him whole.

Penny for the Guy

'Penny for the Guy?'

It was me who asked – Connor was coming up behind – I was going up to anyone who passed to get their money first.

'Penny for the Guy, mister?'

'What Guy?'

I looked over my shoulder, and there wasn't one. There was Connor, and past him the bus stop where we'd got money off people. They weren't there any more, the bus had come and they'd all gone. It was a long way back from there to the corner before you could see round to where it was.

'Round the corner,' I said, but the man shook his head. He had thick glasses and a look on his face like he didn't believe me.

'If you haven't got a Guy –' he spoke quietly so I had to lean in to catch what he was saying, 'that's begging. Begging and lying.'

I was stung.

'What?' It was Connor pushing me out the way, 'What d'you say?'

The man pushed up his glasses on his nose and shrugged, 'Where's your Guy?' He was tall and stooped, his voice was English off the telly, like he was something to do with the cricket up the Oval. He had a tie on, a long coat and thick leather shoes. He blinked, and was looking round like he couldn't see anything and said, 'We haven't let you into this country to beg.'

'*We have got a Guy,*' I almost said, but Connor punched him, shouting, '*Come on!*' and ran off.

He was bent over double, trying to get his breath back where Connor hit him in the stomach, coughing and dripping from his mouth and nose on to the pavement. His face was going purple, and the top of his head was bald and flaking where the grey hair made it look whitish.

I waited for him to come up.

'You all right, mister?'

He pulled his coat in and leaned up against the wall of the shops, steadying himself and wiping his mouth on a handkerchief. There were red sores and brown blotches on his hands. He was old.

'You all right?'

'What's your name?' he said.

I looked at the snot on his handkerchief, I didn't know what to do. It was too late to tell him there *was* a Guy. He could have come round the corner and seen it. A whole gang of us made him out of old newspapers stuffed into a jumper, we put on two cardigans that had holes in, and a balaclava filled up with paper for his head. Manus put on a cardboard mask with elastic that came from a scary Halloween comic to make him a face. He was a skeleton. We sat him up on cardboard under the big factory door at the bottom of the street with the newspaper sticking out the bottom of the jumper and everyone spread out to start getting in money. But that didn't feel right, so Julie went in and got him some old trousers her dad left and a pair of socks with holes in. The socks didn't fit, so he had newspaper sticking out his trouser legs ready to be lit. Everyone's mum and dad gave us money so I thought it was all right. Harry's mum gave us some and his dad was a policeman until he broke his back and they moved in round the corner while they were working out the insurance. I wasn't sure what my mum and dad would think, they'd gone up the hospital in the morning. I didn't know when they were coming back. Would they know what a Guy was? Manus and Connor and Busola were doing it, everyone was, so I joined in and people were giving us money as we went along.

'Where do you live?' I woke up from what I was thinking and the man was saying we'd gone too far, he didn't believe us. He stood up from the wall he'd been leaning on and his hand was shaking. I reached out to hold his sleeve and steady him, but he shook me off, 'You don't belong here. Why don't you just go back to where you came from?'

A bus came and people were walking past, looking. So I left him there and walked home.

I didn't know why all the tramps were coming to live at the bottom of our street and round by the railway arches. As I turned the corner, some of them were starting to bed down in the doorway of the factory. The Guy was gone and there were just scraps of newspaper and cardboard left on the ground. The man with one leg wasn't there. He was gone, and lots more had come – red and black and oily and grey, with bruised faces. People said they looked like a pack of dogs, that they could smell people were moving out so they were moving in. But I could see they were just looking for somewhere to sleep. A woman with heavy bags stopped and crossed into the road to go by them. She looked weighed down, her shoulders were hunched – it was Danny's mum, Mrs Keogh. She stopped her bags again in the road between the cars for a moment and was asking them something. One man shook his head, and Mrs Keogh nodded and walked on. It was all right to talk to them, they belonged in the street. 'They're angels in disguise,' my mum said, you had to be good to them. But my dad said they were like the dead, you had to be careful to give them something if you could.

One of the tramps got up to pee against the wall. His face had gone deep red, he had swollen hands and he was losing his hair. His coat was torn at the back and hanging down, stiff with dirt and trailing like he couldn't help it any more. I looked at him longer than I should have.

'What d'you want?' The old man with the grey beard Mrs Keogh spoke to was picking up cigarette butts over the road. I shook my head because he was drunk, and I shouldn't talk to strangers. He was stooped over and keeping his eyes down, searching the dirt on the pavement, 'I'm looking for money,' he said. His voice was raspy and thick, and he was closed to anything else – he wasn't seeing me.

I looked away.

The streetlights came on, rosy and orange, flickering at the edges. There was no one else on the street, everyone had gone in. I felt a pang in my stomach getting up to our door. I'd stayed out too long and didn't hear them calling *all-y-in!* I thought it was all right to be out if I was with Connor, but he'd run off. I thought about the man, crumpled up by the wall. I didn't know why Connor hit him, but I felt bad about begging. But there *was* a Guy, so he was wrong. But maybe what was wrong was I'd gone too far to be able to show him. And if I'd come round with him, it wouldn't be there, so that *would* be begging.

Connor came round the corner at the top of the street. 'What you waiting for?' he shouted. 'A punch?' He was angry and I didn't know why.

'Where's the Guy gone?' I said.

'They've taken it and they've nicked the money.'

'Who has?'

'How much you give 'em?'

I gave everything I'd got to the two brothers round the corner who were Manus's friends. They said they'd stay by the Guy and look after it. They put the cardboard under it and even had a biscuit tin they put the change in so it rattled when they both held on to it.

'They've run off with the money,' said Connor, 'I've just gone and kicked their door!'

'Won't they give it back?' We hadn't decided how to spend it, so why would they give it back if it wasn't for anything? I didn't really want it any more, anyway.

'They wouldn't come out,' he said.

But that was because they were coming out our house with their dad holding the biscuit tin. Manus was at the door and saw us. 'Come in,' he said. 'Daddy wants you.'

'More dirty toerags,' their dad said as they walked past us with the tin rattling under his arm.

It was a punch. We stood there and watched them go.

I didn't know what had happened. There was an argument while we were gone about money going missing and the brothers had gone off with the tin and taken the Guy. Everyone blamed Manus and he'd gone round while their dad was out and got the money back off them. He'd spent some of it in the shop buying chocolate and handing out bars like he was rich to people who said they'd been collecting. I didn't get any, but by the time I got back everyone had gone in anyway, so he put what was left under his jumper and took it home. My mum was in from the hospital and found the biscuit tin under the bed when she didn't believe him about why he had chocolate on everything, and she took it to my dad. She said he came home with the chocolate melting on his face and his tummy rumbling.

He wasn't good at lying, so they were just getting to the bottom of it, that he'd gone out begging with us, when the door knocked and his friends turned up with their dad saying Manus had stolen the money from them.

That was when me and Connor got home.

'Are you so stupid, I won't find out?' I could tell he was angry from how calmly he was talking to us lined up in the front room. He looked from Manus to Connor, 'Begging in the street?' He looked at me, 'I don't feed you?' And then at Busola. 'And you,' he said, turning to Manus again, 'I have to find you stealing.'

Manus lowered his eyes, 'I wasn't stealing.'

My dad exploded, 'So you bring your criminal friends to attack me? Bring them to my house?' He looked at my mum. 'Did they say he was stealing from them?'

She was standing by to stop it getting out of hand, but she nodded, her face stretched tight and looking sad. He was fuming.

'It was Penny for the Guy –' Connor said, but then he stopped and put his head back down.

'Penny for what?' my dad said, and waited for an answer. 'Begging and stealing? You are all banned from going outside! Go to school, come home, I'm going to watch you like a hawk.

You can forget anything else. And tomorrow, so you can think what you have done,' he was looking at Manus, 'I am going to break a stick on your head!'

Manus started crying. No one moved to stop him. It was what he got from our dad, and no one else did.

'Now go away!' he said, and we trooped out the room.

'Why did you hit that man?' I asked Connor when we were on our own.

'Because he said we were begging.'

'Oh,' I said, thinking that was what our dad was angry about. Was it begging?

'You shouldn't have got that chocolate, we wouldn't have got caught,' said Busola, trying to get Manus to look up.

'They'd have still come round,' Connor said.

'You're all useless!' said Manus. His eyelashes looked wet, bitter and closed, so we all shut up for a bit.

'What happened to the Guy?' I said.

'The head kept falling off,' said Busola. 'We had to put it on a stick.'

'Can we get him back?'

'What for?' Connor said.

I shrugged because I was feeling bad about the man with his head flaking, the way he tried not to fall over, about him not being able to breathe.

Connor was watching me, 'You'll get in trouble, you will.'

'They're gonna burn him on the bonfire tomorrow,' Busola said, looking at Manus. 'They're gonna get a stick and light his toes till his face burns off.'

Manus looked up, and thumped her on the arm, and we all

shut up as her face turned cold and her eyes shut off and the dark feeling came on.

We watched bonfire night inside from the windows. Bangers were going off on the street and fireworks over the roofs. There was the smell of gunpowder. I was all shaken up with the excitement, but I couldn't go out. There was a bonfire going on in the school, you could put your Guy there and they'd burn him for you. You could put potatoes in tinfoil and get them out when they were hot. There was a big crash from the firework display going off in the park but I couldn't see it properly, even from the backyard, so I rushed back up to the front windows. A group of boys threw a banger at a car going down the street and ran. It slammed on the brakes, and moved off again with a man shouting his head off out the window.

'Stupid!' Manus said, sulking back into the room.

'It's those brothers,' said Connor. 'I'm gonna get 'em.'

'You have to get out first,' said Busola. It was the first time she'd spoken since Manus hit her. We looked across at him. 'Go on, I dare you,' she said, looking up from the telly. 'Daddy's not in, he's forgotten about you.'

'You'll tell him,' Manus said.

'Of course I will,' she said, and left the room.

'Why's that?' said Connor. 'Because you didn't give her no chocolate, or you thumped her?'

'Because she was supposed to go out and meet her boy-friend,' he said.

Connor didn't expect it and his mouth fell open.

'She blames me. Everyone blames me,' Manus said.

The door slammed downstairs. We rushed up to the windows

and saw Busola in her coat going up the top of the street. She turned the corner without looking back.

'Does Mummy know?' Connor said.

I rushed to the kitchen and said, 'Mum, Busola's gone out!'

'She's gone on an errand for me,' my mum said, putting her lips tight and rattling the pots on the cooker. 'And you can be minding your own business.'

I put it together in my head that Busola had told about how Manus had thumped her and my mum was letting her out to stop it building up.

'Go on, out of the kitchen, I'm busy,' she said.

I walked down the stairs slowly, away from the others, and lifted the flap of the letterbox open to the street. There was no one out there. It was empty. There was frost in the air, the smell of fireworks drifting in against the smell of the cooking. A stream of cold air blew on my eyes and made them water. It wasn't fair, she wasn't treating us equally, I wasn't stealing, Busola *and* Manus were stealing that money, that's what happened. Was that what happened?

'Did you steal out that money, Manus?' I asked.

'So what?' he said.

Connor looked up at him.

'Not all of it. It was my money, I put the mask on.'

'And you let Busola take some?' I said.

'She wanted it, if that's what she told you.'

'So what about me kicking their door in?' said Connor.

'You're lucky their dad wasn't home,' he said. I thought they were going to fight. Connor was looking at him and Manus was just being brazen, 'What you gonna do about it?'

'What about the money I put in?' Connor said.

Manus went behind the sofa and pulled out a packet of sparklers. He opened it up and gave one to me and held out one to Connor.

'All right?' he said.

Connor shook his head and looked at him, but took it. They sent me into the kitchen to get matches from under my mum's nose. She was cooking, so it was easy.

'Go on, out of the kitchen. Don't go in the cupboard, we'll be eating as soon as Daddy gets home.'

We leaned out the window together and lit the sparklers, waving them in the air and letting the light burn itself into our eyes so they left an afterglow once they'd gone out.

'Don't tell Daddy,' Manus said, and pulled back into the room.

I stayed leaning out with Connor, listening for fireworks, but he was quiet and I couldn't tell what he was thinking. He thought in flashes, he had a temper.

Manus came back with more sparklers and gave us one each and said that was the last. We lit them together and I lifted mine up against the stars and let it sparkle against stray fireworks still going off over by the river. I felt I was holding Fireworks Night in my hands, fizzing and burning and silver. I put my fingers up against the sparks and felt the tingle. The glow went out, but we stayed up at the window seeing who could throw the used wires furthest into the street.

Those boys came back. The brothers were there. They glanced up at us from the other side of the street and hurried on. No one said anything. We watched them all the way up to the corner, carrying what looked like cut-out shapes of trousers and jumpers under their arms.

'Is that the Guy?' I said.

'No,' said Manus, 'they're nicking clothes off people's washing lines.'

I hadn't heard that before, only people stealing things out the shops. The man Connor thumped came into my head, telling me I was stealing, that the sparklers were stolen. I shut him out.

'They're your mates,' said Connor.

'No, they're not,' said Manus, pulling back in from the window.

'Come on, let's shut it,' said Connor, going in. 'It's cold.'

I looked down the street on my own, the tramps were huddled up under the big door but they weren't moving. I thought about those boys flitting up the road like shadows, holding the clothes they'd stolen, stiff with frost, and the echo of them calling out, *Penny for the Guy ...*

'You shouldn't have hit that man,' I said to Connor as I came in from the window, 'just because he thought we were begging.'

He looked at me like I was asking for trouble, but Manus stopped it saying, 'We weren't begging. It's only Daddy doesn't know.'

'You're the one who's stupid,' said Connor. 'We didn't do anything to him. It was Penny for the Guy, and he knows it.'

'But we have now,' I said.

'So shut the window.'

'They can put that Guy on the bonfire,' said Manus. 'I don't care. They can burn him till he goes black.'

Connor pointed his finger at me, 'I hit him because you're too stupid to. Remember that. No one likes you.'

A burst of cold air pushed past me into the room. I shut the window, and it came down with a bang.

Winning The Pools

'Go and bury that cat,' Gary's mum said.

It was outside their door it died, but he didn't want to – he was upset she wasn't telling Julie, who was the one saying it was bad luck and making him be the one to get rid of it.

It wasn't even a black cat. It got knocked down in the wet and crawled on to the pavement and stopped in front of their door with its mouth broken and its ear cut off, and its legs stretched out stiff in front like it was pushing something away.

'I'm not touching it,' he said.

'Get a shovel and take it up the bomb site,' Julie said.

'You do it,' he told her. Gary was waiting for their mum to go so he could thump her, but she was holding on to her mum's arm and getting ready to cry, so he had to look at us and say, 'Who's got a shovel?'

Manus pushed up the front and said, 'I'll do it.' He wanted to be in Gary's gang because they were older than him and had metal studs on their shoes that clicked as they walked down the road. They could strike sparks on the pavement, Manus said. 'Let me.'

Gary's mum went in to get a shovel out the backyard and everyone crowded closer, but the door was left open and Julie didn't back down, 'You think you're it,' she said, 'and you're scared of a cat.'

'I'll do it,' Manus said, and they looked at him like he was getting in the way. 'I don't mind.'

'You haven't even told him,' Julie said, 'you just let him do it. You don't care about anyone but you. Just like your dad.'

Gary's mum came back out with a shovel that was rusty and had a short handle, hollow on the inside. She said it was a coal shovel that she didn't need any more and Manus could leave it there when he finished.

'It's your own fault,' Connor said, because Julie and her mum went in and shut the door, and everyone else followed Gary up the road because he had long hair and was letting it grow.

Manus was on his own with the cat. Me and Connor were the only ones standing there to watch what he was gonna do. 'I don't care,' he said, 'it's not fair on the cat.'

He bent down and started trying to scrape it up on the shovel, poking it and trying to get it on, but the cat wasn't helping, only curling up as he prodded because its body was stiff. He dug in but it only skidded on the pavement, with its legs stuck out. Its fur looked wet and spiky, and one eye was only half closed.

'Wait a minute,' Connor said, and got an empty milk bottle by the door to keep the cat still. I moved back in case it flew off the shovel when Manus lifted it, but it wasn't like that, it was heavy. Connor dropped the bottle as the cat slid towards him. It clattered and didn't break, and Manus had to use both hands on the shovel to stop the body slipping off. He got hold of it but the tail flopped over on his fingers making him wobble until he could get it steady again.

'Where we going?' I said.

'Get out the way!'

I wasn't in the way, I was walking up behind him. Connor was coming up the other side by the kerb. Manus was holding out the cat in front with people getting out the way in case he wanted to give it to them. But they were slowing down as well, as though what we were doing was grown-up and important. 'Mind out!' Connor was saying, and I started saying, 'We're going to bury it!'

'Where you going with that?' The old lady up the top of the street was leaning out her window with her cats on the sill beside her. I dropped back, dodging puddles to go round on to the road, and I didn't look up again till we got to the corner. She was looking out with her grey hair hanging down.

'Where you going?' It was my friend Brian. He ran up behind me and kept up to see what was going on.

'We're going to bury the cat,' I said, 'up the bombsite. You coming?'

Connor looked at us like we shouldn't be there.

'Which one?' Brian said.

I looked at Manus to see where he was going and ran up beside him, 'Can we come?'

'Just get out the way!' His face was scrunched up and his arms were shaking, like it was gonna drop and he couldn't help it.

'What about this one?' Brian was pulling back the corrugated iron on the bombsite that was blocked off round by the pub. We didn't play in there because it was dangerous and could fall in on top of you. Manus rested the shovel up on the metal fence to get his grip, but the cat's head got squashed and he had to lift it off again. Brian pulled the corrugated iron back a bit more to show you could get in.

'All right, in there,' Manus said.

I didn't look at Connor in case he stopped us, I helped Brian pull the fence back and keep it open.

Connor pushed in and went first, Manus went in backwards, lifting the shovel over the wood across the bottom. Brian held it open for me and it banged back into place as he stepped through.

There was a big hole in the ground, with a pile of rubble up against the wall on one side. You could see where a room was at the back with a fireplace, and a fireplace above it. It was two rooms with different wallpapers stuck to the wall in layers, separated by a part of the ceiling that had wires dangling down like a jungle. Bricks poked out from the house next door that shared the chimney.

'Don't fall in there,' Connor said. Manus had one foot down the slope into the hole like that was where he could bury the cat. 'Bury it in the rubble.'

The ground was wet and Manus had to step up twice to get his foot back from the edge where the earth was giving way. 'I can see that,' he said, but it sounded like he wasn't in charge.

'Put it down,' Connor said, using his hands to pull some broken bricks out the pile. Manus was standing there with the cat on the shovel and wasn't moving. Brian put his hands in his pockets and looked away into the hole. Manus was stuck with the cat and wasn't letting go.

'What's the matter?' I said. 'Manus?'

'I say where it goes.'

Connor sat back on the rubble, and wiped the mud off his hands and knees. 'It's your cat.'

Manus lowered the shovel on to the ground between puddles where it was flat and looked round at the bombsite with his hands empty like he wasn't sure what to do.

'Get the shovel,' Connor said.

Manus looked at him, 'You get it.'

The cat was sprawled out and no one was moving. I looked back at the fence in case I could get out quick if they had a fight. I could push it with my shoulder, but that would leave Brian.

'I'll get it,' I said.

'Go on, then.' It was Connor daring me, he chucked a stone into the hole so it made a splash in the muddy water at the bottom.

I didn't want to. The cat was looking out its bloody eye. The muddy tail was flopped down by the handle, its hair splashed out like a puddle.

'See?' said Connor. 'I'm the only one you got.'

Manus bent over and put his hand on a chunk of brick, but Brian was already swinging the shovel loose and letting the cat fall over itself backwards into a puddle, its leg clawing up at the air. It came down with its mouth open in water, a look on its face of not wanting the taste, and a hiss of bubbles coming out.

Connor stood back off the rubble like the cat was gonna wake up and shake off being dead over his feet.

'Gis it here,' Manus said, grabbing the shovel off Brian, and slid down the slope into the hole and started digging in the side.

We crowded round the edge but it didn't feel safe, so me and Brian sat down with our legs hanging over and Connor went round and crouched over the other side to watch what he was doing.

He dug in and shifted the earth into the big puddle behind

him. His sandals were getting splashed. His foot went backwards into the mud. The backs of his legs got spattered. 'I can help,' Connor said, but Manus ignored him.

'Shall we have a funeral?' said Brian.

'No, we're just gonna bury it,' Manus said.

He dug in some more and pushed a big lump of earth rolling down into the ditch, splashing up to his shorts. It didn't stop him, he went on whacking into the wall of earth like it was gonna open up and swallow him.

'Look at that,' Brian whispered, leaning his arm on my shoulder so I could feel myself falling in. I held the back of his jumper and told him don't push me.

Manus looked up at us and scowled as he took a swing but this time he hit a stone and it hurt his wrist. He dropped the shovel and held his wrist up till the pain went.

'Why won't you let me?' Connor said.

Manus looked up at him like it was his fault there was a stone there, 'Why should I?'

'Because you let 'em walk all over you!'

That was it, I scrambled back from the edge and tried to drag Brian but he pulled away from me and nearly fell in, shouting '*Oi!*' Then he fell in, and landed up to his feet in the muddy puddle. His hands and bum were muddy from the slide, he had splashes up to his knees, and a splash in his face. He looked up at me like I'd pushed him.

'Gis that shovel out the mud,' Manus said, looking at him. 'See what we gotta put up with?'

Because Brian laughed and gave Manus the shovel, I went round to Connor to be on his side, but that felt wrong because then Manus tapped to see where the stone was and there was the metal sound of a clunk. He did it again, and it was a clink. He dug round, scraping away, and there was something metal stuck in the mud.

'What is it?' Connor said.

Manus dug some more where it was wedged in to get it loose. It started to come out, he dropped the shovel and started pulling side to side. As he tugged it looked like a metal tray stuck upside down, but then the whole thing slid out into his hands, and he was looking down at a rusty, muddy box.

'It's treasure,' said Brian.

Manus wiped away the mud, and as the metal came out his face changed and his eyes shone.

'Why can't we come?' I said.

Manus folded his arms round the box and gave me the same look he gave Connor up out the hole, like he'd been right all along and it wasn't dirty. But now we were out on the street, they weren't letting me and Brian go with them.

'Cos you can't keep your mouth shut,' Connor said.

'You can't come, you're not old enough,' said Manus, 'they won't let you in.'

Me and Brian had gone up the Imperial War Museum before. There were two giant World-War guns outside that weren't working. We tried to climb up but a guard in a uniform came out and chased us off. Maybe he'd recognise us, but how would he know how old we were?

As soon as he got hold of how heavy it was, Manus scrambled up out the hole with the box and we all had to chase him out the bombsite to see what was inside.

'You can't take it home,' Connor said.

'Why not?' said Brian.

'I found it,' Manus said.

'We helped,' I said.

'Oh yeah?'

I could see what he meant about me. What about Brian?

'Take it up the War Museum,' Connor said. 'Let them give you the reward.'

'Open it up,' said Brian.

Manus stopped like he wasn't sure what to think. He stood still looking into himself like he didn't deserve it.

'We gonna be rich?' I said.

He unlocked his eyes and stared at me, 'Don't you tell anyone. This is mine, I'm doing it.' He turned to Connor and said, 'All right, come on.'

Brian didn't try and help me stop them. Manus and Connor walked off like they'd had a fight but were friends again, and it was only Brian left with mud all over him. But it was me who was left feeling dirty because I'd brought him.

'Sorry,' I said. 'I didn't know, they give rewards up the War Museum?'

'Lucky it wasn't a bomb,' Brian said, and shrugged.

'A bomb?'

'It's a bomb site.'

It took a while to sink in. A bombsite was a playground, a rough place you could play in between the houses – when you could get in past the corrugated iron. I didn't know it was the place where a bomb fell. No one told me there was a bomb under there. Until it burst in my head, and the ground went out under my feet.

It was raining again when I left Brian to go home to his mum and say he'd fallen over playing football. He was looking like it didn't matter, but it did and I was gonna get him some of the reward, so he could go on telling me where the ground was. My mum was home in the kitchen, marking the pools. I was bursting to tell her, but I couldn't. She was going across and down in columns.

'How does that work?' I said when I'd got out my wet clothes and she was still doing it.

She looked up like I'd stopped her working it out. 'It doesn't,' she said, 'but I do it anyway.'

'What's it for?'

She put the pencil down, and did a big sigh and shook her head, like what did I want? But she tucked my vest in for me and said, 'For you. To give you things I can't.'

There was the smell she had when she wasn't feeling well. She leaned back to have a look at me. I wanted to give her the news but I couldn't. I could have told Busola but she was staying over with Nana.

'I'd have to win, though,' she said, 'and that doesn't always happen.'

You could win the pools? Doing marks with a pencil? That didn't sound likely to me. 'What happens if you win? Do you get money?'

'You all get your own room, and everyone gets a bicycle,' she said.

I jumped up and laughed, and clapped my hands. I felt like I'd won already, because we were rich and she didn't know, even though she was watching me. The door went downstairs and I rushed to get it. My dad was coming in shaking out his jacket from the rain.

'Hello, Daddy, Mummy's doing the pools!'

He looked up like he wasn't interested. But he didn't know either. I was going to get a bicycle. I waited for him as he closed the front door and came swinging his work lamp up the stairs after me.

'Mrs Brown of Luton,' he called out, 'has never in this world done well. Millionaire and can't care. Where's the food? And what's all this mud on the floor?'

I'd trailed it in, but I couldn't tell him I'd dug up treasure. Or Manus had. I had to get my mum to tell him about the pools, 'Come and see,' I said.

He looked in over my shoulder at the kitchen door and saw my mum with the pools spread out on the table. He held up his lamp to see even though it was off, 'Poor man's problem solved. The more you play, the more you pay.'

My mum leaned a finger in her cheek with her elbow on the table. There wasn't any food being cooked and she was gonna have to tell him. 'Hope is a fine thing,' she said. 'Keep it alive.'

I looked up and he was slowly turning his eyes to me, he didn't understand the pools.

'We're all gonna get our own room,' I said.

'And your father won't have to go down the tunnels to work, he'll have lots of time to spend with you all.'

'What tunnels?' I said.

He smiled, and put his lamp down and came into the kitchen in his work clothes. 'Under the ground,' he said. 'There are tunnels going everywhere under your feet for the trains.' He put his jacket off on the chair behind him and sat down. 'You can feel them rumbling.'

I couldn't, I stood still trying to feel it.

'Listen to your teacher,' he said, 'and you won't have to follow me down there.'

I looked at his lamp by the door. 'Is it dark?' I said.

'There's a whole world underneath this one,' my mum said, 'but I want you to stay up here in the light. And your daddy's going to make sure of it.'

I climbed on my mum's lap to get my feet off the ground, even though she smelt funny and her skin was clammy. I had my sandals off but my feet were still dirty with mud. My dad saw them but he didn't tell me off.

'When your mother wins the pools, we are going to cry for one whole week, and then we are going on the longest journey we have ever been, all of us together.'

'*Amen*,' my mum said.

I thought about it, because the ground still felt shaky and my dad was looking at me like we still might not be able to afford it.

'Will I get a bicycle?'

It hadn't stopped raining when I opened the door to Manus and Connor. They were drenched and didn't have the box with them. I'd been waiting all afternoon and ran down as soon as I heard them knock to see what they'd got. The rain had washed the mud off Manus's legs, their shirts were soaked to the skin and their shorts were wringing.

'D'you get the reward?'

They didn't answer and pushed me out the way, Manus with his face set and his hands empty, Connor looking at me out the corner of his eye to see if I'd told, rain dripping off his ears and dribbling down his face.

'I haven't,' I said. 'I just told 'em you'd gone up Bedlam Park.'

My mum and dad had gone to bed for a lie-down and only two other people had knocked, the milkman with curly hair catching the rain and the man from the pools in a brown raincoat under a black umbrella. 'She says she's not in,' I told the milkman, 'she'll see you next week.' And I gave the pools man the coupon with the money clinking inside. They both gave me nice smiles and went away. But Manus and Connor were horrible to me.

I looked at the rain coming down and no one there as I held the door open, the splashes making bubbles that floated along in the gutter. The brown envelope of a pools coupon was being washed away. I stepped out to get a closer look. It was a brown baby pigeon being lifted up and put down with its wing spread in the water, and its eye open. We hadn't buried the cat.

I followed Manus and Connor out to the bathroom and watched them having their bath. They didn't say anything, and I didn't ask. There were bubbles on the dirty water as they splashed.

'I didn't say anything,' I said.

They both looked up at me with the shampoo in their hair. Connor raised his eyes at Manus, and Manus shrugged. There was steam coming off and Manus blew it away with the bubbles from his mouth.

'It was Oxo cubes,' Connor said. 'They showed us. It was a Sunday dinner for the soldiers. It crumbled in your hand, they said it was probably poisonous by now.'

'What was it doing there?'

Manus looked at me like I was asking too much, 'They said not to dig in the bomb sites.'

'And if we found anything report it,' Connor said.

I didn't want to look at Manus, so I handed the flannel to Connor to get the soap out his eyes, 'Where is it?'

'We left it there,' Manus said, telling me to shut up.

They were doing everything together and not including me, I still had mud on my feet. I waited until they were getting dry in their towels, 'Was that cat really dead? Was it breathing? Did you go back there?'

'It was raining, it was too dangerous,' Connor said, and gave me a look like he was gonna kill me.

Manus's face went the wrong way round feeling useless and ugly, like a hole inside him was filling up and he couldn't stop the cat drowning in the mud. I didn't want to hurt him, it was too late to take it back, I didn't know how to stop it. It was like he was losing hope, and Connor was putting his arm round him.

'Mummy's gonna win the pools,' I said.

Blood Brothers

'You know we're best friends?'

'Yeah ...' I said, but really I was holding on.

We were sitting on the fence, it was really unsteady. We climbed up because Brian said he wanted to talk, but it wasn't coming out what he meant and we had to hold on with our fingers to stop the fence wobbling and brace with our heels on the cross-wire. I had one hand on the metal support to keep steady, but he was balancing on his bum with both hands gripped to the mesh as it folded over at the top. If he fell, he was going to have to flip over backwards and hang on. I was worried about getting my fingers twisted.

'For a long time now ...'

I nodded.

'We can be friends, but we can't be best friends any more.'

I didn't know what to say, so I nodded and looked down at my feet to get them into a stronger position.

'It's because my dad says.' He wobbled a bit on his bum to get comfortable and I could feel myself tipping forward. He stopped to let me get my balance.

'Shall we get down?' I said.

'If you want,' and he did a backflip over into the playground.

That's when it happened. I put one leg over the fence to climb down but the top of the mesh caught in my shorts. It stung, and

I could feel a warm trickle. I unhooked it, got down slowly, and jumped off the wall at the bottom. He watched me lift back the waistband and look.

'It's bleeding,' I said. Not much, not like a nose bleed, but it really hurt.

'Shall we go up the hospital?'

'Let me go and wash it,' I said. We both knew I was wounded. I wasn't sure how badly.

He held the button down on the water fountain by the sand-pit. I held the waistband open with one hand and cupped water on to it. It was a strange feeling getting my pants wet, but I didn't mind because I could see I'd nicked it and it might be serious. A watery reddish trickle ran down my leg into my sock.

'I have to go to hospital.'

He looked at me like he'd hurt me. It was difficult. We hadn't done anything like this before.

People were looking because I was limping and because I had to go slowly and keep my waistband open all the way there. I minded because even though you feel important when you go to hospital, sometimes you don't want people to see. We were trying to sort it out ourselves.

We knew the way because it was up by the park we used to go with Brian's mum and climb trees. She made us hold on to the pram across the busy roads and sit down on the grass for picnics with the sunshade up for the baby. But when she was trying to get the baby to sleep she let us go wild and run around and climb. There was the big climbing tree with twisted arms that made her scream when she woke up and saw how high we'd gone. She called us 'right little monkeys!' and slapped his bum.

She gave me a worried look. I could see in her eyes she thought he was a better climber than me and she'd have to tell my mum if something happened.

We walked in through the entrance of the children's hospital to where we could see the nurses having a cup of tea and pulled back the curtain to show them my willy. The one nearest coughed out her biscuit and spilt some tea. The others started laughing and it was only the one who got some ointment on cotton wool with pliers and plastic gloves that could see it was serious and dabbed it so it stung. I flinched and she lost her temper with me.

'*Keep still!*'

They burst out laughing again and I looked up, annoyed, and said, '*Ow!*' They stopped what they were doing, took their tea and moved outside.

'Is it gonna leave a scar?' Brian asked as the nurse snapped off the gloves. I hadn't thought of that, but the sting was wearing off and she didn't look worried.

'Be careful next time,' she said. 'No climbing fences.'

I saw the nurses looking at me as we went out, so I stopped limping.

'There goes a very proud little boy,' said the one in the blue cardigan by the tea trolley.

'And very brave,' said the nurse coming out behind us. 'Go straight home and tell your mummy – show her where it hurts.' They all burst out laughing again. Brian's face went red.

'*Why don't you shut up?*' I said, but I don't know if they heard me, so I didn't stop to find out.

We didn't go home. We sat inside the concrete tunnel in the playground and I showed him my scar. It was purple with ointment. I felt proud for being brave and I felt bruised. So I asked him, 'What does your dad say?'

'He says I can't play with you no more.'

I didn't say anything.

'Anyway, those nurses are tarts – my dad says!'

I couldn't see it – how nurses could be tarts – only the way his face was going red again.

'But we can be friends?'

'Yeah,' he said.

'How can we play and not be friends?'

'We can't.'

We both nodded. And it started to rain.

We were playing in the hallway when his dad came in. He came backwards out the rain, blocking the whole doorway, banging and shaking his umbrella. He turned to us at the bottom of the stairs and stopped. He looked at Brian and looked up at Brian's mum who came hurrying out with a tea cloth from the back kitchen. I saw the look that passed between them. I shouldn't be there. He didn't say anything, he just looked.

'It was raining,' she said. 'They had to come in.'

I hadn't been in Brian's house before. All the days we'd played had been sunny up till then. We sat on his front windowsill and minded the baby in the pram with the doors open. We walked with his mum to the park and sat on the grass for picnics. We climbed trees and it never occurred to me I'd never been inside his house. His mum made us sandwiches and brought them out to us. She had a beehive hairdo before anyone else and wore miniskirts which my mum didn't. She put him in long trousers when I was in shorts. I wanted my mum to be like his, but I didn't mind she wasn't because his mum was looking after me. She was standing over us to keep that man off. I'd never seen her scared like that before.

He didn't say anything. He walked round us and went upstairs. I looked at Brian. He looked at his mum.

'Go home now. Run all the way. Don't get wet. Go on.'

I stood up and walked into the rain. I didn't stop to look back. I ran, ducking the moving cars. I ran as fast as I could so the rain would bounce off me. I ran home and pushed past questions, and ran a bath and told my mum she couldn't come in and see me. And I sat in it until it went cold, and looked back at what I'd seen.

'*This is a moonstone my dad gave me,*' he said. '*It changes colour depending how you feel.*'

I looked at his eyes. They were grey, aeroplane grey. They looked steady. I believed him.

I looked at his mum.

'*When you get stung by nettles look for dock leaves and rub them on. You always find the cure in the same place.*' Where she rubbed it on, my skin turned green and it stopped hurting.

I looked at my hand. It was brown. I looked at my willy. It was white at the edges of the cut. I held up the moons in my fingernails, the spongy white where I gnawed my thumb to the knuckle, the tips of my fingers, puffy and waterlogged.

I looked up at my dad coming in through the door and closed my legs.

'Where have you been?'

'Playing in my friend's house.'

My mum came in behind him.

'Stand up,' she said.

I kept my hands in front of me, shivering. She folded the towel around me and let the water out. 'It's cold. What's going on?'

'Nothing.'

She looked at me, pursing her lips. My dad shifted on to the other foot, shaking his head.

'I don't want you in that house,' he said.

I waited, feeling the water trickle at my feet, but he wasn't telling me why or what he meant. My mum helped me step out and started rubbing me dry with the towel. I took it off her to do by myself. He didn't like that. I didn't care.

'I don't want you going there, do you hear?'

I nodded.

'His father's back,' my mum said quietly.

We were back in the playground, in the concrete tunnel. Brian was brushing sand out his ruffled up hair.

'My dad doesn't want me to go in your house,' I said.

He stopped and looked at me. He nodded. We were even. 'That's all right, then.'

'Yeah,' I said.

Then, slowly, he shook his head and I had a pang. We weren't happy.

'Let's be blood brothers.'

We both said it. We nicked the end of our thumbs with a dry stick and closed them together, our fingers clasped, letting the blood mingle. And that was it. We didn't have to be friends to be together. We didn't have to be apart any more.

'We're blood brothers now.'

'What you gonna do when you grow up?' I said. I was gonna tell him I'd be an astronaut, but he said, 'I'm gonna work with my dad.'

I thought about that.

I could remember glimpses of his dad telling us to race to the car. It was a funny race because I wanted to let Brian win so his dad wouldn't mind me. Brian pretended to have a limp too and we ended up leaning on each other and getting to the car at the same time. But I couldn't go with them, and Brian didn't look back as they drove off. I couldn't remember his dad being around that much, and didn't know where they went, and didn't actually know what his dad did.

'I don't remember,' I said, 'what's your dad do?'

He shrugged and opened his hands, 'We're thieves.'

'Oh,' I said.

I started stealing my dad's money. Every time he came home he emptied his pockets out on to the sideboard and I started to nick his loose change. We all did, so I didn't think it mattered. It was where you went to get money for the shops – milk or paraffin, a loaf of bread. When you didn't bring it all back and got some sweets, no one noticed. Until my dad started asking, 'Where's my change?'

You weren't supposed to take half a crown – at the most it could be sixpence, or a shilling. 'Don't take too much!' Manus said. But it was too late – I was stealing, I took all of it.

My dad started checking and testing to find out who it was. He'd leave it on the side like he wasn't thinking, but then he couldn't work it out because we were all doing it, bit by bit, going and coming from the shops, when he was looking and when he wasn't.

'I won't have thieves in my house!' he shouted.

The shouting was getting my mum down, she said, things were hard enough already and it was only coppers, to let it pass. He looked at her furious, and said she could give in, but he wasn't going to tolerate it, he was going to stamp on that kind of sickness before it spread.

I could see he was upset and he really meant it, but by then I wasn't on his side, I didn't want what he wanted. I was going around watching to see what he'd do to stop me. He kept money in his jacket pockets, I'd find it. He'd set traps of money round the house, I'd leave it alone. He'd send me to the shops, I'd bring him his change.

I started stealing ten bob and one-pound notes, spending them on food I wanted and being careful not to bring any of that change back into the house.

'Who is stealing from me?'

Everyone was standing in front of him, looking around like it wasn't them. 'All you bloody bastards!' This was when I took five pounds out the wallet in the bedroom. It was too much. I knew it was. I slipped it behind the skirting in the hall. But now it was all going to come out. I was going to get caught.

'*You*,' he said. My heart stopped and everyone looked at me. It was like a knife at the lump in my throat before I could lie. But then he said, 'It wasn't you. Go and sit down.'

For a moment, I couldn't move. It felt like a relief, but it wasn't. I got myself out the way, but it wasn't going to end there – it was going to get worse. There was Manus and Connor and Busola standing, and me on the sofa facing them as my dad shook the wooden spoon in the air, 'Which of you is stealing?'

Manus said he'd told everyone to bring back the change, but my dad said that was a lie and he was going to beat him twice, once for stealing and once for lying. Connor said he took the money and got himself something because he thought he deserved it for going to the shops, especially when it was heavy gallons of paraffin that made his arms ache. My dad shook his head, tapping the spoon on his palm with a *thwack!* It was the wrong answer, but he didn't say anything and turned to Busola, 'What have you got to say?'

She looked at me sitting on the sofa and pointed her finger, 'He's the thief. He's the one who's been stealing.'

My face started burning. I could see Manus and Connor hating me with their eyes because I'd been singled out to be safe, but I didn't know how Busola could see I was stealing or if she was only guessing, so I looked back at her and said nothing.

'*Liar!*' he said, and told her how much she'd stolen, what she'd bought and when she'd done it. 'You are the one stealing!'

'That wasn't stealing,' she said. 'Mummy told me I could have a shilling for helping her with the shopping.'

My dad looked round at my mum standing by the door. She put her hands up to the sides of her face and nodded. He threw out his arms like he couldn't go on and I thought it might end there, but he whacked the wooden spoon down hard on his own hand.

'Steal again and it's you or me!' he said. 'If I catch you, you'll wish you were never born!'

He put on his jacket, pushed past and went out, slamming the front door. My mum waited until it stopped shaking and left the room without speaking. The others turned and looked at me on the sofa.

I went to find my mum. She was bending over the bath with dirty clothes and the scrubbing board, wet strands of hair falling forward over her face. It was steamy and smelly, so I stayed by the door and let the clouds of air out into the backyard. She looked round at me and used her wrist to wipe the sweat and hair off her forehead.

'What do you want?' she said. 'Close the door, it's letting the cold air in.'

I took a deep breath of fresh air and let the door bang to, going over to hold on to her dress. She shook me off.

'What is it?' she said. 'I'm busy.'

'The others don't like me,' I said. 'Connor called me a cunt.'

'Oh, for God's sake, grow up!' she snapped, and I started to cry. It worked because she sat down on the edge of the bath and held me. 'There ... don't cry. Tell me, what's wrong?'

It was easier to cry than tell her about Brian, or the money, or being in the wrong about getting everyone into trouble, so I burst into tears again. She held me away from her by the sides of my arms and looked into my face. I don't know what she saw but she buckled up her lips and shook her head.

'Ah, no, it won't do,' she said. Then, 'Another fine mess you've got me into.'

I thought she wasn't taking me seriously, I could feel myself getting angry. I tried to shake her off and get my arms free but she wasn't letting go.

'He's turned them against you, do you see?' she said. 'And he's going to take five pounds out of the housekeeping. There'll be less to eat. We can't afford it,' she said. 'And neither can you.'

I couldn't cry any more, and I couldn't pretend to be on my own side. I felt like I'd lost weight, I was floating. I heard myself say, 'It wasn't me,' but the thought came in my head, *so who was it?*

She pulled me close and held me. 'It's not your fault,' she said, 'you don't know.' Her clothes were wet against her body, she was hot. I looked down at the clothes in the bath behind her. We were all there, climbing over one another in the muddy water – trousers, arms, socks, kicking and struggling. The collar of my dad's shirt was up on the scrubbing board, by the plughole I saw brown stains on a pair of my underpants.

I was running up behind Brian's mum as she was pushing the pram and dragging Brian along in her other hand. She was telling me not now, we could play when we got into school. She kept looking over her shoulder, back at the house, but I'd been watching for them to come out and his dad had already left with another man. I ran up when I saw Brian and gave him a hug and jumped around to show how much I wanted to be with him.

'Don't do that!' she said. 'Come on, we'll be late for school.'

Brian gave me a quick look, 'My uncle's in,' he said. 'He's not well.'

'What's wrong?' I said when his mum dropped us off inside the playground and hurried back. The bell was ringing but we hung back in the arches under the school caretaker's house.

'My uncle got beaten up,' he said. 'He's all bloody.'

I asked what happened and he said it was all because of his dad coming out of prison and there was a lot of trouble and they might have to move. I could feel my stomach dropping out from under me. The bell stopped and we were alone.

'I want us to be friends,' I said.

He looked at me with his grey eyes, that looked dark, the

colour of kerbstones, and a bit frightened, and leaned his forehead on mine.

'We're brothers,' he said.

I took the five pounds out from behind the skirting and tucked it in my underpants.

'What you doing?' Busola said, leaning round the stairs on the banister. 'Is that where you've hidden it? You can't hide it there no more.'

'What makes you say I'm stealing?' I said.

'You are,' she said.

'So are you!'

'You have to catch me first,' and she hopped down some stairs. 'No one likes you because you're no good at it. You don't even know what to spend it on. You can't spend five pounds on sweets, you get sick.'

'Then how do you know how much it is, then?' I said.

'Mummy told me, so I knew you did it. You're stupid.'

'I'm going out,' I said.

'Don't get sick,' and she jumped down the last stairs.

I got in behind the corrugated iron across from Brian's house and peered through the gap to see what was going on. I saw my dad walking up the street on his way home and leaned back out of sight with my heart thumping, trying to stop it being so loud. Some people walked by on my side of the street with their heels clicking on the pavement. A car turned the corner and went past. I kept still against the wooden post of the fence. A cat came up out the bomb site and had a look and slipped past my feet and stopped and looked back and went on, sniffing the weeds and peeing against a bed frame. The hole in the ground was spread out from under my feet and I could feel myself tipping forward on the slope like I was standing on the edge of a crater. There was a rusty tin bath upside down, a burnt mattress with springs, a broken television set. It was like being on the moon. The cat looked back at me and disappeared into the weeds. Everything went quiet. I had the feeling I shouldn't be there, standing in someone else's house, the shadow of the stairs going up the wall, brick fireplaces on the different floors and rooms up in the air with layers of wallpaper peeling off. A door opened and closed shut across the road. I heard steps running towards me and the corrugated iron being pulled open. I crouched down. It was Brian, breathing like someone was after him.

'I saw you from the window,' he said.

I got out the five pounds and gave it to him as he got down beside me.

'What's that for?'

'For you,' I said, 'for going away.'

He shook his head and held it back to me, 'It's your money, you keep it.'

'It's not,' I said. 'I stole it – from my dad.'

He blinked at me and put his head on one side. 'You can't do that,' he said. He put the money in my hand and steadied himself on the wooden post. 'I didn't tell you to do that.'

'I don't want you to go away,' I said.

It was half dark, the light was going. We looked round at the rubble of broken bricks from the house that wasn't there any more, at the gaping hole that was full of rubbish people had thrown out. The empty space between the walls had tall weeds growing up into it. We were on our own.

'My mum says people got killed in this house,' he said.

He picked up a pebble and threw it down on to the tin bath, making an echoey metal sound snake up the walls. We listened for anyone moving on the street.

'How's your uncle?' I said.

'He's got holes in his hands.'

I looked at him because – 'What?'

'They banged in nails,' and he pointed his finger into the middle of his palm. 'My mum has to take off the bandages and look after him. I've seen it. A man comes round and gives him injections.'

I looked at the fiver in my hand. 'What shall I do with this?' I said.

'Can you give it back?'

I shook my head. He nodded.

'What would you do with a hundred pounds?' I asked.

'Run,' he said, 'because they'll come after it.'

We both smiled. I tucked the note back in my pants.

'Maybe you can leave it somewhere they can find it?' he said.

We froze because something moved. It was down in the hole. It wasn't a cat. It was inside, tugging at the mattress. My stomach went cold and suddenly we were scampering across the ledge to the opening and got out.

The lamp posts had come on. We looked at each other to get steady. Brian had a cut on his arm and licked it with some spit. It was there, but he could close it up. We both nodded not to say anything and turned for him to cross the road and me to run home.

Grey Blue Green

'I found this, Mum.'

'Don't tell anyone,' she said, tucking the fiver away in her purse. 'They don't need to know.'

'Why not?'

'That's grown-up business,' she said, putting her finger to her lips to say keep out of it. 'And where have you been?'

I thought I was going to say something to make her not listen and forget, but what came out was, 'I was hiding in the bomb site with Brian.'

'Why were you doing that?'

'Because you don't want us to be together and his mum can't take care of me,' I said. 'She's looking after his uncle, he's got holes in his hands.'

She looked at me close up. I couldn't remember which one was her glass eye, the one that was more grey, or the one that was grey-green and blue, because they were both glassy and moved over my face in the same way.

'And how's Brian?' she said.

'Why don't you like him?'

'You like him, that's good enough for me.'

'He told me to give it back.'

She gave me a look like lots of questions at once. 'Go and be with him, but don't go to his house.'

'Why not?'

'They don't want you there,' she said. 'They've got things to hide.'

'His mummy likes me.'

'Yes, I know. They love you.'

My chest swelled up but I felt out of breath and confused. They didn't want me and they loved me. I shook my question back at her in my face – *what should I do?*

'Wait until his father goes away,' she said. 'And don't tell yours.'

'What's that fuckin' black cunt – ?'

We thought his uncle was asleep upstairs, but he was sat in the front room with the curtains closed, bandages on his hands and a black nose where he got beaten up. He stood up and chucked his drink at us, we rushed back to the front door and got out on to the street.

Brian's mum and dad had gone out but gave him a key to let himself in. The baby was asleep in her pram at the bottom of the stairs, and woke up as his uncle hopped out after us to the front door. We could hear her crying as he shouted after us running down to the corner. He was fatter and shorter than Brian's dad, and had that voice street traders used that rang out round the corner, '... *come 'ere ... fuckin' ... bloody ... kill yer!*'

'Sorry,' I said, wiping beer off my face with my shirt. My shirt had got wet as well.

He only had a bit on him, but wasn't wiping it off because he was thinking with his tongue between his lips. 'It's all right.'

'Is your sister all right?' I said.

He looked at me and frowned. 'They've gone down ... to see a policeman down the pub. They'll be back in a minute.'

We'd gone in his house to see the bags and boxes packed up and get out the Johnny Seven gun he wanted to give me, because even though it'd lost all its ammunition it still made noises when you fired it.

'Shall we run and get 'em?'

He shook his head. 'Nah,' he said, 'my mum's trying to sort it out.' He looked down at the ground and it was like there was a lump on his shoulders where he was bent over.

I touched his arm.

'We haven't got enough money to run,' he said. 'And I'm in school. It's my dad who wants to go, he says the council want us out anyway, and my mum says we don't have nowhere else to go.'

'Is your dad like that?' I said. 'Like his brother?'

He got his knuckle and wiped some beer out his eye. Then I saw it wasn't beer, he was crying and forcing it back.

'He's my dad,' he said. 'I love him.'

I put my head down. We walked on and sat up on a wall at the back of the London City Mission. We got turned away from there when we turned up at Christmas together and they said we hadn't come to Sunday school so we couldn't have any toys they were giving out. We used to climb up on the roof instead which was slanted and roll over, but we weren't going to be doing any more climbing. We didn't do anything for a bit, we just sat there.

'It's not like you and me,' he said. 'They're grown-ups. My uncle's scared they're gonna come back and get him. He blames my dad for not giving them the money and my dad says he hasn't got it. My mum doesn't know what to do.'

'Is your dad going away?' I said.

Brian looked up at me like I wasn't on his side. I felt caught out and couldn't look at him because I wanted his dad to go and leave us alone even though my mum said to wait.

He shook his head, 'I don't want him to.'

'What's gonna happen?'

He shrugged. 'I've got to look after my mum.' We looked at each other. We were losing everything. And we couldn't stop it. 'I can't stay with you,' he said.

I nodded.

'I've got to go back.' His eyes were like grey submarines going down black into water and there wasn't any room there for me. He jumped off the wall on to his feet and gave my legs a hug. I didn't get down – I hung my head and watched him walk off down the road and round the corner.

'Your friend Brian's gone,' my mum said, taking her coat off and putting her bag down. She was coming in from her early cleaning job and putting her arm round me. She smelt wrong, like she'd been sweating and it was stale. I had my spoon in my mouth from a bowl of cereal. It tasted like cardboard and metal. I took it out and didn't say anything. I didn't think I was going to be able to eat again. My throat felt like it was closing up. I felt my bottom lip go over my top one to keep it warm, and just nodded.

Busola looked across in a scowl. 'You can cry if you want,' she said. 'But don't think you're special just cos your cornflakes go soggy.'

'Shut up,' my mum said.

'No,' she said.

My mum picked up a cornflake and threw it at her.

'See?' Busola said. 'He doesn't even care about me and you don't, either.'

'I saw them on the way to work,' my mum said. 'It was still dark and his mother's sorry they couldn't say goodbye. They had to load up this morning and go. She's not sure if they'll be coming back.'

'Where have they gone?' Busola said.

'Will you eat your cornflakes?' my mum said to her.

She put a spoonful in her mouth and chewed, looking at me. I sneezed over my bowl, which brought the tears to the back of my eyes, but I didn't want to cry in case I flooded everything. I started shaking and my mum held me tighter, saying, 'It's for the best.'

'He's not coming back,' said Busola. 'What's good about that?'

'Sometimes I could murder you,' my mum said.

I passed his house on the way to school. The net curtains were up but it was empty. I came back and it was dark. No one said anything at school. A teacher came up after a few days and said, 'Do you know where Brian's gone?' I shook my head. No one said anything in the playground. It was like playing on my own and being deaf. I didn't want to know what anyone said. I sat under the arches in the playground and watched everyone playing out in the sun.

After a while I passed his house and it was like only I knew anyone ever lived there. It was like a bomb had hit it and everyone had gone, and it was just the walls standing. It was dark and it felt dead, but I still had to get up and walk past it on my way to school and come back, past all the bomb sites where people used to live but no one knew who they were any more.

My dad gave me some money to spend on comics and on a model aeroplane with a pot of glue and a pot of grey paint. I left the plane out to dry on newspaper in the backyard and Manus accidentally trod on it and threw it in the bin. I got it out and tried to piece it back together with the glue, thinking maybe I could cry about that. It didn't work and I threw it away myself.

I was in the bathroom, trying to get the glue and the grey paint off my fingers, and think why things I made always got broken. I squinted at the flecks of paint on my nails in the running water, and made them go grey-blue in the light coming from the window. I thought about his eyes. We were up in the big tree, climbing out on to weaker branches that dipped under our weight. He had his knee over one branch and was holding on to the one above while he looked at me and put a finger to his lips and pointed down to his mum asleep on the grass beside the baby. I couldn't remember the baby's face, and I couldn't move because my shorts were caught on a twig. He put his foot on my branch and pressed down to release me. I got my knee up and joined him and we hung for a moment breathing in the air through the leaves. It was going to rain, you could hear it spatter the leaves at the top, his mum was going to wake up, there was wind in the branches of the tree, they were moving, and I was feeling it was going to be a long way to fall.

Custard Out of a Tin

My mum was gone and my dad was looking after us. He gave us fried bread and you had to eat it, oily out the frying pan, and cold corned beef mashed into lumpy boiled yams that dried your mouth out and you still had a long way to go. He couldn't cook. He boiled milk and forgot about it until it bubbled over and burnt at the sides – then let it cool down with skin forming on the top and you couldn't leave it. He sat there and told you it was good for you so drink it. Busola looked at the skin and started being sick, burping up air from her tummy and trying to vomit up her tonsils. You had to get it from the cup into your stomach without it touching your tongue or the roof of your mouth, or letting it get stuck in your throat. It was boiled, slimy and stale. 'What's the matter?' he said. We looked at each other. 'It's not too fresh,' Manus said, trying to get rid of his tongue. It rumbled inside my stomach, then gurgled, and rushed out my mouth on to the oily bread. I looked up at him, and wanted my mum back.

He got a cloth and wiped it up. I had tears down my cheeks and snot running out my nose. I wiped it all off on my sleeve and used the back of my hand to wipe the milk off my chin. He used the dirty cloth to wipe my mouth, and sat down and stared out the window.

No one said anything. It was too much food and it was bad.

He didn't know what to do. We knew he didn't. He needed my mum back. 'OK, you can go,' he said.

She'd walked out, but she'd left us too, so we had to look after ourselves. We weren't blaming him, but he was trying to clamp down on us because he wasn't in control.

'What we gonna do?' Manus said.

'Make him drink it first,' said Connor.

'Get Mummy back,' I said.

Busola wasn't saying anything, it was all her fault anyway. She was the one who wasn't going to give in.

It started when she came home one day and told everyone she was Kate. *Katherine, Kathleen, Kitty,* we'd all heard, but *Kate* was new. And anyway, her name was Busola. But everyone stopped a minute and thought about it.

'You're not English,' was all Connor said, and walked off.

'That's as maybe,' my mum said, smoothing her dress down over her knees, which was saying your skirt's too short, and putting her hand up to her chest which meant you were showing too much up top, 'but if God wanted us to go naked, He wouldn't have invented clothes. So, girls –' we always blushed at that and left them to it, *'smooth down, cover up.'*

But Busola said she was going to choose her own clothes from now on and she didn't care what anyone thought.

'You've been doing that for years,' my mum said.

Manus shook his head and got up, like he'd heard it before, 'Why d'you always have to cause trouble?'

'Why don't you go on lugging an African name?' Busola said as he went out. She turned on my mum, 'None of them do!'

'What's wrong with your name?' my mum said.

'It's *bush*,' she said.

I wasn't sure what she meant. Like it was rubbish, or she was tired of it? I could feel it, but it could be she got the word wrong. All of us had African names. *Jimoh* for me, Manus was *Yemi*, Connor *Yinka* – only our dad called us that any more. When we stepped out the door to go to school they switched our names and said, *By the way, you're Michael.* You had to get used to that being your name when they called the register and your mates called round for you to play. But Busola didn't change. She went on being Busola. You had to go round her. My mum said because she had a strong will. Only Nana could call her *Kathleen*, or *Kit*, or *Kitty*. But Busola gave my mum a hard time, even calling her *Alannah!* which all of us were when we fell over or got hurt. My dad said it was because they were just like each other. My mum said it was because she was like him, a daddy's girl, it was him who called her Busola. Anyway, she was changing now.

'Bush?' my mum said, looking at her.

'African,' she said. '*Backward.*'

'Where did you get that idea?' my mum said.

It turned out Busola was getting teased at school. Some of the girls asked if her dad had a tail on him from Africa. Could you see it coming out the back of his trousers?

'And what did you tell them?' my mum said, as if she knew it was going to be difficult.

'I said *he did*.'

Busola smirked and fell over backwards off the sofa on to the floor and rolled over trying to get her breath back. My mum pursed her lips. I could see but Busola couldn't, my mum wasn't trying to stop herself from laughing even though it was funny.

She was watching Busola roll around on the floor and her eyes were still.

Busola got her breath back and went on, 'I said *he did* –' but she lost it again and struggled. She took a deep breath, '... but it wasn't at the back of his trousers, *it was at the front!*'

I could have told her, *Please, Busola, stop!* but she wouldn't have heard me, she was arching over on her back. And then she did it in an Irish accent, '*It's at the front, not the back!*'

She got slapped. My mum reached out and bent down and slapped her hard on the side of the cheek, 'Wipe that smirk off your face!'

It was only when I felt the slap I got the shock of what it meant – *at the front* ... Everything stopped.

Busola sat up. 'You slapped me.'

'Oh God, no, I'm sorry!'

'You slapped me.'

For a week, longer, it was my mum begging and my sister getting revenge, 'You slapped me.'

'I won't do it again.'

'You slapped me.'

But then Busola got into one of my mum and dad's rows, when he went out slamming the door. I wasn't there and had to hear about it from Manus and Connor, but I could imagine it because I'd seen Busola get up my mum's nose with a finger and twist. She told my dad what our mum said when she was crying on the floor after a row, and he'd gone out. We were pretending it wasn't happening and she said we were siding with him, we were all *niggers!* and she was going to walk out on the lot of us. Because she'd lost it, and she wasn't allowed to, we all said, *Oh, Mum!* and waited for it to blow over. But Busola told him. He threw up his arms and stormed out. Without warning, my mum jumped on top of her, scratching Busola's face with her nails – they were short because she bit her fingernails like me – and said, 'You're-not-nice-to-know!'

There was trouble going on and my mum's sisters were in the kitchen boiling the kettle for tea and smoking cigarettes.

'Jesus, Bridie, he leads you a dog's life,' Tess said, and turned to Annie who was telling my mum to leave our dad and come with them. I wasn't sure if they were saying for us to come too, or where they thought we'd go.

'Excuse me,' everyone turned to Busola, 'that's my father you're talking about.'

'Oooh ... Aren't you the daughter?' But you could see in their eyes they hadn't seen us or thought we counted.

'Go on, go out and play!' my mum said, 'It's too steamy in here for you!'

It was raining, no one was going anywhere outside that teary, steamy, sob-filled, smoky kitchen with the teapot and the kettle on the boil.

'And if it goes on any more,' Busola said, 'I'm going to tell him what you've said.'

That stopped them. Annie mumbled about putting poison down for the rats. Tess swore she hadn't a thing to apologise to the dog's bollocks and flicked her ash at me, so I had to shut up and think about it.

But Busola wasn't finished, 'And what's more, that's your husband they're talking about. You've got to stop them!'

My mum went bright red.

'Jesus, Bridie, put a stop to that!' Annie said. 'Look how she's talking to you!' And she stood up to show she'd take her leg off and brain you if she wanted – she had a bad leg from falling over her husband down the stairs. 'The sheer, bloody mood on her!'

'And look at you,' Busola said, ignoring everyone except my mum, 'your eyes all red and puffy. You look like a lobster!'

My mum tried to quieten her down.

'You're just like them!' Busola said.

'I beg your pardon?' Tess was standing up to the row that was brewing by stubbing her fag out on the saucer.

'Drinkers!' said Busola, wrinkling her nose up.

'What's wrong with that?' said Tess. 'Sitting down to a cup of tea?'

But Busola was making for the door. She'd seen something I hadn't – before she could slam it my mum had her off-balance, holding tight on her wrist, 'You're so *common!*' She spat it out so Busola had to think about it a second. '*Aren't you?*'

That gave Tess and Annie the chance to laugh at Busola. But my mum opened her eyes wide and switched sides away from them. 'This is *my* marriage. His people don't want it, out there they don't like it, if my own people can't support me, they can go. Is that clear?' She was still holding Busola by the wrist and digging her nails in. '*You,*' she said, 'are *not* to come between me and your father.'

But that's what Busola did. She told him my mum spoke to the priest about a separation and my dad blew up and told her she could go back to her family. She got rid of my mum and we blamed her. Connor punched her in the playground and she tried to get him to punch her in front of our dad. When he wouldn't, she called him a coward and went on hunger strike saying he'd punched her in the stomach and she couldn't eat.

'Did you punch her?' my dad said.

'No.'

'Did you see it?' he asked me.

'No,' I said, in front of her, 'they ran into each other.'

'Yemi?'

Manus shrugged, 'I wasn't there.'

Busola could see we were all against her. She'd got rid of her mum but we hadn't told her she could get rid of ours. No wonder she couldn't eat. We felt like killing her. She was gonna have to change, or she was gonna have to starve. She was gonna have to go on drinking stale milk.

But then my dad spent money on tins of Fray Bentos pies and Ambrosia cream custard you couldn't get wrong if you followed the instructions. Big tins of it got passed round with a spoon until it was gone. It was a reward and she didn't deserve it. If my dad wasn't there, Manus was allowed to open it and Busola got none. It was a feast and she wasn't invited. But if he was, she forgot she had stomach ache and ate the custard out the tin. It was smooth and cold and creamy and delicious. It was almost as lovely as our mum, but she was warm.

'What you gonna do about it?' Manus said. The tin ran out and there was no more custard. We hadn't given her none. We'd given her the spoon to lick.

'I'm gonna make sure Daddy finds out you're on her side,' she said, licking the spoon handle. 'And I hope he kills you.'

She was tough, Busola. No one was gonna try and beat her up any more. She had all the power, she wasn't gonna give in. But she didn't have the power to bring our mum back.

My dad started making her do the washing-up. We were

running out of clothes and he was showing her how to wash them. She wasn't allowed to go out after school and she could feel him breathing down her neck frying eggs in the pan, she wasn't doing it right. She hadn't thought about that. She was gonna have to take our mum's place. She looked embarrassed when he told her to bring him his *gari*, which was like porridge in cold water with lemon juice. She squirted the whole of a plastic lemon in the bowl and he poured it down the sink with a disgusted look on his face. She'd bitten off more than she could chew, and we were satisfied. But he wasn't, 'Do it again.'

He made her walk with him up the market and carry shopping bags, which my mum made us do because we were boys and it was heavy lifting. He chose clothes for her that looked like they came off a jumble stall, I almost felt sorry for her having to try them on in front of us to see were they the right size. They weren't, they were too big. But he nodded and made her keep them. She tried to break the zips, but he warned her to take care of her clothes because there wasn't any more money. She started to look worn out, and her hair went wild because my mum wasn't combing out the knots. Then one day my dad took us round to the barber and made him cut off all our hair.

Busola thought she was coming along to get her own back and see us get our heads chopped, which was what happened when our hair got too big. But when we were finished he made her sit up in the chair and get her hair cut short with all of us looking on in the mirror. It fell off in big lumps on to her shoulders and on the floor and I could see all our faces staring in the mirror at what was going on. It was what Busola brought on herself, but getting her hair shaved by the barber wasn't funny. My mum did it with scissors and they spent hours looking at it, keeping the curls in the towel before washing her hair and saying about the little girl, *who had a little curl* ... Busola's hair was theirs, they loved it and they sang to it. The barber was a man from Cyprus with lots of *u*'s in his name and black hair growing up his cheeks and flowing off his arms, who chatted away to my dad and didn't seem to notice Busola while he was killing her.

I looked at Manus with his mouth open. Connor was frowning at her curls on the floor. My dad was trying to get a job lot price from the barber, and he was telling my dad where to get wallpaper cheap in East Street market. There was rain in Busola's eyes and her hair was falling.

'That's enough.' My dad looked at me. The barber looked up in the mirror, and I spoke to his reflection, 'That's how she likes it.'

The barber looked at my dad, who didn't react but then nodded, 'Just even up.'

Busola's face had changed. Her nose looked big and her eyes were bulging. They didn't have a great big bush of curly hair to hide them, there was only an inch left all round and she looked bald. She looked hard at herself in the mirror and said, 'I'm ugly.'

My dad didn't say anything, he watched Busola and glanced at me as he paid the barber whose hand was shaking as he lit up a cigarette. Manus and Connor weren't looking at anyone as we got out the shop. On the street, my dad gave Manus the keys to go home and said, 'Go on, I'm coming.'

We walked back on our own.

'It's your own fault,' Manus said as we turned the corner.

'My head feels cold,' said Connor.

'Your ear's bleeding,' I told Busola.

The barber had cut her and she hadn't said anything. She put her hand up and saw a bit of blood on it. 'I don't care,' she said, 'I don't feel it.' She'd made her choice and she was gonna stick to it. She was just like my mum.

'You look like a boy,' Connor said.

She stopped in the street as we walked on, and burst into tears.

My dad came home with fish and chips, full of salt and vinegar, and we wolfed them down with the paper soggy on the plates. Busola's eyes were like swollen wood, dark and wet. She looked around at everyone as though we couldn't see her, watching our mouths move as though there were words coming out. All we were doing was eating. My dad coughed and she looked at him as though he'd just said something. He picked up a bit of fish and ate it, careful not to see her staring as he put some on my plate. She was wearing a wig she got out my mum's wardrobe drawer. It was attached by a comb to the top of her head where it bunched up and wasn't the same as her hair, it was shiny black and came down the back of her neck in long twists.

'Your mother is coming to pick up her things,' my dad said.

Manus's mouth was full and he stopped chewing. Connor's jaw did a slow sideways move like he'd got something stuck in his teeth. I looked at Busola's wig and tried to remember my mum, but it wasn't really her and made my stomach feel empty even though it was full. Busola turned on me, 'What you looking at?'

My dad stood up from the table and left.

'You,' Connor said.

'Why don't you fuck off back to Liverpool?' That was what Connor said to her as we were cleaning the stairs with dustpans and brushes. The dust was swirling up and getting into my eyes and nose and up the back of my throat. 'Don't breathe it in,' Manus said when I showed him the black snot on my tissue. But I didn't know how not to breathe, it was hard kneeling on the stairs getting the dirt out.

'Top to bottom,' my dad said as he went out to get new curtains. It wasn't until Manus got the windows open we started to feel we were getting the house clean. The dust was really thick in the air and I could see we were all getting coated in it. Busola's wig was starting to go grey because she wouldn't take it off.

'You look ridiculous,' Manus told her. She whacked him hard on the back of the leg with her brush and I had to hold his leg to stop him kicking back down the stairs at her. Connor got hold of his arm from the top because Manus was gonna throw his brush at her, and we all slipped down the stairs together.

That's when Connor said she should go with our dad, 'It was all right till he came, you fuck off back with him!'

But Manus wasn't having that, 'You shut up!' he told Connor. They were gonna fight – Connor let go and stood up on the stairs, 'Make me!' But they didn't because the door knocked and Busola ran down to get it. It was Mr Adebisi and he'd come to help. He told us all to go and have a bath and put on clean clothes to get ready, he'd finish off the cleaning but we'd already done a good job.

Busola wouldn't have one with us because she said we were dirty and Mr Adebisi had to come and help her clean off the dark rings round the bath before she'd run a new one and get in it. He told her she shouldn't take the wig in because it would get wet and she'd get a cold and to leave it on the side. We left her to it and ran with our towels through the backyard up to the bedroom with Mr Adebisi helping us choose new clothes because our mum was coming.

'How is Busola missing her mummy?' He was putting his finger on my crossed laces so I could tie up the bows by myself. I looked up at Connor, and Connor looked at Manus. We didn't know how he knew what was up, but Mr Adebisi knew things just by feeling them.

'He started it,' Manus said looking at Connor. 'He told Daddy to go back to Liverpool.'

I didn't know that. Connor didn't say anything. He pulled his socks on like he was getting ready to kick someone and he wasn't gonna take it back.

Mr Adebisi looked at him. 'Yinka?' But Connor shook his head. 'Come on, let bygones be bygones. Your mother is coming. You don't want her to come?'

'Why does he have to shout?' Connor said.

Mr Adebisi took a deep breath and nodded and let it out. He sat back on the bed with his hand on the metal support and his head up against the springs of the top bunk, his face in shadow, and the metal frame creaked under his weight. He looked like he was in prison.

'He's angry, and he takes it out on us,' Connor was saying. Mr Adebisi's breathing was already calming it down. He nodded like he knew what Connor was saying and it wasn't just to get round him. His eyes went to Manus and he tilted his head to listen. 'And you?' he said.

Manus nodded.

'Tell me.'

'It's all on my shoulders,' he said. 'Just because I'm the eldest, I'm not old enough to stop it happening.'

'Don't worry.'

Manus shrugged, but his face was doing something different. He looked crushed.

Mr Adebisi leaned forward and gave me a hug, but his eyes were already moving on. He went over to Manus and picked him up and took Connor by the hand to the window, 'What do you see?'

I went up on my own and looked out at the backs of the houses, the bomb site and the top of the church over on the main road. I couldn't see what he was showing them and Manus's shoe banged against my ear, so I moved back.

'The backyards,' Connor said, and Manus just hugged Mr Adebisi round the neck.

'London town. In Liverpool your father was studying to go back home. He doesn't see any future here for him. He's doing this for you. And your mother can be near the hospital. That's a big, heavy something he's carrying for all of you, and he's shouting out. Help him.'

I crowded up to the window under Connor's arm, and saw someone opening a window across the way, an aeroplane going over, my own breath on the glass, and downstairs in the backyard Busola coming out the bathroom in a big towel, one hand holding up the wig slung over sideways on top of her head.

My dad was back and Mr Adebisi was helping him put up new curtains in the front room and bedrooms, banging in nails and cutting new wire. The curtains made my skin feel itchy so I left Manus and Connor holding them ready and went to look for Busola. She was combing her wig out in the bathroom mirror. I wasn't sure I should go in, so I stood with one foot out in the backyard and one against the door keeping it open.

'What d'you want?' she said, changing the way the wig was attached and combing it down long at the back.

I didn't know what to say, so I said, 'Did you know Connor told Daddy to go back to Liverpool?'

She looked at me, reached over and dragged me inside, shoving the door shut with the comb in her fist. 'Who you gonna go with?' she said.

It was too quick, she was holding the comb over me, I didn't want to get it wrong, and I didn't know what it meant, so I said, 'What about you?'

She pushed me away against the door and said, '*Coward!*'

I wasn't ready. It felt like I'd closed the door on my dad and shut out my mum, but no one properly asked me or told me what was going on, and they all knew. Why wasn't she telling me? I wanted to grab her hair and pull it out. I wasn't scared of her.

'You look ugly,' I said, 'I'm not going with you.'

She looked over her shoulder and flashed her eyes at me, 'You're not going anywhere, you've got to help me.'

'Why?'

She turned her back on me and looked in the mirror, passing the comb over her long twists.

'Make him get her back.'

There was a woman helping Mr Adebisi pack away things into a suitcase in the front room. I looked round the door and saw my dad watching from the sofa with Manus and Connor on one side of him but they weren't getting up to help, so I looked across at Mr Adebisi to see what he was doing. The woman was bending over the suitcase and the backs of her legs were fleshy with creases because she didn't have anything on them. She was tall on wobbly shoes and her skirt was up short over her bum. She stood up and I couldn't look, so I looked down. There were red shadows round her knees – I didn't know what my mum's knees looked like before, but I was looking at them. She was in a miniskirt on high heels, and her hair was bunched up on top in a twisting hairstyle so she looked taller, and she had white lipstick on with thick white eyelashes curling up. I didn't recognise her. But she'd come back.

'Who's that?' Busola said, coming in behind me.

My dad turned and said, 'That's your mother, look at her.'

She was lovely. She blinked at me as she sat down and I felt shy. She was dressed like that for him. But how was I going to get my mum back from being a stranger? I looked at Manus and Connor, they were stuck flat to the back of the sofa beside my dad. Not even their hands were moving. And their eyes were glued to her. She was sitting down the other side of them from my dad on the sofa and asking them how they were. Mr Adebisi was sitting on the floor in front of them. They couldn't get out. And they couldn't say anything.

'How have you been?'

They looked at my dad, they looked back at her, and they shook their heads. She had her arms tucked in and her hands over on her knees like she was trying to cover them up. My dad was picking his nose and flicking it over his shoulder like he didn't care. It was Busola was the one who had to say something.

'Busola,' my dad said, 'fetch me *gari*, and not too much water.'

'No,' she said, 'that's Mummy's job.'

He couldn't open his mouth before she shook the wig off her head, and held it out to my mum, 'Do you want this back?'

My mum looked away from Busola's cut-off hair down at her own bare knees. So did my dad.

'Look what they've done to me,' she said. And when my mum looked up, 'When you coming back?'

Mr Adebisi thought that was good, because it was in his eyes when he told my dad, 'Go there, take her things and come home.'

My dad wouldn't budge.

'Look at your children! It's not for fear of losing her that you can lose her for them– it's your wife, and the mother!'

'If she wants to go, she can go,' my dad said, 'I don't care.'

So it was all right, because she was ready to stay. But my mum didn't say anything. Then he spoilt it by saying, 'Go, they are your people, they don't want us. Look how they are treating you. They have nothing to cover them?'

My mum stood up quickly and stumbled on her shoes putting her bag over her shoulder and went to pick up the suitcase. I ran over and got on top of it, holding the handle so she couldn't lift it up, and looked at her. She was crying into her lashes, the strap of her shoulder bag fell off on to her wrist as she bent down. She picked me up but I didn't let go the handle. She tried to get my fingers off and I didn't let her. So she dropped her bag and I let go the suitcase to be in her arms.

'What's the matter?'

'I'm hungry,' I said.

'Isn't he feeding you?'

I shook my head and looked into her face, 'I want you.'

'*Sh*,' she said, rocking me in her arms. Manus and Connor were on the sofa looking at us like we were in a film. Busola was holding Mr Adebisi where he'd stood up to help my mum. My dad was sitting tight because it was all going on.

My mum put me down. 'I have to catch my bus,' she said.

Mr Adebisi put his hand in his pocket and threw his car keys on my dad's lap, 'You are driving her.'

Looking for Monkeys Up in the Zoo
(Je t'aime ... moi non plus)

The next day there were lots of cars and my mum came back. Everyone came, Nana and my aunts, some of the cousins and Tess's husband, Uncle Eamon, carrying the bags up to the bedroom. My mum was back in her normal clothes and looked fresh like she'd been having a good time. My dad was helping them bring things in from the cars. They had bottles of Guinness, egg-flip for Nana and lemonade that all went up into the front room, and Annie had some records to put on the radiogram. Tess got me first, 'While the cat's away, eh? What you been up to?' I was standing in the passageway out to the backyard, watching people go up and down the stairs to the front door. I got out her way as she went to the loo. 'I've got an eye in the back of my head for you,' she said, yanking open the back door in a hurry and leaving it ajar. I went over and bolted it shut and ran upstairs.

A strange man was upside down in the front room, standing on his head with his feet up against the wall. My mum was smiling at him from the sofa, looking shy with her hands on her lap and her feet crossed. I didn't like him, he was in the way, so I went to push him over but he was too heavy. He just looked up at me with the blood rushing to his red face and his jacket hanging down. My dad pulled me away and held me as the man pushed himself off the wall and stood up facing us. 'I had to do that,' he said.

'Then please, you are welcome,' my dad said. 'Sit down. I won't be long,' and my mum echoed him, making a space beside her and saying, '*Ejoko* ...' My dad rushed out the house taking Manus and Connor with him.

I was on my own. My mum was sitting with that man, I didn't know where Nana was, and Eileen and Carmel were fighting over what records to put on the radiogram. Barry was twisting open the lids on all the lemonade bottles so they fizzed up and squirted everywhere while his mum, Annie, was trying to stop him and light a cigarette at the same time. Uncle Eamon put his head round the door, 'Look at you, smoking in the rain, you'll get a cough.' Annie blew out her match and gave him a look as he said, 'Give us a drink.' She nodded at the bottles, 'Thirsty? Mine's a Guinness.' He looked over and said, 'Bridie, have you glasses?' My mum looked up and shrugged, 'Blind as a bat. Try in the kitchen, is Nana there?' Annie caught my eye, 'Go and get an opener.' I didn't move. 'Or I'll use my teeth on you,' she said, 'Barry, stop that!' Eileen shouted at Carmel, '*Oi!* You're putting your grubby fingers on it!' 'They're my records I'll have you know,' Annie said. 'Barry!' He was shaking the lemonade for extra fizz.

It was too much. I ran out and dodged into the bedroom and shut the door. Busola was sitting there in the bunk bed listening. Tess was out in the backyard banging and shouting up. We heard the bolt go and the back door open. 'What you doing?' Eamon said. 'It's a terrible long queue, you've to wait to get out of that toilet,' she said. 'I told you it was haunted,' he said, and they went in.

Busola looked at me. We didn't say anything. We heard Nana's voice in the kitchen – she'd wait till our dad got back before she'd drink anything. Maggie, our eldest grown-up cousin, was saying the kitchen was a mess and really dirty. Uncle Eamon was calling up the stairs to tell her get down on her knees then and clean it, and Tess was telling them *shush*. Maggie came out on the stairs and shouted up, '*Mum! Mum!*' But the radiogram came on with a breathy French song, and Tess passed our door saying, '*That's pure filth, get that off.*' It scratched and went quiet. Then there was a burst of laughter and it went on again.

'Don't be a coward, go in,' Busola said. 'It's your house.'

She had her wig on. She didn't have shoes and her toes were dirty. She was the one sitting there in the bottom bunk with her back to the wall, trying to hide.

'It's you,' I said. 'You're saying it's me – it's you.'

She gave a big sigh.

'Yeah,' she said.

We walked into the living room. They all had their shoes off and were dancing on the carpet to the end of that song. The carpet was clean. I cleaned it. There were spots of lemonade drying. My mum was still sitting down with that man.

'Who's that?' Busola said.

'That's your uncle, Gerry, say hello,' said Annie, going on dancing slowly so you couldn't see her limp.

'And who are you?' he said, sitting forward on the sofa.

Busola looked at him a long time and didn't answer. The music faded and the record span off into silence.

'She says her name's Kate. It's still Kate?' Tess asked.

Busola took off her wig and held it out so the comb came up

like a claw out the fur, 'No, it's like that,' she said, 'Kat.'

'Oh, she'll claw your eyes out!' said Annie.

'Ah, kitty cat,' Eileen said, reaching out to touch the wig. Busola whipped it away from her.

I liked the way Eileen and Carmel both moved back.

'Then everyone's to call you Kat,' my mum said. 'This is my brother, Gerry, and this is my daughter, Kat.'

'Why don't I know you?' Busola asked.

He looked at my mum who blinked at him with her hands folded and let him answer. 'That fella,' he said, and he pointed at me, 'saw me stand on my head. I've had my differences. Now I'm back on my feet.'

Busola looked at the wig, 'What changed?'

'Time changes things,' my mum said. 'We're back now.'

'Have you got children?' I asked, because they'd be cousins.

'No,' he said.

My mum cleared her throat, 'What do you want to do with that hair?'

Busola looked at her, and handed back the wig, 'You look after it.' Then she looked across at Gerry. 'I'm Kat,' she said, 'but my real name's Busola.'

My dad came back with whisky and crates of beer, cherryade which only Manus liked, more egg-flip, and fish and chips for everyone. I couldn't eat mine, I still felt shook up from everyone coming, so I held on to Nana's arm in the kitchen while she ate hers. There was music coming from the living room, and Busola was running with the girls up and down the stairs. The record changed and it was Chief Ebenezer Obey, one of my dad's Nigerian ones. Tess raised an eyebrow at Annie who was standing smoking by the sink. Annie listened, took a puff and made a long face. I looked at Nana who was having trouble with a bone in her teeth and not noticing. Uncle Eamon saw me and said, 'Are you listening?'

I nodded.

'If you're not eating, I'll have that!' And he grabbed my plate and pulled it to him.

'Leave that!' Nana said.

'When there's only bones, I will.'

Nana looked at me, 'You not eating?'

I shook my head.

'And when he's only bones,' he said, 'I'll finish the job!'

I didn't mind him eating my fish and chips, or tapping his foot loudly out of step to the music when he couldn't keep up with it going double-quick. He was fierce but he was keeping Tess and Annie quiet and making Nana laugh as he grinned over a bad chip and chucked it on her plate, 'That's for you!'

'Go on,' Nana said, knocking the side of my ribs with her elbow, 'see if they're finished in there.'

My mum and dad were dancing to the music, going down really low and lifting each other up again. Manus and Connor and Barry were on the sofa with their plates empty on their laps and their mouths open watching Gerry doing a mad dance of his own in front of the window. Maggie was looking at the album cover by the radiogram where she'd taken over, 'Funny music, in't it?' But no one listened to what she was saying. Carmel came in behind me and looked round the room. 'Can you wiggle your bum like that?' she said. I looked at her, because the last time I saw her she didn't say two words to me. 'No,' I said, 'you have to be a girl.' I looked over her shoulder for Busola, but my eyes dropped when I heard her down in the hall with Eileen and remembered she was calling herself Kat. 'Your mum's nice.' I looked at Carmel again, and felt jealous she'd had my mum off me. But it wasn't her fault and she'd brought her back. 'So's your dad,' I said. She looked at me. Her face was soft and white like bread and anything you'd say could hurt and leave a mark because she took it all in and her eyes were half closed trying to stop it. She looked at me from a long way away, seeing who I was, and then suddenly switched off and turned away and I could feel it was me who wasn't being nice to her. I felt a pang about pushing her away. 'Do you want to dance?' I said. She turned and looked back at me as I bobbed up and down. 'No,' she said, 'dance with Uncle Gerry,' and went down the half-stairs to the kitchen.

'Come and join us,' my mum said, holding her hand out. It was the first time she'd noticed me and my knees locked so I couldn't bob any more. She went and forgot about me. I was gonna fall over because my legs couldn't move from pulling in different directions, and I wasn't strong enough to keep my balance. Connor called out from the sofa, 'He can't dance.' My dad came over and picked me up. I hung on to his neck and buried my face in his shoulder while he swayed. 'What's the matter?' my mum said, putting her hand on my back, but it was too late, the music ended and Maggie took the record off. I clung on to my dad. He was still swaying, and she said, 'Give him to me.' I wouldn't let go as he tried to take my arm off his neck. 'Come on,' she said. 'This one's for you, Gerry,' Maggie laughed. He was collapsed in a heap on the floor, his back against the wall by the windows. '*The British Army*,' she said. '*Oh no*, not that!' my mum said.

Maggie giggled and put it on. It was The Dubliners, and it went straight into singing about monkeys up in the zoo. Gerry sprang up and did a madder dance with his knees up, stomping round like he was gonna break the floorboards. My dad got out the way and gave me to my mum, and everyone pulled their legs up on to the sofa. Maggie was bobbing her head by the radiogram and my dad stuck his knees up in the air and ducked down and went mad as well. He was stomping round, linking arms with Gerry so the two of them were turning in the room like giants smashing everything in the way. '*Ouch*,' my mum said, because I was grabbing her too tight, 'Mind those bottles, you'll knock the table over!' Busola and Eileen stuck their heads round the door, with the needle scratching and jumping on the record, pushing each other to go in. 'Go on, now, the two of you,' my mum said, 'out the way.' She carried me out and into the bedroom, closing the door as the music ended with a big crash like everyone had jumped on the floor at once and sent the bottles flying.

There were scurries outside as my dad sent Busola for the dustpan and brush, and the next song came on like it was spreading ripples softly over everything and letting you breathe. My mum was listening as she sat down with me on Manus's bed and gave me a hug. She smelt like the fat roses up by the houses on Kennington Lane.

'Mum,' I said.

'Yes?'

I shook my head because I didn't have anything to say. She put her nose up under mine and lifted my head so she could see me. I looked into her eyes and started sobbing.

'*Alannah, alannah!*' She hugged me tight, 'Don't cry, I'm back.'

People were going up and down past the door so I held it

down as she rocked me and rubbed my back. But then it burst out again and my whole face was wet with feeling stupid. I could feel my chin wobbling and pushed in to her to get warm. She let me for a while, until I calmed down, and then she wiped my face with her hand and said, 'Have you had something to eat?'

I looked up and her eyes were different colours of sky. I touched her face and her skin was warm, it was like Carmel's, like milk. She had Nana's high forehead and her hair was brushed back and shiny in the light from the window. I grabbed her jaw and squeezed. She took hold of my hand and kissed it, but then I felt trapped so I pulled it away.

'Was it Daddy's fault?'

'*Sh*,' she said. 'No one's. It just happens.'

'Was it Kat?'

My mum shook her head, 'She'll tell us herself what her name is. It'll all be fine.'

'What if it happens again?' I said.

'I've just got back. You can't be pushing me out the door.'

I had to smile, but I couldn't let her put me off. 'I want to come with you,' I said.

'It won't happen. I'm not going anywhere.'

It must have looked like I couldn't see that far in the future, because she said, 'Look at my wedding ring,' and held it up to the light. 'I'll never take that off. He'll have to pull the house down on top and bury me in it. I'm staying.'

She sounded like Kat.

'What makes – ?'

I stopped because they were pushing Nana up the stairs past the landing to the front room to get her to dance and she was saying she wasn't ready. Uncle Eamon was saying she was too old to be standing on the shelf.

'Who's Gerry?' I said.

'Uncle Gerry to you,' and she blinked at me. 'That's a long story and we'll leave it for another time. Now, are you ready?'

I didn't want to go, but I nodded.

She put me off her lap and said, 'Stand there, let me see you. Are you presentable?'

I took a deep breath, and she wiped my chin with the back of her hand.

Everyone was singing while my dad danced with Nana round the room. It was late and people were drinking Guinness. Gerry called it the blonde lady in the black skirts, telling the story of what happened to their uncle in New York who got taken in by the Salvation Army and ended up dying with a few pennies tucked away, only for a woman who wasn't there when he was drinking himself to death to come and take it all. My aunts shouted him down saying he'd got it wrong, but then they were all singing *her hair hung over her shoulder, tied up with a black velvet band* for Nana, and it was connected but I wasn't sure how, except they were drinking and I could see the woman standing there when they sang *her eyes they shone like diamonds*. Nana reached up and gave my dad a kiss on the cheek and sat down. Then it was my mum's turn to sing with Busola sitting on her lap and everyone looking to see what would happen after she stopped trying to say she wasn't going to. She turned and praised my dad, she said he was handsome and an education. And she thanked him for it. She hadn't expected this in her life. She was going to hold on to it with all her strength, but would he leave off telling himself she was older than she was?

I hadn't thought about my mum being old before. I didn't know how old she was. She'd always been there. 'You're young till you aren't,' Tess said, 'come on, give us a song.'

'Will you sing it with me?' my mum said to Busola. Only she was talking to Kat because that's who squirmed in her lap and tried to slide off, but my mum wouldn't let her.

'Jaysus, will you look at that,' Uncle Eamon said. 'You'd think the holy water touched her.' He shook his fist under her chin, 'You'll sing or I'll murder you with this!'

It was Kat who started, and my mum joined in. They sang and my dad filled everyone's glass. Nana had her egg-flip and she joined in, swaying her glass from side to side. And by the end Maggie and Tess and Annie and Eileen were singing as well, *A mother's love's a blessing*, with Tess looking tough at me for the bit that went *Keep her while you've got her, you'll miss her when she's gone* ... I was watching Busola, looking down at the floor under her dark eyelashes. They all had the words a bit different and were spilling over each other, but Busola wasn't listening to them, she wasn't even really singing any more, she was leaning back against my mum and talking to herself ... *For you'll never miss a mother's love till she's buried beneath the clay.*

It ended and a cheer went up and a mood came down that something was missing. Uncle Eamon leaned into the middle and cupped his ear, 'What were you singing?' Busola looked up, and shook her head. 'If you could remember the words, you could put a tune to it,' he said. Tess slapped him on the arm, 'Bit less of your lip.' I could see Busola keeping still – I thought she was going to say something, but she didn't. 'No, I've a question,' he said, 'for Kat. Did you choose those curtains?' They were drawn closed across one window and pulled open from the other one to let in the air. Everyone started laughing, and didn't stop. 'Did you?' I didn't know what they were laughing about. The only people not laughing were me and Busola and my dad. Annie came off her chair and went down on one knee for breath. My mum was laughing with a hand up shielding her eyes, and Manus was hiding his face behind Barry's back who was laughing because everyone else was. 'They make your skin itch,' Connor said when I shook my head at him. '*Fibreglass*,' said Annie, trying to get back up on the chair and slipping and falling over. The laughing went on again. Nana wiped her eyes behind her glasses, holding her egg-flip up in one hand until Maggie took it off her to stop it spilling. 'It's the same colour as this, in't it?' Maggie said, making a face at the sticky yellow as she put the glass on the table. Nana went into a coughing fit and my mum started patting her on the back then thumping it. 'You could choke on the custard,' Uncle Eamon said, stirring it up all over again. I looked at my dad, he wasn't saying anything but it was the way he had his face tilted up, he wasn't pleased. '*Arrah*, I've seen worse on a skirt,' Gerry said, 'but at least it's up over their heads.' There was a pause, and Annie said, 'What would you know?' The laughter changed and ran through them like they were shocked at what she'd said. I looked at the curtains again, they were made from material that crackled when you touched it. But I didn't see how that could make people laugh. '*Slow down*,' Tess said, 'there's children about.' Carmel was frowning, so it wasn't just me. Eileen had gone back to sorting through the records and looked up, she didn't get it either. Eamon raised his glass, 'Ah, it's only a bit fun,' he said. 'Curtains to die for,' and he looked at my dad. 'Did you dye them that colour?'

'You're just being rude,' Busola said, and she was looking at Uncle Eamon. 'And I don't like the way you touch me.'

Suddenly the room was empty and everyone was gone. My mum and dad were downstairs seeing them off into the street, with the windows and doors open so I could hear the voices outside. Just me and Busola were left with the drinks on the table and on the radiogram and beside the chairs, so we were quickly tasting them all. The egg-flip was sticky and sweet, but had a strong smell of paint so I left it. When I put my tongue in the Guinness it was horrible, like licking the end of a battery, and I said, '*Eaeuch!*' Busola looked up at me with a glass of whisky and giggled, 'If you don't like it, don't drink it.'

'Is your name really Kat?' I was thinking how easily she could break up the evening. It was like she'd got a stick to an ants' nest and you could see them all running about trying to fix it – but you'd have to drop the stick and move back. She didn't, she sat up on my mum's knee and looked at everyone. No one told her off, but it could have gone really wrong. Carmel said she was tired and wanted to go home. Tess and Nana were out the door putting on their coats, and Connor had to run after them with Nana's hat. Manus helped Maggie and Eileen with Barry and sorting the records, while my dad shook Gerry's hand and Annie went out to the toilet. Uncle Eamon went down carrying Carmel half asleep in his arms, then my mum got up from holding Busola and threw back the curtains and opened wide the windows. The night air came into the room and smoke started clearing in the draught. I could smell rain outside and the stale smell of beer. My mum went downstairs with my dad and Gerry, and everyone was out in the street.

'It really is,' she said.

'What do you want me to call you?'

She took another sip of the whisky, and cleaned her teeth with her tongue. 'Call me Kat.'

'Who's that?'

'Try the whisky,' she said, 'it's nice.'

'You'll get drunk,' I said.

And she laughed.

One by one the cars started up, and I had a quick go at the beer. It was stale, so I spat it back in the glass and shook my head. Connor came in and saw me, 'Don't let him catch you.' And he looked at Kat, 'What d'you do that for?'

'She doesn't need them,' she said, 'she's got us.'

'You think you're clever.'

'You don't have him touching your bum.'

'Why does he do that?' I said, and they both looked at me.

'Because he thinks he can,' Kat said.

'You're making it up,' said Connor.

She just looked at him.

'Why d'you have to spoil everything?'

She didn't answer, she just tilted her head sideways and waited. 'See?' she said. 'You don't wanna know.'

I didn't want him to punch her so I moved in the way. He saw me but he was listening to my mum and dad calling goodnight on the street and the cars going.

'They don't come for us,' she said. 'Let 'em go to the pub and get drunk.'

His eyes came back from the window, 'What about Nana?'

'She can come on her own.'

Manus came in and put a finger to his lips, 'No one say

anything.' The front door clunked shut downstairs. 'Look like you're tidying so we can go to bed.'

I could hear my mum and dad moving about. They were clearing, going up and down to the kitchen, and taking empty bottles out the back to the bins. From the bottom bunk I could hear Manus and Connor breathing but I couldn't hear Kat, so I poked my foot up against the springs, 'You awake?'

'No,' she said, leaning over the top.

'*Sh.*' It was Connor.

'Shut up,' Manus said, '*listen.*'

I locked my ears into the sounds from the front room. They'd stopped what they were doing. She was crying, he was asking questions. I couldn't hear what he was saying. Manus got up and stuck his shoulder into the corner by the door so he could hang his head down and listen like my mum when she was worried. I got up and put my ear down to the gap under the door where light was coming in from the landing. Kat scrambled down the ladder and put her arms round Manus's middle. Her ear moved to the keyhole. Connor sat up on the edge of his bed and told me to stop breathing. We all listened.

'*They'll close their doors.*' It was my mum. I thought of the car doors slamming again.

'*They are your people?*' His voice was on her side, telling her what to do. '*You have to keep them.*'

'*How can I?*'

There was a pause as the front door banged opened downstairs, and voices of a man and a woman came into the hall. It was Mr Ajani but I didn't know who the woman was. They went talking into the back room, then the front-room door swung open and I saw my dad's shoes on the landing. We all made a big noise stampeding back into bed. He didn't come in, he just called out, *'Go to sleep.'* The front-room door closed shut behind him and it went quiet until the music went on and then got turned down low. It was their song, the one they played and danced to themselves, *Don't forget who's taking you home, and in whose arms you're gonna be ...*

'They make me sick,' Connor said.

'Who asked you?' said Manus.

'Did you smoke a cigarette?' Kat said.

'No,' said Connor.

'I did, with Eileen in the bathroom,' she said.

'And I had beer and cherryade with Barry,' Manus said.

'And I drank the Guinness,' I said, 'and the beer. And Kat had the whisky.'

'You shut up,' she said.

'Who's Kat?' It was Manus, and she didn't answer.

I pushed my foot up against her back on the top bunk but she didn't move.

'Who you gonna be?' Connor said.

She turned over in the bunk, and I could hear her taking a deep breath. 'I'm Kat,' she said. 'I'm Kat outside, and Busola inside.'

There was a grumpy snort from Manus.

No one said anything. I could hear the music going on quietly, *Oh darling, save the last dance for me ...*

Manus shook in his sleep and half woke up, *'What's that?'* But he sighed and carried on sleeping.

'Drunk,' said Kat. 'Better not tell Daddy.'

Connor turned over in his bed, 'You will anyway.'

'Why don't you run away?' she said.

He didn't move, I could feel my heart beating fast but he pulled the covers over his shoulder with his back to us, 'You fuck off back to Liverpool.'

My face was hot and I felt shaky. The sheets hadn't been changed for a long time and felt grubby. There wasn't any air under the blankets so I got up out the bed and went over and held open the curtain on the window. The moon was up over the backyards, clear of the rain and bright, with clouds going across, dark in the middle and silver at the edges. I put my forehead on the cold glass to cool down and looked into the backyard where a light was on in the downstairs kitchen, then went off. I pulled my head back because I'd forgotten the curtain was itchy on the side of my face, making my eye sore and sticky. Manus was snoring and Connor's back was silver in the moonlight with the sheet folded over the blanket. I took my hand away and let the curtain close, feeling my way back to bed. I listened for my mum and dad but I couldn't hear them, the music had stopped. I heard laughter downstairs. Then it went quiet. I got in the sheets and covered up, trying not to shiver. Busola turned over in the top bunk.

'Anyway, you can't split 'em up,' she said. 'I've tried.'

Sunday, Sunday

'What you reading?'

Marie looked up and moved her hair back over her ear with a finger from where it was falling from her face to the page. The strands were long and black, and catching light from the tall window up to the top landing. The stairs were where she went to be by herself, but she let me sit beside her if I kept quiet. I wasn't supposed to speak, but I could see she was coming out of the dreamy spell when only her lips moved, with the one finger she used to curl over and turn the pages.

'*The Count of Monte Cristo*,' she said. She was older than me, she knew how to read really well. I could see the words but they weren't real like the streaks of light in her hair or the pale skin where the hair parted in the middle. Her wrists were long and skinny and so were her fingers, when she pointed at something on the page it felt like she was there and happy in what she was reading. I didn't want her to stop. 'Look and see if it's clear.'

I scrambled down the stairs and looked over the banister to the hall and scrambled back up to tell her there was no one and she could run down without being seen.

I sat up on my own after she'd gone and thought about her. The dust was still swirling from where she'd stood to run back to her room at the bottom, the book under her arm and her hair swaying from the awkward way she stepped from side to side going down the stairs like she wasn't used to how long her legs were growing. I could smell the soap she used and feel the warm patch on the carpet where she'd been sitting. *The Count of Monte Cristo* sounded like numbers and reading at the same time, I wanted to be able to see what she was thinking and what was making her face look so still and her breathing soft.

It was Sunday morning and everyone was having baths, only I hadn't had mine because I'd been sweeping the top stairs down to the front room. Busola said I had to do that landing too, but that was her job, she had to do it along with the front room and the bedroom on that floor. My mum told her to jump in the bath because they were going to church and Busola dropped her brush and ran, so I had to do it when my dad came and shouted at me and I was fuming. By the time I finished, Marie and her dad were going to the bathroom and I felt sticky and dirty and had to wait as he waved his soap at me in the hall. He was tall and gangly and looked like a gangster in the films with hairy arms and shoulders in a white vest tucked in to high-waisted trousers. Even his toes were hairy in his flip-flops. Everyone thought he was handsome, my mum said it to Marie's mum, but he had a lot of hair and it flopped over on one side of his head where he combed it to a point. It was thick and glossy and black, and made the smile of his teeth look really white as he waved at me with his head leaned over on the same side as his hair. I wasn't sure if he kept his head down because he was shy or because he was too tall for the doors. But when he was drinking he lifted up his voice and his arms and told stories and argued with people who weren't even there.

Marie said he was West Indian from Guyana and I knew her mum was Irish like mine, but he got on with my dad and my mum liked him except when she went down because he'd stormed out and left them, and my mum had to talk them out of packing up and going as well and not telling him. 'He'll rue the day he'll look and ye're out of his reach,' she said, 'but leave it to God.' Marie's mum cried a lot and so did Marie. Their room had boxes piled up against the walls and wardrobes and they sat on the bed crying because there wasn't much room to move. My mum cried too when they killed Bobby Kennedy, sitting on the bed with Marie's mum, but a man came round with framed photographs of the three Kennedy brothers smiling and one got hung up in the room in a gap between the boxes. We had one too, so it was always smiles and tears when I thought about Marie's mum being married to Jimmy Singh and my mum talking about the sacrifices you had to make to be with a man you loved.

When Manus put his head round the stairs and said it was our turn to have a bath, I told him to go first and Connor because I was still on the top stair sulking. I knew it was going to be lukewarm and have dirty rings round it after them, but it served my mum right if I turned out dirty because she shouldn't have let Busola get away with just running off. But that's when Marie came up – her mum had gone to church without her.

'Can I stay here and read?' she said.

It was only my stairs because I'd swept them, but it made me feel good that I could move out the way and let her sit where it was clean.

'Can I stay with you?'

She nodded and sat down two steps where the light could fall on to the book, and I sat beside her.

'What's that?' I said, but she put her long finger to her lips and started reading. I could have waited until the bath went cold with her reading and hooking her hair back behind her ear and the strands falling one by one slowly back on to the page.

'I'm going to get my revenge,' she said, shutting the book when I told her it was clear to go down. And that's how she flew downstairs, with her hair swaying from side to side.

Tunde came again with his dad. It woke me up from thinking about Marie. I heard the front door and my dad called out from the front room, '*Answer the door!*' I just listened and let Connor come out the bedroom and go downstairs to get it. I thought I could quickly go down and get in the bedroom, but my dad came out and saw me on the stairs and frowned. I still had my dirty clothes on and he told me, 'Go and wash.' Tunde and his dad were on the stairs with Connor coming up behind them so I stood back in the bedroom doorway to let them pass. Mr Lawal came up on to the landing with a suitcase and did a stoop to kneel to my dad and Tunde came up after without looking at me and went past to follow them into the front room. He was younger than me and dressed in Nigerian clothes with a hat that was too big for his head and sleeves that covered his hands so he had to keep folding them back on to his arms. He had a watch on his wrist. He looked weighed down and it served him right. Connor was trying to push past me to get in the bedroom out the way and finish dressing. My dad leaned out the front room again before he could get away and said, 'Yinka, bring beer,' so he had to turn back and go to the kitchen. Then my dad looked at me and said, 'What are you still doing? Go and bath!'

The water was cold and all the towels were damp. I put my hand in and swirled it round and the black marks stayed stuck to the side, so I pulled out the plug and sat down on the towels. They left the bath in so I'd have to clean it up. I always had to do everything. Florence and Mr Babalola weren't even up yet, and I didn't know where Mr Ajani and the others were, so it was just me cleaning up for everyone else and watching the flat, soapy grey water sink down in the bath. Marie said I could look at her books when she wasn't reading them, but I couldn't go and get them because I wasn't allowed in her room. Only my mum could go in, and I had to try and follow her, but then she told me, 'Don't touch anything.'

The whirlpool was starting to form over the plughole. I tried to put my finger in without it touching the sides. There was one book with a picture of the Three Musketeers looking like a fairy story with hats and curly feathers and buckled shoes, but I couldn't turn over the page to see what was next because Marie was in there looking at it and closed its cover on the bed. My mum was marking the rent in a book and Marie's mum was counting money out of a small bag and saying she'd get the rest back off Marie's dad as soon as she could, and they set off talking again. Marie wasn't letting me see what was in the book, she was twisting a strand of her hair in both hands with her long feet poking off the edge of the bed and frowning. 'Can I look?' I said, and she shook her head looking angry. It wasn't even at me, it was at her mum saying it wasn't her dad, it was those other fellas, he'd got in with a bad crowd, an Indian fella and a black fella, they were leading him astray, and there wasn't room for drink and a family, he'd have to stay out, but he'll lose that job, then where would they be if she hadn't her own little trickle of money coming in, out of time and out on the street for the price of her own self-respect and stupidity. 'Soonest mended,' my mum said, because when she looked up from the rent book she saw us. Marie was scowling and her eyes were wet to the brim, angry and lit up. The look changed suddenly and she kicked my hand off the bed where I was leaning like she was blaming me.

The door banged on the latch and made me jump. The bath water had run out and it was Mr Babalola trying to get in, '*Ah! Everybody's at home? How long now?*' He knew it was me and I could hear Florence in the background talking up to someone in the top kitchen from the backyard, so I said, 'Out in a minute! Just rinsing!' There wasn't time for a bath so I got undressed and cleaned the tub from the inside, crouching down and splashing some water over me and using one of the damp towels to dry off. There was lots of water on the floor, so I put another towel down to wipe it up and got dressed again in my old clothes. 'Coming!' I said, and undid the latch and swung the door open. There was no one there, so I let it bang shut and quickly cleared the towels up in case they complained and I got in trouble.

'Take your time,' Florence said as I got in from the backyard. She was sitting in the downstairs kitchen with the door open, and Mr Babalola in his pyjama bottoms and vest boiling a pot of water for breakfast. My mum said they weren't married, but they looked like they were. He smiled at me and flicked water from the wooden spoon he was holding under the tap, because that's what he did when he wanted your attention. It got me in the face and dripped down my front. 'Number one, *omi ko l'ota*, you can't fear water,' he said. 'Number two, godliness will go together with cleanliness. Number three, how are you this morning? Number four, greet your mother for me.' I bowed down and was going to go when Florence said something to him in Yoruba and he shushed her. I wasn't sure about her, sometimes she was nice, when my dad was there, but sometimes she said things and you couldn't tell what she was saying, even in English. My mum watched her and didn't ever say anything. Florence laughed and bit down on her chewstick, using both hands to fold her wrapper up under her arms. 'Don't mind her,' Mr Babalola said, banging his wooden spoon down on the edge of the pot of boiling water, 'she's just jealous.' She waved the stick out at me in one hand then clenched it back between her front teeth and smiled, 'You can go.'

I had to get changed, my skin felt itchy. Upstairs in the bedroom Manus was going through my mum and dad's things in their drawers and listening to the voices in the front room. Mr Lawal was being loud, telling my dad a long story that he wanted Tunde to come and stay with us again. *'He can clean! You can clean, abi?'* Manus was looking at my mum's jewellery, holding it up to the light. One of us had to go and sit with Tunde while my dad and Mr Lawal were talking and I didn't want it to be me, so I didn't say anything. I got open our drawers and got out clean clothes. They smelled of mothballs as I put them on the bed. Connor was already there in the front room with them, I could tell from the way Manus was keeping quiet and ignoring me and not getting dressed properly. 'What d'you think of these?' I looked round at Manus standing up on my mum's high-heel shoes, his face set like he was going down a steep slide and he didn't care what happened when he hit the bottom. He looked tall and bossy, so I ignored him and got undressed and put on the new clothes thinking I could get out quickly to the backyard to see if Marie got let out. But Manus jumped out the shoes and up on the bed in his underpants and jabbed his finger at me, 'You're gonna have to squash up with him!'

I didn't want Tunde to stay, there wasn't room. Now there was rain coming in to the big room upstairs, our bedroom was my mum and dad's, and we were squashed up to sleep in the front room, so he'd be in there with us and no one liked him. *'Just one, two, three weeks, I will come!'* Mr Lawal's voice was growly, the words exploded out of his chest in English and sounded like they were laughing everything off in Yoruba. I didn't like him. He always dressed in smart English clothes, with dark glasses and a big parting in his hair that looked like two cliffs wedged into his head. My mum said he was a playboy, he didn't want to look after Tunde because he was too busy running around. He talked a lot when he wanted everyone to be on his side, but then he sat around being silent and moody. I did like him though when he smiled, he looked like a shark and he knew it, and he'd do it for you and you wouldn't let him near you, even though he always kept his teeth together to keep you on edge. I felt sorry for Tunde when he came because he lost his mum in Nigeria. He didn't know where he was, he only knew us. On the first day he went round the back of the television set to see where the man was, and kept wanting to play with the ice cubes in the fridge. He was all right until we realised he was staying and he wet the bed. He couldn't really speak English until we started teaching him *Bob's yer uncle* and *cor blimey* and *thingamajig*, but my dad said no swear words, and then without anyone saying it he started *fuckin' this* and *fuckin' that* and smiling that he could get us in trouble. *Slag! Shit-'ole! Cunt!*

It started coming out, but he couldn't say everything. *Wakka!* 'What?' *Wakka!*

I didn't like the way he kept following my mum around. We had to share our food but he kept picking bits off the side of our plates with his hands and he didn't know how to use a knife and fork. Once, when we were all using our hands to have *eba* and *okra* with tripe and cow's foot from shared plates, he picked his nose and put it on his side of the *eba* to stop us taking it, he sucked up the pepper off the tripe and put it back, and that meant we couldn't eat any more, but he denied it when my dad came in and made us finish the leftovers. He made it so you couldn't like him. And his dad kept not turning up, so even his dad didn't like him. Connor kicked him playing football when he kept getting in the way to stop the game, but that left a bruise and my dad whacked Connor on the bottom for it. So we started spitting in his milk, but he didn't care, he still drank it. '*For God's sake, are ye animals?!*' my mum said. She found out what was going on when me and Busola pushed him off the bunk bed and he went head first into the potty she put there for him to use. He came up crying with the pee dripping down and the potty covering his head, so when my mum heard the bang and came in she found us laughing from the top bunk at the way the sound was muffled. She lifted it off and some blood started to drip down his forehead. '*He's someone's child!*' She slapped me hard and that frightened me. Busola said it was his fault for pinching us and my mum picked him up and hugged him and kissed his head to get him quiet and searched his hair for the cut. He clung on to her with his arms and legs and I stopped and held my breath at the thought he wanted her, she kept him alive, and it was my fault he nearly died, and that I was afraid of him and hated him at the same time.

But it all changed when Mr Lawal turned up with a woman in tall blonde hair who was nice but nervous and smoked all the time with two fingers missing under the two she held the cigarette in. I asked her what happened to them and she said she lost them in a factory she was working in but she got the money and Sunday was going to live with them in their place – Tunde's English name was Sunday. My mum was friendly and chatted to her a long time, but I never saw her again. Tunde left and didn't say goodbye to any of us, only my mum, and his dad was being moody. But now they were back again and the woman wasn't around.

We heard the front-room door open and Manus jumped down off the bed. We held our breath, hoping they'd go past to the kitchen or downstairs, but the bedroom door swung open and I started pulling on my socks. Connor looked round, holding the door handle, and said to Manus, 'You have to get dressed. Daddy wants us to take Sunday down the park.' Manus made a face like it was Connor's fault for dragging him into it and he should have kept quiet. Connor shrugged and said, 'They're going to send him back to Nigeria.'

'*Yemi!*' It was my dad calling Manus from the front room. 'Yes, Daddy!' He started grabbing his top and pulling it over his head and trying to step into his trousers but tripping up on them. '*Yemi, come here!*' Manus did a hop to get his legs in and move towards the door, and tucked his top into his waistband by stretching up on tiptoes in his bare feet and pushing it down inside, 'Coming!' Connor moved out the way for him and looked at me and put his finger to his lips. Just then, Tunde squeezed past Connor and stood inside the bedroom. He looked like he was trying to find my mum, his eyes didn't even see me. '*Ah, there you are!*' my dad said, and switched back to Yoruba to speak to Mr Lawal. I gave Tunde a nod by lifting my head up and his eyes focused on me. He was smaller than I remembered, and more frightened. Connor turned and went back into the front room leaving the doors open, so I could hear my dad say, '*Eh-heh, they are all getting big. As you can see, there's no much room.*' He wasn't going to let Tunde stay. '*Ni ile Baba mi, now,*' and I could hear Mr Lawal was still pleading. Tunde blinked and his eyes flicked round the bedroom like he was trapped into listening. His hands had disappeared under his sleeves and he looked wrapped up like he was already back in Nigeria and there was no one to take him in. 'Wotcha,' I said, and he looked at me once more with almost black eyes like I wasn't there and darted back into the front room.

I slipped on my other sock and got in my sandals and crept out and down the stairs to get away. At the bottom, Marie's door was shut but I could hear them moving about and the bed creaking. I didn't feel I could knock, so I coughed by the keyhole and said, 'I'm going out the backyard,' loud enough for her to hear but not so it would go upstairs.

I waited outside by the back door a long time and no one came. The sun was warm and the backyard was full of flies from the bins round the back, lazy and buzzing off the walls and the concrete. They looked fat and blue or green, with brown blunt heads and black hairy bodies, wiping themselves down in front and kicking up their legs behind to clean under their wings. I couldn't stop myself doing it even though I felt it was wrong, but I picked up one of the wooden scrubbing brushes by the buckets and started squashing them down hard where they were thickest by the drain. The bristles made a spongy thwack on the ground as I flicked the brush quickly before they could get away, and even though they lifted off and started to make a louder buzzing sound, they settled again, and there were always more that didn't seem able to move. Soon there were little squashes of brown blood dotted all over the backyard and up the walls by the drainpipes. It was only that my wrist started to ache that I slowed down to do them one at a time and look at their squashed bodies with sometimes a wing waving out from the mush. I picked a wing off and held it up close to my nose. It was so small and see-through and brightly coloured that when it blew away I started only to do the bluebottles. They knew I was coming and kept hopping out of reach so I had to creep up on them. I got one on the bathroom step and the latch opened and Mr Babalola's face looked down at me from inside the door. He didn't say anything, but he'd caught me red-handed and looked at my brush and closed the door again. I put the brush behind my back and moved off to sit on the upturned metal bucket my mum put over the red rock by the backyard wall, only bringing the brush out if a bluebottle came in reach, but they knew it was there and flew off as soon as I started to move my elbow.

Marie came out and looked at me. She didn't see what I was doing, so I dropped the brush behind me and pretended I was just sitting there, even though it made a clatter on the side of the bucket. She moved a broken stool with a wobbly leg over beside me and wedged it up against the wall and wiped the seat with her hand and sat down.

'What do you want?'

I wanted to rescue her, but I didn't know how, so I said, 'Let me look at your books?' It wasn't meant to but it sounded like a question.

'I did,' she said. 'I let you read over my shoulder.'

I shrugged, 'I can't read that fast.'

She looked at me like I was smaller than she thought, 'You should.'

We didn't say anything for a bit. I got worried she'd start to see all the flies I'd done, the black, red-brown splodges everywhere on the ground and some on the walls. I got ready for it, that she wasn't going to like me. I spoke to try and put it off, and because I didn't know why I'd done it.

'What's revenge?'

'I'm going to get lots of money.' That's what she said. 'And I won't have to live in your house. I'll have my own house. And then anyone who wants to come in will have to ask me.'

I thought about it, and wasn't sure. It felt like she was talking about being a grown-up, so I said, 'You gonna grow up?'

'No,' she said, 'I'm going to be rich and I'm not going to be shut up. I'm not going to depend on you to get upstairs and read my book. I'm not even going to let my mum and dad in if I don't want.' She made a frowning look with her eyebrows that were thick and black over the pale skin. I noticed the hairs in between them where her skin was rumpled. She had no freckles, so when she didn't frown her skin was completely smooth. But now she looked really pale in the shadow under the wall and her brown eyes looked reddish again as though she'd been crying. 'I don't care if it hurts.'

I wanted to know but I didn't want her to tell me, so I didn't ask. But then it came out, 'What about me?' She looked away and shook her head. 'But I want to rescue you!' I said.

She turned round to me and leaned forward with her head on one side to make sure I could see in her eyes. I could, they were blaming me again. 'It's because of you we're shut up in that room. It's your house.'

She was too old for me, I couldn't follow. It wasn't my fault she was squashed up, I was squashed up. It only hurt if you got pushed out. But I couldn't make her like me if she didn't want to. The Three Musketeers and the Kennedys and the all the grown-ups arguing crowded into my head, all the squashed flies lying on the ground and the ones buzzing around them, and it was my fault. The window opened from the bedroom on the first floor and we both looked up as Tunde leaned out. His hat fell off and bounced on the ledge of the ground-floor window. Then his leg came over with his white trousers pulled up as it scraped the ledge and he was hanging from one arm off the bottom of the window frame looking down at the ground.

'*Tunde! Tunde!*' My dad's voice came down the stairs and out the back door, and from upstairs through the open window. Tunde let go and the white shirt he was wearing ruffled up as he fell.

'*Oh.*'

He landed on his feet like a cat and his knee came up and banged off his mouth with the horrible sound of a clack. He stood up stiffly with blood on his lip and limped past us to the bathroom door. It was locked as he pushed at it because Mr Babalola and Florence were in there, so he went round the corner up the passage to the toilet and the bins. I could hear Mr Babalola in the bathroom shout, '*Kilode? What's going on?*' as me and Marie both sprang up to follow. He bolted the toilet door from inside and wouldn't answer as Marie banged on it, 'Sunday?' I saw his feet move through the chink in the door at the bottom, then I raced back to tell my dad where he was. Mr Babalola came out the bathroom and looked at me sprinting past, but I didn't stop. I bumped into Mr Lawal coming out the back door and fell back on my bum as his leg lifted over me. I could feel I'd sprained my wrist but I picked up Tunde's hat that was lying there. My dad came out and the air came out his chest as he saw me lying on the ground. 'I'm all right,' I said because he froze and Mr Babalola was picking me up in his arms saying, '*Kilode?*' I told them I could stand and wriggled my legs down to show I wasn't hurt. Jimmy Singh came up behind my dad in the doorway and half pushed past and half held him round the shoulders as though my dad was going to fall over. It was all wrong because it was Tunde who'd fallen and it was Mr Lawal pulling and banging at the toilet door to try and break the bolt. 'Where de noise?' Jimmy Singh said, and I could see Marie had come away and was looking back down the passageway with Florence who was leaning out the bathroom wrapped in a towel. 'Tunde! Come out! Open the door!' Mr Lawal wanted to break the lock but he couldn't.

'You useless man!' Florence was out in her towel and took her flip-flop off and threw it down the passageway to hit Mr Lawal, 'Leave him!' He came charging back down the passageway at her, and Marie gave a little scream as he knocked Florence over the metal buckets and brooms against the backyard wall. She scratched him back on his face, keeping one hand to hold up her towel and spitting at him in Yoruba, '*Oniranu!*'

Jimmy Singh got there first, and Mr Babalola let go of me to join in pulling Mr Lawal off Florence and hold him while she went on shouting and trying to hit him with a scrubbing brush. It got Jimmy Singh on the back and he had to duck his neck down under the blows, 'You are the worst man and the worst father! Good-for-nothing you!' My dad moved in to calm it down, and I saw Marie duck down and go back up the passageway to Tunde. '*Otito!* Please, that's enough!' my dad said. He looked up as the bedroom window opened some more and Manus and Connor both leaned out, 'Go inside! All of you! Close the window!' They banged it shut upstairs and I went in the back door, peering back round to see Mr Babalola bundling Florence back into the bathroom and holding the handle shut as she kicked and pulled it from inside. Mr Lawal looked like he was in tears pleading with my dad as Jimmy Singh was holding on to his arm and rubbing and patting him on the back. My dad took off his glasses and rubbed his eyes and was shaking his head. I heard the sound of tapping and Marie's voice down the passageway saying, '*Sunday, Sunday ...*'

I couldn't sit up on the stairs because Florence would have to come past in her towel when they let her out. Connor was shouting down out the front window to his mates that he couldn't get out, Danny had a ball, go and knock on his house, and Manus was peeking down through the curtain in the bedroom to see what was going on. He didn't want me there in case I saw what else he was doing, so I went back down the half-stairs and sat on my own in the upstairs kitchen. The tap was running like someone had been waiting for it to turn cold. I knelt up on the stool and turned it off. The voices came up from the backyard of Mr Lawal and my dad trying to talk Tunde out the toilet. I couldn't hear Marie any more, even though the window was open at the bottom and I could feel a draught on my face when I put my ear up against it. There was a shuffle of feet and Mr Babalola said, '*It's a bad business.*' Jimmy Singh made a puffing sound and said, '*It have de devil in de boy?*' I shut the window and sat away from it round the far corner of the table where it was dark. The room looked long back to the closed door with the gas cooker beside it and the blue cabinet with plates and glasses squeezed into the corner. Stacked along the side from that corner to the sink and the window, the knife and fork drawer, pots and pans and the food cupboard were all in the dark too, with the white side of the sink catching light from outside. The ceiling folded over and sloped down to the window on that side so it felt the kitchen was getting smaller. I checked the door that it wasn't closing in and felt like I was in a tunnel. All the chairs were squashed in round the table and it was only me there. It felt lonely and crowded at the same time. The picture of the Kennedys was up on the wall above me, smiling down. I couldn't imagine me and Manus and Connor like that, we never played together. And then without knowing how it happened, I was outside myself looking down at the crowded table with the breakfast things still on it and me sitting there, and I thought this was something I should remember if I could just grab hold of something that could tell me why looking down at myself in the kitchen was important and how come the ceiling was folding over so my shoulders were having to hunch round. Marie didn't like being squashed and I didn't want Tunde to have to go back to Nigeria even though the room was getting cramped. And then I told myself, I had nowhere else to go.

The Thames

Everyone told us not to go down by the Thames. Manus said the scaly fish wrapped round the lamp posts would come alive if the water splashed them, they were dredged up from the bottom, that's why they were black. They had open eyes and fleshy mouths that dripped and glistened in the rain. It made them look like they came from the river. I knew the water was dirty, that you couldn't swim, you'd get pulled under.

'Don't go to the river.'

'All right, Mum.'

The way down was dank and slippery, and I was always down there where it opened on to a bend in the river. The water came in and out, and slopped with the tide on to the steps, or dropped below a shoulder of mud and shingle. There were old wooden posts sticking out the mud. It smelt old going down, which was one reason for going, it was where you grew up. Everyone said don't go, but the river pulled you. You just found yourself there, where no one ever looked for you.

At low tide there was a rope slung under the bridge. You could go on the knotted tyre if you felt you could hold on. I didn't like the green slime on the bricked foreshore, or the slow swing out over the river. I wasn't going to risk going near the current you felt would drag you under as soon as you touched it. But some did – the brave ones, or the ones you knew something was wrong by the strangled laugh that hung there under the arch as they swung back.

They said there were rats that wee'd on the shingle and gave you diseases, that you could get sucked in the mud, or cut by bits of glass and broken pottery that washed up, that there were ghosts that clung to the steps and no one would hear you if you got into trouble. No one ever said you could watch drowned animals float past, or stone bits of driftwood that turned into table legs.

We were in morning assembly when Thaddeus's mum came in with the headmaster. She was shaking, the way light does on water, going to and fro unsteadily. He told us she was going to talk to us about not playing down by the river – we all turned to look at her – that Thaddeus had drowned and ... I didn't hear any more because of the surge of sadness and shock that came out of us. We were all sat there cross-legged on the floor, we knew that river and knew what it meant – I felt the rush of it in my ears and held out against breathing, but we all gulped for air.

I knew Thaddeus hadn't come home. The police had been round, but that was because he was always in trouble and going off. He was in my class and always getting told off for mucking about and not listening. But he was all right, he had a mop of hair like mine, bushy and reddish, that all got tangled, and made the girls like him because he pulled faces and made them laugh. We got on because we looked like brothers and we knew we weren't. He had lots of brothers and sisters at home and was always following his mum around, but because he was small he couldn't always get to her so he'd wander off with a set look in his face like he was going to find her somewhere else.

I watched his mum as she leaned on the headmaster's arm to speak and nothing came out. She stood there shaking, in floods of tears, coughing and trying to breathe, but no words coming, just the struggle for air going on in front of us. The headmaster slumped in his grey suit and hurried her out of assembly into the corridor. The doors banged shut and we heard a wailing sound as she was being led away that felt like someone being dragged where they didn't want to go, where there was nothing to hold on to. No one said anything, the teachers moved us quickly back to our classrooms, with the sound of people's legs moving and the squeal of the chair legs as they sat down.

The next day she was at the school gate. It wasn't a change, she always brought her children to school and talked to the other mums. It was where she used to tell them she could do childminding. She was always nice to us and chatty, pushing a baby in a pram. I never knew exactly who was hers and who wasn't because she had lots of children with different dads and they didn't all look the same. I knew Thaddeus, and he looked like his sister Sandra, but then her house was full of children she was looking after, and you didn't know who she was just minding. At school she had her hair scraped up in a bun and didn't smoke, but when she was home she kept looking for a space to put a fag in her mouth and have a smoke so she could get a break. She looked at me once, watching her, and said, 'You've to steal a life sometimes.'

She was there under the black iron gate of the entrance, pushing a pram backwards and forwards with a baby in who was looking up at people with its toe in its mouth. Her face was crumpled and she had lipstick on which made her look even more pale and washed out. The other mums didn't want to push past her, so they drew their prams up and pulled their toddlers in close.

'I've got too many children to look after,' she said.

A big crowd was gathering and keeping quiet, and no one was going in. After a while, some of the mums went up and spoke to her, and nodded, and came away. She pulled her pram back and they all started going past into school with the baby looking up at them.

I hung back, and slipped in on the other side of a pram with my head down.

She was on her own after that. People stopped sending their children to be with her after school, and her clothes were dirty and her face started to look craggy and thin.

'She's drinking,' my mum said. 'And who'd want to risk it after what happened to ... you know.'

She came round one evening and asked to borrow some money to tide her over. My dad came straight down to the door and gave it to her.

'I've got no one helping me,' she said.

After she'd gone, my mum was crying. 'It's more than money she's looking for,' she said.

My dad shrugged, 'Life's let her down.'

Her house was a few doors down on the same side as us, she lived in the rooms on the ground floor. She'd looked after us sometimes – usually just me and Busola who got on with Sandra.

'Your mum works hard for you,' she said when I kicked her front door wanting to go out. 'You have to wait until she gets back.'

I don't know what happened, usually we played out in the backyard with the others and got on with it, but I was bored and upset and I wanted to go and run outside. Busola joined in and there was a fight with the two of us screaming and shouting that she couldn't keep us locked up. She had a front door that closed on the top latch and we couldn't reach it, so we started kicking and thumping against the door. Someone upstairs shouted about the noise so she came out into the hall and tried to talk to us.

'Where you going? Your mum's not back from work yet.'

She tried to move us away from the door but we didn't care, we ganged up on her. Busola scratched her and I kicked out with my feet as we struggled to get past. It felt wrong to be doing it but we were screaming and something came out of us that we couldn't stop. She was keeping us prisoner and she shouldn't. We were supposed to be free and our brothers were out. She was a witch and we'd tell our mum. I spat at her. She stopped, swore at me, and walked off saying, 'Break your fists on the door for all I care.'

We stood there breathing in the hall as the people on the stairs went back up, and Sandra and Thaddeus who were looking at us from the back door with the other children turned away to the backyard where their mum could watch them playing from the kitchen window.

I looked at Busola, and got down to let her climb on my back to open the latch. It clicked, we got out and Busola slammed the door shut behind us.

'She's a witch! And she's got too many children!' Busola said, but then she looked at me like it was my fault we'd run away in the first place.

'What we gonna say?' I said, because I wasn't sure any more. It didn't feel right to be out, there was no reason for it, or the reason just drained away. There was no one playing out on the street to tell it to, everyone had gone in. So we wandered around getting our breath back to normal until we came to the river.

A tug boat was making waves along the wall of the embankment. We leaned over to see the splashes reaching up. They were a long way down, but you could feel the thud as they lifted. The lights were on along the river and the water was dark and glittering across to the other side.

'Shall we go back?' I said.

Busola shook her head, she was looking out over the water as though I wasn't there. I got off the wall because it felt too close to the lamp posts and the monster fish even though they weren't moving.

We didn't look at each other, then she said, 'Let's go and find Mum.'

We knew she worked in the laundry which did the sheets for the hospital, and that we could find it by the brick chimney with the steam coming out the same colour as the sky. It looked like a cloud factory but we knew it was a laundry for getting blood out the sheets and stitches, and it felt a long way off because we hadn't tried to cross over those roads from the river on our own before. The traffic was busy with all the headlights on. It was because of that we held hands.

Our mum came out to the big doors in the yard. Her arms were red, and she was flushed and sweating as she took a wet bit of hair off her forehead and wiped her hands on a cloth.

'What's happened?' she said.

We said we'd come for her to take us back home over the busy roads. That we'd had to fight to get out and Thaddeus's mum was too busy to look after us.

She went back in to get her coat and we set off with us holding on to her arms as she buttoned up. We told her we'd run away because there were too many children and it was too rough. That what Thaddeus's mum gave us to eat was mouldy bread and margarine. She'd made us share a big can of baked beans with one spoon to go round everyone, and one of the children had spat on it to stop us having ours. She'd grabbed us with her bony fingers to stop us getting out the door. We didn't want to go back, her house was dirty and they had nits –

'Stop it!' she said, and shook us off. We'd gone too far. We walked the rest of the way home in silence.

'Wait now till your father gets home.'

There was a knock on the door. It was Thaddeus's mum, with Thaddeus and Sandra there. She stood at the door and told my mum what happened, that she'd sent her two out to look for us but they'd come back because we'd gone. And then she apologised to us.

'I'm sorry it hasn't worked out. I didn't know what I could do.'

Sandra was pulling on her mum's coat to make her come away and Thaddeus kept looking off down the street. Their mum was worried because she was biting her nails, some of her teeth were missing and her fingers were shaking.

My mum said she'd got a shock when she saw us, but now she understood and it wasn't anything to worry about, we were safe.

She told my mum she'd had to wait until the other children

had gone before she could put on her coat and come out, and she'd left some of her own alone so she'd have to get back. She asked Busola and me not to be upset with her.

My mum told us to say sorry. Busola nodded and said, 'See ya tomorrow.' to Sandra who nodded back. I couldn't look at Thaddeus because he wouldn't look at me. I couldn't look at his mum because I was ashamed, so I just looked down and mumbled, 'Sorry.'

'No, you're not.'

I looked up, Thaddeus was looking at me. His face was blank – it was pale and red at the same time – his eyes were dark and glossy, almost crying.

'Come on, Mum,' he said, and pulled her away by the hand. He loved his mum and I'd got her in trouble. It was my fault she had to stand at the door and say sorry. It was all bottled up and something broke in his voice. 'Don't worry,' he said.

'My children are waiting for me,' his mum said, and they went.

My dad heard us out. My mum said we'd told her a pack of lies. Busola blamed me and I blamed her. He asked if Thaddeus's mum had looked after us properly, or if anyone had hurt us. I said yes and Busola said no, and we both hung our heads.

He made us stoop down, balancing on one finger and one leg until the snot came down and we fell over, so we could change legs and he wouldn't notice. When both our legs were dead and the tears were burning our eyes because our heads were upside down, he told us off for trying to balance on more than one finger and waved the wooden stick over us as our legs collapsed under the weight on to our knees. After that, our mum asked him please let us up, we'd been stupid but enough was enough, she forgave us, we were only children and we'd learnt our lesson, it was crowded at Thaddeus's mum's and she couldn't really cope.

We could tell he was angry because he told her off for coming between him and dealing with us. He told us to get up and wipe our faces. When our mum had given us something to eat, he told us to come back in and face him.

'False report,' he said, 'is no child of mine.' He looked at us like he didn't know who we were, and didn't like us. 'Are you listening?'

I nodded, and burst into tears.

'Shut up,' he said, and I stifled them. 'Never let me hear you spreading lies. The woman is trying to feed her family. If you think you can run wild in the street and I won't find out, if you ever do anything so stupid again, I will break your head! Do you hear me?'

We nodded. Busola gave me a sideways look so he could see she still blamed me, but I didn't look back.

'Now get out before I punish you!' he said.

The next day at school, Thaddeus wouldn't speak to me, but with Sandra and Busola it didn't seem to make any difference. They still played cat's cradle with the string passing backwards and forwards between their hands and fingers. I saw him digging in the playground on his own because he'd been told off in class for not paying attention and wandering off, but I avoided him. I didn't know what to say. He kept digging his hand in the sand and flicking, digging and letting it run out through his fingers, like he was trying to dig his way out of having to talk to anyone. I left him alone. He dug down, crouched in the sandpit holding on to sand, and never spoke to me again.

The Thames was flooding and the sirens opened. The sound came in waves, we'd never heard them before. There were the dark air-raid shelters by the flats that were full of rubble, and we played on the bomb sites, but we didn't know that warning sound that came from everywhere and emptied the streets. The school closed and they told us to run home with the wailing sound following us all the way.

I was one of the fastest. There wasn't any traffic past the London City Mission, past the shut-up shops, down Auckland Street which was empty of cars, around by the main road, under the railway arch and across to the silence of the embankment.

I got up to the river and put my foot on to the ledge to look over and see the flood. It was at the top of the wall, running level with my eyes all the way across to the other side. A slop of water splashed on to my face. It lapped at the monster fish round the lamp posts. I felt the pull of the water, the swirl of the current – that I was being dragged away.

I stood down, and I was alone on the pavement. No one else was coming. The sirens were sounding like slow panic, the river was above me and Thaddeus's voice was pounding in my chest, telling me *run!*

Lambeth Walk

'Come on,' my mum said.

I was stamping puddles on my own in the backyard as she leaned out the window. She was changing the rooms round now Marie had moved out with her mum and her dad had gone back to Guyana. Marie's room down by the front door was my mum and dad's, and that was where my mum told me to come when I bent down and shook my head. She was gonna ask me to carry the shopping with her and I didn't want to.

She sat on the bed with the door closed and pulled me down beside her in a cuddle so I'd have to give in. The room was still crowded with the stuff she hadn't packed away, and the curtains were pulled so it was half dark, but now her Kennedys were up on the wall beside the Nigerian army calendar and underneath was a picture of the sacred heart, its blood on fire. I hardened myself up to stop her getting round me.

'I've been watching you,' she said. 'What's the matter?'

I shook my head. Even my dad was going easy on me and I could feel they were thinking I wasn't well, but I just didn't have anyone to play with. There wasn't anything to say, only a feeling that I couldn't carry any more and if I did I was going to burst.

'When I was growing up,' she said, 'there was a girl, and whenever her mummy wanted her you could hear her name being called, *Precious! Precious!* And you should see the pretty dresses, because she had relatives in America sent them over in boxes. But one day she became sad. She used to love playing out, skipping along the road, and hadn't a care in the world. One day she was happy and the next she was sad, and we didn't know why. No one ever told us. But her mummy went on calling, *Precious!* What do you think of that?'

I shrugged.

'Can you say?'

The thought of Marie saying it was my fault she was sad came back and I squashed it, but not completely. 'What happened to her?' I said.

'She caught cold and died of pneumonia.'

'Are you making this up?'

My mum shook her head. 'In those days people didn't know. They should have been cooling her down, but they wrapped her up and she overheated and died.'

'I don't want to die,' I said.

'Then you shouldn't dwell on it,' and she looked into my ears to see were they clean. She scraped her nail in to see if she could dig something out, 'You may have to do without me one day.'

'You just want me to carry the shopping on my own,' I said. 'You never ask them to do it, always me.'

'Who's them?'

'Connor and everyone.'

'They're not moping around the house with nothing to do,' she said. 'You are, and I'm not going to wrap you up in cotton wool. You're a big boy now.'

There was an edge in her voice that she was getting ready to push me over and I had to cling on to something, so I clung on to her. She took off my arms from round her waist and said, 'Ah no, you're not getting round me, come on.' She held my hands up between us and said, 'God knows what's in your heart, even if you won't say. So what's it to be? Are you going to help me or are you going to be idle?'

It was my chance and I grabbed it. I was going to do whatever my mum told me, so I nodded, 'Can I have a treat?'

'You're my treat,' she said, 'so I can be yours.' I must have looked disappointed because she bent over and got one of the bags up off the floor. I leaned over to see what was in it – the bag was silver and had four handles and looked heavy. She got out a coin, with a chain attached, and poured it into my hand. 'That's yours,' she said, 'don't lose it,' and she started to get ready to do the shopping. I looked and saw a man with a beard up to his legs in water. I moved it around in the half light from the window, and there was a baby on his shoulders, frowning, the water was up to the man's knees and he was leaning on a crutch. I wanted to know was that me, not wanting to carry the bags? 'Do I have to wear it round my neck?' I said. 'What is it?' I looked up and she was facing me, pale and white by the window. 'To keep you safe,' she said.

The market was up Tyers Street at the top of the road, round past the shops then a long straight stretch between the blocks of brown flats on both sides of the road. All the blocks on the Vauxhall Gardens Estate were good for playing run-outs up and down the stairs and round the balconies, but it was a long walk anywhere if you had to lift shopping. My mum had the wicker trolley and she had me, so she was jollying me along and swinging my hand in hers, getting me to sing *Oh, I am a jolly ploughboy* as we went. There was a pub up the top on the corner with Black Prince Road before you crossed over into Lambeth Walk called The Jolly Cockneys. It was always busy with people spilling out on the pavement in between doing the shopping, and I liked it because the man and the woman with hats and feathers and white buttons sewn all over their clothes were doing a dance on the painted sign over the door, and my mum said they were the Pearly King and Queen. Because not everybody thought we should be holding hands, my mum let me go and walked ahead, only holding my hand again to cross over the road into the market. But then because I was looking back over the road at the sign and dragging my feet, she had to go on keeping hold. 'Come on,' I said, and she knew I wouldn't move until she sang with me *Any evening, any day* ... She didn't want to because lots of people were going past looking at us and she thought it was silly. I dug my heels in and slid on the wet pavement and caught hold of the lamp post on the corner with my other hand so she couldn't go in under the awnings between the shops and the wooden stalls.

'Will you come?' she said, stamping her foot.

'*You'll find them all ...*' and I looked at her.

'*Doing the Lambeth Walk*?' said Lottie. It was her and Charlie, our neighbours, on their way home with Charlie pulling the trolley. Charlie grinned and said, '*Oi!* You should be helping your mum, not dragging her back!'

My mum shook her head at them and let go my hand. She didn't want people to notice us but the man on the first stall was peeling off a cabbage and looking at her.

'How are the boys?' Lottie said. They didn't have children and Manus and Connor were their favourites.

'Fine,' my mum said. 'Not as much trouble as this one. Not long now?'

'Two weeks,' Lottie said.

'Sorry to see you go,' my mum said. 'Will I get them to write?'

She shrugged and said, 'We'll be staying with Charlie's sister first down in Swindon, until we get our own place.'

'Shame it's all going,' Charlie said, looking back at the market.

I didn't know they were moving. They'd always been there, two doors down from us. They had the whole house to themselves. And even though they were old they both had pearly teeth and their clothes were clean. They made you feel they were always going to be happy living there and watching you play.

'It's easy for us, just renting,' Lottie said, 'We haven't got to sell up and deal with that council.'

'You going?' I said.

Lottie looked at me, but I didn't know what she was thinking because she said, 'You look after your mum.'

'Look at that,' Charlie said.

They all looked up where he was pointing over the tops of the awnings at the houses. Most of the windows were empty and boarded up like some of the houses round by us. Some trees were growing out the bricks along the roofs, their top branches almost touching the low clouds moving like grey smoke across the street. A gust of wind shook the awnings and spilled rainwater on the pavement, and another one came down and made the striped screens of the stalls flap like boats.

'They don't care,' Lottie said, but I didn't know who she was talking about. Charlie looked back at her and shook his head, 'End of an era.'

'I must be getting on,' my mum said, 'before it rains again. Say goodbye to Charlie and Lottie,' she said to me.

I looked at them and said, 'What's it the end of? Why you going?'

'Come on, we'll be late!' my mum said.

Charlie scratched his head, and Lottie shook her head at me and looked at my mum, 'Life goes on.'

As my mum pulled me along, I looked back and saw them holding hands and watching for cars going across, Charlie was limping and pulling the trolley. Manus said he was a soldier in Italy, and he had to change his leg when it hurt, but I didn't know what to make of that.

The market was full of noise in a tunnel under the awnings, and I liked the way they were filling out and blowing in the wind. The light made it look like a long room everyone was in, with crowds going in between the shops and the stalls. The traders were calling out loud and fast in that way of talking that moved their jaws a lot and sounded like yawning. 'Keep up,' my mum said, and she let go my hand. I felt alive and started to enjoy it, watching all the people talking and shopping. I ran ahead to keep up and then wanted to know why we were rushing, so I stopped, 'Is the market closing because it's late?' She stepped by me and said, 'It's closing because it's closing.' She had a tight way of walking which wasn't like her, so I shut up and kept close. 'Wait here,' she said, going into a butcher's she liked. She gave me a penny because there was the boy outside the shop who was blind and I could put the penny in his box. We used to be the same height but now I was taller than him and his paint was flaking – he had a white shirt, blue shorts, black shoes, yellow hair and orangey-pink skin. 'You'll always be the same and never grow up,' I said. His eyes were shut and he didn't know what to do with my pity. I shook my head, 'There's something wrong with you,' and dropped the penny in the slot. As soon as I did, I wanted it back to put in a slot machine for bubblegum, but he wasn't going to give it. I looked around to see if anyone was watching and gave his shoulders a shake. An old lady went past and said, 'Stop that!' I knew I was in the wrong, so I didn't look up and said, 'He's my friend.' As soon as I said it I could feel she thought there was something wrong with me. She walked off, and I didn't know why I was acting like that, except I always did. I looked at the boy again, he was blind and I was stupid. He wasn't real and I couldn't go on pretending I was like him.

'Come on,' my mum said, walking on ahead with the extra meat the butcher gave because he liked her. He always did and she moved off because she didn't want me to see her counting up the money. She waited for me two shops up and put the meat in the wicker trolley. 'Mum,' I said, 'can I have my treat?' There were only two shops I wanted to go in, Micklejohn's, the blue toy shop on the other side of the road, and Sainsbury's because there was sawdust all over the floor and big mirrors up on the walls, you could see everyone from different angles. But she said we were only buying vegetables from the stalls and to look at what was being dropped on the floor because all those greens got eaten up by the rats, which was what made their coats so glossy and black and I should eat up my greens. She stopped to look at onions and carrots, but moved on while I was crouched down trying to look underneath the stall to see what was going on. The man standing in the road behind came round through the gap between the stalls and jingled his money, saying, '*She's a looker!'* I stood up and saw he was wearing a leather pouch on a belt in front and talking to the old man with white hair on the pavement looking after the fruit stall. The old man pulled him round by the elbow to look at me, 'That's hers.' It took me a moment to realise he was connecting me to my mum, and the man with the pouch let his mouth fall open and looked down the stalls at her, 'Fuckin' black man's mattress ...' I looked at both their faces, it was me standing there but they were ignoring me, one with his hands in his pouch looking at my mum and the other one turned back to his fruit stall. It was like I was a wooden post. They were treating me like I wasn't real. They were treating me the way I treated the blind boy, as though I wasn't a proper person. I didn't know what else to do, 'I'm a real boy,' I said. They both turned to look at me, but it didn't make any difference, they looked at each other and shook their heads and turned away.

I was looking in the window of Sainsbury's, thinking about it. I wasn't worried what they thought. Both of them had weaselly faces and I thought of saying to the vegetable man, *'You look like a rat!'* But it was my face I was looking at ghosted in the window. I pressed my nose up against it. People were passing behind me. I wasn't like them, but it didn't matter I was small, I was big enough to see my head in the window. I saw my mum go by and turned, 'Mum, my treat?' but she swerved into the shop and I followed her in because she was gonna get me a cream cake or a custard tart. The sawdust was trampled in with wet feet, and there were gaps where you could see the black and white marble pattern on the floor. 'What do you want?' she said. 'What you get me!' I said, because that was what was gonna get the most, and she laughed. 'All right, wait here,' and off she went.

I was standing on my own in the middle of the shop. It was a big hall, and the people serving had long white aprons on. I looked in the mirrors and saw crowds of people going round the counters, with me keeping still and holding heavy bags of shopping in both hands. Everyone was going round me and not looking, and the smell of the sawdust was rising off the floor, and the noise was bouncing off the walls and ceilings. I looked round and could see myself from lots of different angles in the glass, but no one else could because they didn't see what I saw. I was growing up and my paint wasn't flaking. I was staying still because everything was moving. I was invisible but I could see everyone. And what I saw in between the mirrors was a boy with brown bushy hair and blinding eyes being watched by the best mum in the world.

Susan

'*Mind out!*' I was at the top of the street balancing on the kerb, and trying not to step on the cracks. I stopped on one leg, but I wasn't sure she was talking to me. It was the old lady who watched everything from her doorstep, and spoke to people as they went past. She caught you off balance, leaning out with her arms folded. My mum didn't like her and said she was common. In the summer she sat out on a chair in slippers, and always wore thick stockings on her legs and a scarf on her head, knotted at the back with stringy grey hair hanging down the sides. She used to work in a factory and still had the apron on under a cardigan with its sleeves rolled up so she could fold her arms up under her chest. She kept her arms up and just moved from her elbow to touch her scarf into place, or lift her hair back over her ear. Mostly she talked to the other women, but when she wanted to find out something she got you over with crisps and started, 'The woman down there – red door –. your mother – Irish girl – with the black fella. What's that about?'

I kept away from her part of the pavement because even when she wasn't there you felt she was, leaning out on her arms, or looking up from her chair and catching your eye as she chatted to someone with the cats on her lap. She had cats everywhere, on her windowsill and on the sills of her first-floor windows, round her feet and over her shoulders, coming in and out her house. They moved about looking mean and ugly and brown-striped and black and sometimes grey round their mouths. When they reached up and scratched her legs she'd slap them away, and when she wouldn't they'd get interested, their eyes would go scary and they'd start to make a racket until she got up and grumbled about having to feed them. I was scared of her and kept away but Busola didn't – she said the lady had brown stuff dripping off her teeth and wasn't always nice about people. Busola made me go up close and look. I only did because I was trying to see in her house where she lived on her own and never let anybody in – through the door it looked like a black cave.

'What's that about? Such a lovely girl. How's he treating her? Is he staying? You never see that in my day. Black fellas coming over. Getting everyone in trouble. Does he beat her? If he does, you come to me. I'll listen to ya.'

That's how I thought she was a ghost and she wasn't really seeing us, because why would she talk to us about our mum and dad like that and not think we'd run home and tell?

'Well, she's not a ghost,' my mum said. 'She's old. We have to look after the old. And she's very old. Go down now and keep an eye open and see is she all right.'

'*Mind out!*' I was stood behind Busola, balancing one foot on the kerb, listening but keeping out the way. '*They bite.*' Busola was feeding a crisp to one of the cats trying to claw it off her. 'Where's your mum been? I was gonna get flowers. Tell people he'd done away with her.' My mum had been lying in the hospital, and Busola had been saying you could catch things off people there. But she was home now getting some rest. 'Men, they wear you out. Don't worry, I been watching him. Looks after you, though? All clean clothes.'

'She's been in hospital,' Busola said, and pulled her hand back because the cat's claw caught on her finger. It drew blood and she had to put it in her mouth to stop it bleeding.

'Told ya. End up eating me, they will. Always hungry.' And she gave the cat a kick with her slipper, '*Get off, yer!*' It spun round and hissed at her with its teeth and slunk off. I didn't like it and wanted to go, pulling Busola by the sleeve. 'Wanna plaster? I can go in and get you one?'

Busola shook her head and shook me off her arm. 'I don't wanna catch what you got. You got too many cats,' she said to the lady, 'and you're not nice.'

The lady shrugged like she didn't care what Busola said, 'I don't know what's gonna happen to 'em when I'm gone. They'll be the last ones living here when they've cleared us all out. Outlive me. No one'll feed 'em.'

'Let's go,' I said.

'Is he your brother?'

Busola shook her head. I didn't know what was going on with them pretending they didn't know who I was. She knew who Busola was. Maybe she couldn't tell me apart from Manus and Connor. But then I felt she could hear me because she lifted up her hair over her ear and said, 'Yeah he is, I can see it in his face. Bet you can't tell my cats apart, can ya?' And she laughed, 'Wanna feed 'em a crisp?'

I stepped back off the kerb on to the road and shook my head. They were teasing me. 'She *is* my sister,' I said.

'Come here and talk to me. Know how old I am?' I shook my head again. 'See 'em land on the moon?' I nodded. 'Not in my day. I was here before the war. Knew everyone. Now look at it. All the black people moving in.'

'Who lived in our house?' Busola said.

'Down your end, those people would still be here if it wasn't for the war. Lotta people didn't make it. Come out the shelter, it's a flying bomb, they're all dead in the park, it's all burning.'

'She don't know,' Busola said.

'Oh, no – I know. You've had fire trouble, ain't ya? It's not the first time. There was Madge lived there. Lost her husband, hadn't she? Didn't wanna go down the shelter. Too smoky. All those rough old men feeling yer. I told her, you had to. House up on the corner got hit. Come out the shelter, walls bombed flat. Her house on fire. Don't know they ever found 'em. Be nice they were still alive. Her and her daughter, her Susan was lovely. All the fire engines. Couldn't walk down the road for rubble. See an 'and sticking up there was people had the ring off it. Not like it used to be.'

She went on about how she went deaf and got cut when another bomb exploded the windows. But I wasn't listening properly because I saw Busola go stiff when she said about Susan and I wasn't sure they weren't still teasing me.

'... Irish fella stood here, digging out the road, wanted water – couldn't understand him – what's he saying? – sounded like grunts to me. Shook my head, said *I can't speak Irish*. Didn't mind though, let him use my tap.' She leaned forward and laughed with her shoulders bouncing, 'No one else to.'

Busola was walking away.

'You're not frightened of me, are ya?' The lady was looking at me in the road and ignoring Busola, so I shook my head and ran. '*Your friend, Susan ... Is she a ghost?*' Busola looked up at me, and turned over and didn't answer. Manus and Connor were still at my aunt's, so it was me and Busola on our own. I was in Connor's bed and she was in the bottom bunk in the dark. My mum and dad were sleeping in the front room because he moved up while she was in hospital to be near us and she didn't want him to change back till she was strong enough to sort out their bedroom and help him do the wallpaper that was falling off. There was a strip of moonlight in our room coming down over the edge of the curtain where it sagged and another smaller one on Busola's side lighting the floor where the curtain caught on the ladder and didn't fold back properly. It wasn't completely dark, but I didn't want to move because it was me lying on my own and I didn't want anything to come and get me. I didn't want to be on my own. I wanted someone to talk to. '*You know she's not real.*'

Only I wasn't sure. What if it was the Susan who burnt in the fire? I bit my finger to tell myself it wasn't true, but I had to pull away because my teeth were sharp and I suddenly wasn't sure it was me. I couldn't sleep any more because I'd have to close my eyes and I had to keep them open in case anything moved. What if the handle turned and the door opened? I was straining my eyes in the dark.

'Susan's gone,' Busola said.

I looked but she was still facing away from me to the wall.

'She's not coming back.'

That's all she said. Even when I asked her, *Why not?* She wasn't answering. I lifted up on my elbow to see what she was doing. She wasn't moving. It was just me and her in the dark. There was scratching going on, but that was mice. I looked up at the crack in the curtain and got the moon in one eye. It was high and white and blinding.

I lay back in the bed and blinked so there was the ghost of it on the inside of the curtain. I tried to imagine it was Susan's face, but I couldn't see that it was, I didn't know what Susan looked like. I blinked some more and it faded. It was pale and it was going and the old lady came. I tried to blink her away, but she was standing up by her front door, looking at me and lifting her grey hair over her ear. I shut my eyes and she was still there, waiting for me, so I had to look. I looked at her eyes. They weren't doing what I heard her saying, they were bright and lonely, telling me they weren't in the same place as I was but they could see me.

I opened my eyes up and she wasn't there any more. There was a flash in my mind. Now Susan was gone, the house wasn't going to burn down. It was her doing the fires. She was gone and she wasn't coming back. The lady was looking and telling me.

'I was watching the smoke because I thought it was a witch coming under the door.' It was Busola, I lifted up and looked across at the bunk bed – she was on her back looking up at me. 'But the door opened and the man came in to rescue me.'

'What?'

'I was worried about the smoke of the witch coming under the door. But the man across the road came and lifted me out the bed. I thought he was saving me from the witch, I didn't know what else he was doing there.'

'What witch?'

'It wasn't, it was smoke. He wrapped me up in the blanket and I could see downstairs everything was smoke because he jumped over the banister and the stairs were burning. I felt the fire, but I didn't think it was happening to me, I thought it was happening to Susan.'

'They threw you out the window,' I said, because it didn't make sense what she was saying and that's what I remembered.

'You're talking about the other fire,' she said, and turned over to face me. 'I'm talking about the one with Susan where she told me not to breathe. It wasn't her it was happening to, it was me. I don't want her no more. I want to breathe.'

I didn't like the way it was going or the way Busola looked in the dark, in shadow at the bottom of the bunk bed. I wanted my mum to come in and turn on the light. So I said, 'Where was Mummy?'

'I don't know, in hospital.'

It sounded like Busola again, like she was thinking about it. I looked across to see if there was anything coming under the door but the light was off on the landing and I couldn't tell. I didn't want Busola to leave me. 'Where was I?'

'You were outside.'

'What was Susan doing?' I was trying to keep hold of Busola in the dark. 'Were you haunted?'

Busola lifted up on her arm and looked at me like I didn't know what I was talking about. 'Can you keep a secret?'

I nodded.

'Mummy told me not to tell you. It's not me who's haunted. You know who it is, don't ya?'

I shook my head.

'*What if it's you?*'

She watched me from the shadow.

'It was you lighting fires,' I said, 'you and Susan.'

I wasn't sure any more who I was talking to, because she didn't answer until her head moved towards me and said, 'You tell me how then.'

I couldn't. I was trying to imagine myself lighting matches, or dropping them like Manus into the dome of the paraffin heater so it lit up with different colours, or being the one who poured water on to damp it down, so it rose up in a big orange flame to the ceiling and spread out down the walls to set light to the curtains, but I couldn't. I only saw me watching and jumping up to run outside.

'See, can't, can yer?'

I could tell her about Manus but she'd get him in trouble. Wasn't she there in the room with us? Why did I think she was the one doing it? 'You went funny when that lady said about Susan,' I said.

Busola didn't move. I couldn't make out her face properly, I had to imagine it. She just kept still.

'She was real, wasn't she?'

'Susan's gone now,' she said. 'So we're all right, aren't we?'

'Yeah,' I said.

'Remember, you started it,' and she rolled over on to her back.

I wasn't sure what I started, but we listened to our mum come out the front room and go down to the toilet, and after a while our dad come out on the landing to look for her. They whispered on the stairs. Then came back up the steps slowly. The door opened and they looked in on us. We both pretended we were asleep.

The doors closed behind them. Busola turned over, 'Mummy's ill,' she said, 'I think she's going to die.'

I sat up in bed with my back stiff and my eyes open wide.

The Face of God

It was my mum, grief-stricken, my aunts, soaking with tears down their faces. The man on the cross was someone dead in the family, and Good Friday was when he died. I was there too, crying at the foot of the cross because I was frightened and the surge of the crowd separated me from my mum at the funeral. Then the words stopped, and everyone went wild. It's hard to be without God. Everyone was pressing forward, all the statues covered in black. I looked up at the cross, dripping blood from the thorns and nails. My dad turned up his nose and wouldn't go, he called it 'the blood and wig-hair melodrama'. Strangers groaned and my nana wept. A hole opened up in the middle of my chest and I clutched at people I didn't know to stop it pulling me under. A bell rang and stifled it. I pushed back against the wetness of the bodies, sobbing until I got out the church.

Buses were passing, the street was still there. The shops were closed, the sun was shining. I was on my own.

'Never again!' I said out loud. A passer-by over the road glanced at me, I was shivering. I'd seen Jesus crucified and I didn't want to be there ever again.

'Are you going to do your first communion?' I nodded at my mum because I had to. Everyone was busy opening out the Guinness and fish and chips and beer and lemonade and being noisy coming in from church. I didn't want to tell her I'd already gone up when she was in hospital and tasted the wafer and wine they gave you when you kneeled at the rail. I wasn't supposed to, but everyone else did and I followed. I kept my head down and my hands together while I tried to see my way back to my seat and if I'd been found out. I had to step over Busola who was kneeling with her eyes closed in the pew. 'That's a *sin*,' she said, without even looking up at me, 'you'll go to hell for that.'

I thought if I did my first communion it would make up for it. I'd only meant to get the taste, but it swallowed down the wrong way when Busola tripped me up and I'd gone into a coughing fit. People turned round in the pews and looked, '*Sit down and shut up*,' Busola said, '*for God's sake!*' I could see a smirk on her face even though she kept it closed, like she was going to be an angel and I didn't even believe in God. I gave her a kick and she opened her eyes. 'You're a *pagan*,' she said. I didn't know what that was, so I ignored her and put my hands back together and my head down and tried to think who God was.

'Don't just nod at me,' my mum said. 'Are you going to do it? Do you want God in your life?'

'Yes,' I said, standing in front of her with my hands in my pockets and my fingers crossed. *Yes*, because God washes away your sins, and sin divides you from yourself, and who wants to go to hell?

'About time,' Annie said. She was my aunt and I had to be nice, so I gave her a blank look.

But it meant I had to do Saturday mornings with the nuns. They didn't know who I was. They weren't my aunts but they wanted to smack me like my mum. They wanted to get up close, and

cling to my hair like bats in their black clothes. It was too much.
As soon as they came flapping into the room I was on the run, I
had to do my catechism on the hoof. *Who loved me? Who died
for me? Who do I owe?* I never asked for anyone like that. I wasn't
stopping for it, I wasn't going to be grabbed.

Anyway, they didn't like me, turning up to their classes not
knowing anything at my age.

'How old are you to be coming to catechism?'

I said nothing.

'Are you baptised?'

I had this way of not saying anything in case the answer came
out the question and I could work them both out together. But
the question was enough, they were telling me I didn't belong.

'Cat got your tongue?'

It was the best way of making them lose interest. I didn't want
to be there. The questions were in bold type and the answer was
plain it wasn't going to be nice with the nuns.

'What's a boy your age doing in this class?'

I looked for the door. If I made a dash for it, that would get
back to my mum. The best I could do was make myself invisible.
Say nothing, don't let them see what I'm thinking.

'What the devil are you playing at?'

It wasn't going well. So I did the next best thing – I put my hand
up to ask for the loo. They ignored me, I was already invisible.

'God moves in mysterious ways ... *and so does the devil.*'

Holding my arm up in the air, I watched as they tried to drag
us down into Hell to meet him, and dangle us there, *Here you
are – he's burning – what do you want? Do you want to end up
with him, or do you want to come back with us?*

He'd always be hanging about afterwards anyway, in case

you changed your mind. Only there wasn't much difference between him and the nuns. The devil could be nice to you, and they could be nasty.

'I want the toilet, miss.'

'*Sister!*' she hissed. 'See you wash your hands with soap.'

The last door on the left of the corridor was further than the middle on the right where the entrance was. I hung about, looking out the glass doors on to the brick wall in bright sunlight, sounds of traffic echoing down the passageway from the street. There was the sound of a flush and the toilet door opened. The caretaker came out doing up his belt, saw me and frowned. A bald Irish man burst in through the entrance, banging the doors and shouting, 'Where's the priest? Where's the fuckin' priest!'

I ducked and bolted, not breathing till I reached the street.

'How was catechism?'

'I've got too much homework, Mum.'

She looked at me and sighed. I looked to my dad.

'They can choose when they're older,' he said, doing that burrowing thing with his thumb in his ear that meant he couldn't listen to any more of this.

I settled in to watch the telly, but my mum picked out some coins from her purse and folded them into my hand, closing my fingers into a good grip.

'This is to put in the box for the collection next week,' she said. 'God gives everyone something in this life. He gave me my children and I want them to know Him.'

My dad stood up, shaking his ear with his thumb, and left the room.

'Don't mind him,' my mum said. 'He's a *heathen.*'

'What you doing?' Connor shouted across the road.

It was Saturday morning, I was hanging back at the bus stop instead of going over to the church. Manus came out the sweet shop behind me and gave me a shove in the back, 'You're going to church,' he said.

'No, I'm not,' I said. 'Why aren't you?'

'We're going to Saturday morning pictures.'

'Come on!' Connor shouted, walking off on the other side of the road.

'I haven't got any money,' I said.

Manus looked at me like I was stupid and shook his head. 'Jump!' he said.

'What?'

'Jump!'

I did and the change for the collection jingled in my pocket.

'There it is.' And he smirked at me, licking his lolly, and went off after Connor.

I didn't know everyone else was doing Saturday morning pictures. It was a long walk once you got over the busy cross-roads down Nine Elms to Battersea. It was hot and dusty. My legs started to ache, but then they got excited as we got nearer and crowds of children were pushing and shoving to get in the cinema – hundreds of them yelling and calling and whistling without their mums and dads there.

Manus and Connor put their shoulders in and I came up behind, pushing to stay together. We all gave Manus our money as he reached out to the kiosk. He kept the change and gave us melted ice poles from the popcorn counter that dribbled over my chin as I watched the first film. Charlie Chaplin was pushing and shoving people in through a door and they wouldn't fit

– everybody laughed. Then he gave the crowd a kick up the bum, and the house fell down with everyone laughing. But the main film was about a man chucking the big stones of the Ten Commandments down at our feet.

'Who's that?'

'Charlton Heston,' Manus said, his eyes reflecting the screen.

'Moses,' Connor said, chewing on bubblegum.

'God,' said the boy next to me, his face squeezed up tight over his knees from his feet up on the seat.

I looked up at the white beard and bushy hair. He looked angry like God, coming down off the mountain to see the Golden Calf. There was a burning bush where he had to take his shoes off. He opened the Red Sea and drowned the Egyptians. There was thunder and smoke. Screams for Pharaoh's son. He was a murderer. His big stick shook with lightning and turned into snakes. *'I am who I am!'* He wasn't telling you his name but you had to believe him.

'*Hold on*,' said Manus. He looked up at the flats in case anyone was looking, pulled his pants down and sat over a low wall. There was a gargle then a stream of poo came out his bum.

Connor made a face and walked off, 'I'm not with you.'

'I had to. Get me that chip paper,' Manus said. There was a twist of newspaper with the smell of vinegar still on it under the wall. I handed it to him and he wiped his bum.

'Run!' he said.

An old lady was looking at us off the balcony. We ran past Connor and kept on going. My hands felt dirty.

'Why d'you do that?' I said.

'Because I couldn't hold it in.'

I hung back and let Manus go on. We all walked back on our own. Up the road, Nine Elms cold store, the big building with no windows, looked like a dead pyramid for people who didn't believe in God. Even the river when I got up close and looked over was swirling and muddy like the Red Sea. I thought of Manus being flushed away as he pulled up his pants from the poo. The old lady was shaking her head at me as I looked up to stay afloat, but she wouldn't grab hold of my hand to pull me out because it was dirty.

Connor caught up.

'What's Mummy gonna say?' I said.

He leaned up against the wall over the river for a rest because the sun was really hot and made you feel tired. 'Who's gonna tell her?'

'I mean about Saturday morning pictures.' I looked down at the water again and sighed, 'She won't like it.'

'Everyone else is going, why not us?' He shrugged, 'No one's forcing ya.'

'Does Busola come?'

He took out his bubblegum and chucked it in the river. 'That's different,' he said. 'They're not letting her off.'

'Why not?'

He looked at me like it was obvious, 'She's a girl.'

I shook my head and he saw I didn't get it.

'She's gonna be a nun,' he said.

'That's stealing!'

'It was a Bible film,' I said quickly, wishing I hadn't told her, 'Mummy won't mind.' We got home and my mum and dad weren't back from the market. Busola was playing in the backyard and I wanted to tell her about Saturday morning pictures, what a big screen it was. 'Manus and Connor were there, too.'

'It's not about them, it's about you. You stole – *you* did. That wasn't your money to spend on yourself.'

'Mummy gave it to me.'

'That was money for the starving people in Africa! For the collection! And you spent it on the pictures. I'm gonna tell on you.'

'Just because you want to be a nun!'

She stopped. 'Who told you that?'

'No one,' I said.

'Good,' and I could feel talking to her was over.

'Mum,' I said. She'd got back and left my dad in the downstairs kitchen to start up cooking for the people who were coming. 'Manus did a poo in the street.'

She looked up from the shopping bags round her feet in the hall. She was counting up to make sure she had everything and hadn't been cheated. 'What are you talking about?'

'I went up Battersea with him,' I said, 'and he did a poo walking back.'

She shook her head, 'What were you doing in Battersea?' She looked at me sideways, trying to work it out. 'How was catechism?'

I hadn't thought it would lead back so quickly. I had to make her believe me, so whatever Busola said, Manus pooing in the street would be more serious than the money. 'No, really, he sat on the wall and it came out. He said he couldn't hold it.'

My dad called her from the kitchen. She shook her head at me, 'Stop telling tales.'

'He did, he wiped his bum on a newspaper,' I said. 'My hands feel dirty.'

'Now, you're not making sense, go away.' And she pushed me off and went down the corridor to the kitchen.

Manus and Connor were upstairs watching the wrestling on telly. I sat with them, watching Mick McManus and Giant Haystacks bang into each other. I was thinking if Busola told on me, she'd have to tell on everyone – but if it was Manus who found out it was me who told on him ... *Ouch!* Mick McManus had his arm twisted back in a half-nelson, slapping his free hand on the floor, '*Not the ears, not the ears!*' ... when the door knocked and my mum called out for someone to answer it. Manus and Connor were frozen in the fight so I had to go out slowly backwards to see what happened, which meant Busola got there before me and opened the door to Canon Byrne.

'Kathleen, is your mammy or daddy at home?' I was halfway down the stairs trying to turn back and hide but he saw me and peered in, 'Who's that? Connor?'

At least he didn't know who I was, so I nodded.

Busola turned and saw me but her eyes went to my dad coming out the downstairs kitchen along the side of the stairs. 'Father!' he said, 'Come in! Long time no see!'

'Ah, now, that's the truth of it,' Canon Byrne said. 'And that's what I'm here about!' He grinned and they shook hands.

My mum came out, wringing her hands on a cloth, and said, 'Won't you come in, Father, for a cup of tea?'

'No,' he said, pointing at all the shopping bags in the hall, 'I can see you've your hands full.'

My dad looked up at me, 'Go on and put the kettle.'

I turned to go upstairs to the kitchen and heard Canon Byrne behind me, 'Will Connor not be coming to catechism?'

I scrambled up fast, banging my knee on the top stair, which slowed me down as I tried to absorb the ache. 'We've the future Bernadette Mary here,' he was putting his hand on Busola's head as I glanced back, 'doing great things with Sister Anne, but not so much as a glimpse of Connor or ... Manus, is it?'

I got into the kitchen as fast as my knee could come along, and put the kettle on. There was a soft explosion of gas because I couldn't get the match to light but when it did a blue puff of heat blew into my eyes to tell me what it would be like in Hell and that I was getting close. I crept back to the door and peeked down the stairs to see what was going to happen.

There was nothing happening. They were looking down at one of the shopping bags. I saw the bag move – all by itself. It moved and made a scratching noise. I put my head out on to the landing.

'What's that?' said Canon Byrne. 'Hiding another child away from me in there?'

My dad laughed and said, 'That's the one we are eating for supper.'

My mum was pale as paper and shaking. She had the dishcloth folded over one hand and tucked across under her arm, the other hand was covering her eyes not to look while my dad unzipped and pulled a white chicken struggling out the bag. My mum crossed herself.

'Just chicken!' my dad said.

It goggled its eyes, twisting its neck round like it was surprised to be there.

'That's a cock,' Canon Byrne said. 'You're going to kill it yourself?'

'Take that one to the backyard.' my dad was trying to give it to Busola, but she hid behind Canon Byrne and didn't want to touch it. 'What's the matter? It can just run round!'

The white wings fluttered and settled back into his hands. My dad shrugged as if to say it wouldn't hurt, but the chicken looked round to see what would happen next.

'You've definitely your hands full,' Canon Byrne said. He turned to my mum, 'I'll have that cup of tea.'

We were sitting in the upstairs kitchen, my dad banging pots downstairs and the grunts of wrestling coming off the telly in the living room. Busola was leaning on my mum's arm, sucking her thumb across the table from Canon Byrne who was blowing on his tea and not drinking it. I put the milk in my mum's cup and pushed it across to her, thinking I might be able to slip away, but he started before I could get the sugar out.

'Bridie, they're to be brought up in the faith. That was the understanding.'

My mum winced and nodded her head, 'Yes, Father.'

'What's going on?'

'Well ...' She was lowering her voice so my dad couldn't hear, 'I've to deal with his people. He's not very sympathetic.'

'Is that all you're telling me? I'm an old hand, Bridie. I've been with the White Fathers in his part of Africa, and I know what a white cockerel is. It's a sacrifice, is it?'

'Oh no, it's not black magic at all ... *oh, Jesus!* I didn't mean that. I meant the Muslims, Father. He says they've to let out the blood and pray over it.'

'That's as may be,' said Canon Byrne, 'but you've the three children and that's a responsibility – to God, to the Church and to them.'

'*Four*, Father,' she said, lifting her head up.

'Is it?' he said, looking at me, like I was going to become two people, but I could see he was on the back foot from the way my mum wasn't having any of him not knowing who we were and set her shoulders back, and closed her lips.

'Well, there's Connor here –' he said, and my mum flashed her eyes at me like he'd just made it worse but I shouldn't say anything. My face went hot and flushed and I felt my ears burning.

'He doesn't know who we are, Mum,' Busola said with her thumb still in her mouth.

'*Sh!* you!' and she shook Busola off her arm, even though Busola didn't budge and grabbed it back and leaned on it.

'Now, Bridie, you're doing your best. You haven't been in the best of health and you've a big family. I know the sacral burden falls to women, and that's good for Kathleen, but that's no excuse not bringing Connor into the Church, is it? He's not in catechism.'

'Bernadette Mary,' Busola said, taking her thumb out her mouth and giving him her scary blank stare. 'And Jesus loves me. Sister Anne says.'

'Now, go on, you two. Go and watch television,' my mum said, but I was stuck and Busola wasn't moving.

Canon Byrne wiped the bald top of his head with his hand and nodded, and gave a big sigh. He looked at my mum, and at Busola and at me. 'We'll have to start again,' he said. 'How is it the chickens are not coming to church? *Oh, for God's sake!* The *children* aren't coming? And is there anything I can do to help?'

He took a big gulp of his tea and put the cup down gently on the table, giving my mum a long look, and making peace. 'I'm old now, Bridie,' he could see an opening, 'and I can't for the life of me pin a name to every last chicken I've on my conscience. Truth be told, I'd want to go home. Knowing full well I'll never get back there. Couldn't tell you the way. And why would I want to leave you and your beautiful children when they never loved us enough in Ireland to keep a hold? Isn't that where we are?'

'It is,' she said.

And that would have been good, because they liked each other, and he gave my mum lots of support and she said interesting things to him I never heard her say otherwise, but Busola pointed at me and said, '*He's* the one who's missing.' They all looked, 'He spent his collection money going to the pictures.'

I thought the ground was going to swallow me up, but it didn't. I was still there, my face burning in front of them.

'You?' my mum said.

I looked at her and didn't say anything.

'I'm the only one who goes,' Busola said.

My mum put her head in her hands. She looked at Canon Byrne and said, 'What am I to do?'

'Was it a good film?' he asked.

'It was Moses,' I said.

He laughed. Still holding her head in one hand, she shook her fist at me, 'Ye'll go to the devil, all of you! And you'll never see the face of God!'

It was my turn in the backyard, digging up earth in the cracks and watching the cock in its white feathers poking about in the corners. It moved in behind the bins and came back in jerky slow motion, trying not to notice me. Canon Byrne was upstairs, laughing with my mum and dad who'd brought up bottles of Guinness.

I was frightened. I wanted to see the face of God and I wasn't going to. The backyard looked grey, like the bins, and the crumbling bricks along the backyard wall looked sooty and black. The broken concrete on the ground made me feel there wasn't any colour anywhere, just the dirt in the cracks. Only the cock's bright red bits on its head looked like drops of blood. I looked up in the sky, the blue had gone overcast and grey. It was hot and heavy, with spots of rain falling and drying up before it could get wet. The beady eye fixed on me and scratched its claws on the ground. When God turns away from you, there's a wind and you feel someone else is watching. The clothes pegs shook on the washing line and there was a white ruffle of feathers. The back door banged shut, I was on my own. I looked up for God and couldn't see him. I lifted up my arms to the clouds floating over the roof of the church, and remembered that's what Moses did. For a moment I thought I *have* seen the face of God. It's Charlton Heston. I had to cross myself because it wasn't true. He was Moses, a murderer. I glanced at the cock and it was walking away from me past the upturned metal bucket, so I thought I better keep on going. I turned up again to the heavy grey-white clouds and saw a dark smudge forming above a lip, then eyes and the white face of Charlie Chaplin, looking detached and kind and helpless. I couldn't make him look down at me, he drifted away into the clouds.

My eyes were welling up with tears.

Why are you crying? I said to myself.

Because the devil had won.

Canon Byrne was gone and my mum had switched off the telly to tell us off. My dad was standing by the door, half in, half out, and stood back to let me through, his hand on the back of my head pushing me gently into the room.

'There he is,' she said. 'And who took him the wrong way?'

Manus and Connor didn't even bother to look at me. They knew it was my fault. I sat down as quickly as I could.

'And what happened on the way home?' she said.

That's when Connor gave me daggers with his eyes and Manus looked at the floor.

'Are ye animals, or have you no fear of God?!'

'*Ah-ah!* Calm down,' my dad said to her. 'Just talk to them. They are children.'

'The curse of God on the child brings the devil to this house!'

My dad stopped it. 'That's enough! God is not cursing any-one here,' he said. 'They will choose for themselves.'

'How can they choose if they don't know? If you won't let them?' she said, on the edge of tears and shaking.

They'd been drinking so it was unsteady. I didn't want it to get out of control, but there was nothing I could do except hold on tight to the arm of the sofa.

'I'm not stopping anyone,' my dad said. 'Let them think.'

He was holding on to the door handles but my mum was standing in front of us, trembling from the chin, as though it was her who was on trial and losing the struggle to speak up for God.

Manus looked at me like he wanted to gob in my face. I looked away and saw Busola standing in the corner by the win-dow, flicking the curtain open from behind and looking down at the street. I hadn't noticed her before. She was better at disap-pearing than me.

'I think you've got a nerve,' my mum said, 'bringing your *juju* into the house!'

We all looked at my dad. His eyes clouded, 'You are confusing them,' he said.

'God is good,' and that was everything out in the open – they were going to fight. 'Whose side are you on?' she said to us.

No one answered.

Connor closed his eyes. Manus looked down again. Busola looked at my dad like it was his fault, even though I knew it was mine.

'I turn my back in the hospital, and you've turned them against me,' my mum said.

And he said, 'You are ambushing them.'

She had a look on her face that wasn't disappointed. It was a look of being on her own, expecting to be wounded. We were betraying her and moving away from God, and it was a way of being strong. She faced my dad, 'You're poisoning their minds against me.'

He flew off the handle and into the room, making the floorboards creak under his weight. Connor jumped up on his feet and got in the way. 'Who is poisoning who?' my dad was shouting. 'Look at Busola!' We all looked at her trying to disappear behind the curtain. 'She won't go to bed without knicker! And why?' My dad was screwing his face into a fist, 'She doesn't want Jesus to see her without clothes, and he's always looking!' The look on his face curled up in disgust, '*Always looking!* Who are you putting with her in bed?'

'The blaspheming ... !' but she didn't finish, she just took her rosary and started praying.

'*Son of God*,' he muttered. 'God has no son to embarrass you with knicker ...' but he didn't finish, either, because he'd gone too far. She was glaring at him, and he left the room.

There was the click of the rosary, the whisper of *blessed art thou among sinners* and Busola let out a stream of pee, running down her leg by the curtain and pooling on the carpet before it soaked in. Manus picked a towel off the drying frame and started mopping it up, moving the curtain around her feet as she stood there looking out the window. Connor shrugged and went back to turn on the television but stopped as my dad came straight back into the room.

'Keep Busola,' he said, 'the boys can come with me.'

My mum wasn't looking at him. He followed to where she was staring down at Busola by the window with Manus stooped over drying her feet.

Off to See the Wizard ...

The first thing I saw were glittering red shoes filling the whole screen because my dad made us arrive late and there wasn't hardly anywhere left to sit. Manus and Connor found their own seats so I had to climb up the back in the dark with my dad saying '*Excuse me*' to everyone because he couldn't see he was the only grown-up there. The red shoes were on the end of a witch a house had fallen on top of, so only her feet were showing.

My dad sat down beside me and wiped his glasses. He let out a gasp when he saw there was a wicked green witch with a sharp nose and pointed hat trying to get her fingers on the shoes. He looked round like we weren't supposed to be there and I got ready to go but he saw by the electric sparks coming out the witch's hands that the cinema was packed with children.

'What's going on?' he said.

'*Sh.*' people behind him were craning their necks to see past his head. He looked up at the screen, reflecting in his glasses, and shrank in his seat.

My mum wasn't speaking to me. She took Busola to church and brought her back, making a fuss over the frilly gloves she was going to wear for first communion. Busola clammed up and didn't say anything, until Nana turned up out the blue. I was leaning out the window, wondering where Connor was after

Manus went off with my dad, and I saw the shape of her coat coming up the street. She had a load of bags and I ran out the house to jump up and take them. In no time there was bacon boiling in the pot and bags of broken chocolates from the factory where she worked.

'What's your favourite?' I asked Busola, who had chocolate smears all over her mouth.

'Yum! Yum! Pig's trotters!' she said, making a nose like a pig and cramming a whole fistful in from the bag Nana gave her. She looked at me, munching her way through, and said, '*You're a pig.*'

I moved away and went to sit in the kitchen. Nana was at the table peeling potatoes and talking to my mum at the cooker, but they stopped when I came in.

'Is it you, the troublemaker?' Nana said.

I didn't know what to say to that, so I looked at my mum but she just rattled the pots like she didn't want me there. I sat on the edge of the chair next to Nana.

'Well, I'm the peacemaker,' Nana said, 'and you've to answer me this. Do you believe in God?'

'Yes,' I said.

'That God has made you and he'll not let you go?'

I frowned at her and looked at my mum.

'And if I give you Connor's bag of chocolates will you answer?' she said. I nodded. But then I thought that was like being a pig, so I shook my head. 'There, now, Bridie. That's what I call a normal little boy with no more self-control than he should have. And putting them on the spot doesn't help.'

'*Kat!*' my mum called out. 'Come and show Nana your gloves!'

I wasn't sure how it happened but it put Nana on my side. She gave me a knife and let me cut the potatoes into chunks. Busola came in with her white gloves and showed them to Nana with my mum looking on. Her hands and the gloves were covered in chocolate. She threw them down on top of the potato peelings and walked out.

The bacon bubbled away and Nana and my mum looked at each other.

'That'll wash off,' Nana said.

The wrestling was on again, Connor was out but Manus was back and watching it with a bag of chocolates on his lap. I was feeling a bit sick and the thump of the wrestlers' bodies banging into each other was making me queasy. I went out the room past the kitchen where my dad was at the table talking to Nana. They had bottles of Guinness on the go, but my mum wasn't drinking, she was crying.

'Look at their children, and look what he's doing for yours,' Nana was saying. 'They're only jealous. There's no nun in this house, and there doesn't need to be. He's getting them an education.'

I stuck my head round the door to see my mum standing by the cooker. Her eyes were rimmed with red and she was blowing her nose with a tissue. Nana and my dad were at the table, and she was taking his side. I didn't know how to take my mum's. She wasn't talking to me.

My dad waved me away, 'Go and play.' I looked back at my mum and she nodded, raising her eyebrows at me, 'Go on,' she said.

Going downstairs I heard Nana saying, '*God doesn't think less of these children for the lovely tan. There's nothing wrong with them.'* I froze on the stair, seeing the chocolate stains on the white gloves and feeling sad I couldn't say my prayers.

Mr Ajani came out the downstairs kitchen along by the stairs and went into his room. He was closing the door, holding a saucepan, and saw me. My dad burst out, '*No, I did not say that!*'

'Are you listening?' Mr Ajani said.

I shook my head and felt dizzy.

'Your sister is in the backyard, go and play.' He gave me a smile that was wicked and kind at the same time and closed his door.

Busola was playing hopscotch on her own with a piece of chalk. I sat on the upturned metal mop bucket and watched as she stooped on one leg to snatch up the chalk on her way past.

'Can I play?' I said.

She looked at me, jumped two squares and one again on one leg and said, 'No, you have to grow up on your own.'

She got her balance, jumped and span round on to two feet facing away from me.

I didn't know what to do, so I kicked the bucket with the back heel of my sandal to say I was still there, but she ignored me.

'Mummy thinks there's something wrong with us,' I said.

She let out a laugh and launched back along the squares to the beginning and span round again. She was getting her chalk ready for the next square.

'You can laugh,' I said. 'That's why she takes you to church.'

She looked up at me, frowned, then threw her chalk and got it on the next square. 'Jealous,' she said, like that's what she expected.

'No I'm not. Daddy takes me to Saturday morning pictures.'

'I'm not your mum,' she said, 'I don't care,' and she skipped up to the chalk square.

'What they making you do?' I said.

She stooped to pick her chalk up. 'You know, you were there.'

'Are you a nun?'

She stood up straight, lifting on one leg into the air, 'No.'

'Then why you doing it?'

'Helping Mum.'

I thought about it as Busola skipped to the end and span round. I could smell the bacon still bubbling in the pot upstairs.

'You peed on the carpet,' I said. 'There *is* something wrong with you.'

She turned her head and looked at me over her shoulder. It was a smile like Mr Ajani's – but it wasn't kind, it was pity. 'I couldn't hold it in,' she said. 'What's wrong with that?'

She skipped fast all the way back and span round to face me. 'If it's all right for Manus, it's all right for me.'

'Manus helped you wipe it up,' I said. 'You wouldn't piss in front of the nuns.'

Busola looked at me across the empty squares. 'God is watching you,' she said.

I looked up, there was no one watching from the windows, they were shut. Even if someone was standing behind the net curtains they couldn't hear us.

'Mummy's wrong,' I said. 'The nuns don't love us.'

She stood holding the chalk, with one hand on her waist like she didn't care what I said. I looked up again to make sure no one was there.

'They don't have to love you,' she said. 'Jesus does. Sister Anne says.'

'What if she doesn't even like you?'

Busola shrugged, 'She wants me to be a nun.'

'Because you'll give in?'

She pointed her chalk finger at me, 'She wants to stop me being like you.'

I didn't like the sound of that. I couldn't remember which one Sister Anne was, but I didn't want any of them to know who I was. I didn't know what Busola had told them.

'Being like me what?' I said.

'You don't believe in God, and you're scared.'

The game was over. But I wasn't ready to let it end, I didn't want her to win. She didn't believe God was watching her being cruel to me. She wasn't doing it for my mum. She was doing it because she was horrible, and the nuns understood about being wicked. And my mum was making her do it.

'Mummy doesn't trust you,' I said.

'You shut up,' she said. 'Who asked you?'

'You can't shut me up.'

'I can.'

'How?' And I put my jaw up and had my hard face on, I was going to hit her in a minute.

'You're the devil,' she said.

'Who's the devil?'

My dad looked at me over the edge of the book and pushed up his glasses, 'The angel who refused to bow down to Adam.'

'Who's Adam?'

'Adam and Eve,' he said. 'What do you want to know?'

'Is he bad?'

My dad shrugged and shifted in his seat. Busola was in the bottom bunk next to me in her pyjamas while Nana got ready for bed upstairs. I could feel Busola getting ready in case I tried to get her in trouble. 'That can depend,' he said.

'On what?' Busola said.

He put the book down on his lap and leaned back and put his finger up his nose like he was digging around inside for something to say. He made a big popping sound in his nostril and folded his arms. 'When God made Adam,' and he put his careful voice on, 'he wanted the angels to bow down and worship him. Iblis refused because he would bow down only to God.' And he shrugged. 'He could say he was the first good Muslim.'

'But God doesn't like him?' I said.

'Who's Iblis?' Manus said from the top bunk.

Connor was yawning across from my dad on the single bed with the covers up to his neck because he wanted everyone to get out and go to sleep – he'd been playing out all day with his friends on top of having gone to the pictures.

'The devil,' my dad said. 'But there are lots of names for someone who can play tricks on you and let you down and change shape,' he said.

'He's been around longer than people?' I said, because I wanted Busola to hear I wasn't old enough to be the devil.

'That devil doesn't exist,' my dad said, which wasn't what I was expecting. 'It's just misunderstanding.'

'He does,' Busola said.

'There's no devil going to walk in this room and turn on the light when you're sleeping,' he said, trying to listen to everyone.

'I'm sleeping upstairs with Nana,' she said.

'There *is* a devil in the story, though,' Manus said.

'Let's get on with it,' said Connor, and we knew he meant get it over. It was *Rumpelstiltskin*. We didn't want to tell my dad we already knew it, because reading at bedtime was part of the new way of looking after us they'd agreed with Nana.

My mum looked in for Busola. 'Go up and say your prayers,' she said. 'Nana's going to bed.'

'Daddy says there's no devil,' Busola said.

'*Rumpelstiltskin* is my name ... !' my dad said, reading on and not waiting for any more trouble.

'Why can't the devil be a girl?' I said.

'What's this?' my mum asked.

'Can I let Daddy finish the story?' Busola said.

My mum gave us five minutes and left the room to listen outside on the landing. 'Tell us the other story about the devil not being there,' Manus said, 'we know this one.' My dad shrugged and said loudly, 'Are you listening?' And this was the story he told us.

The devil, he said, was a singer, he sings. He jumps up and down and dances. When he was up there in heaven he organised all the choirs. But when he was cast down to this world there was only silence.

'Is that when Lucifer turns into Satan?' Manus asked.

'You know,' he said, 'we don't where I come from have any wicked being. We think of him as someone who disciplines people.'

'When they do something wrong?' I said.

'When they don't tell the truth,' Busola said.

But the devil still liked to do what he was doing before, my dad said, only now he went round keeping people quiet so there wouldn't be any singing and no one would tell the truth. So what we had to do to keep the devil off was not *shut up* but speak up.

'That devil's sneaky,' Manus said.

'Like the Wizard of Oz?' I said.

Connor lifted up and shook his head, 'He's only hiding because he's frightened.'

'What's he frightened of?' I asked.

'Himself,' Manus said.

But we'd be safe from him, my dad said, because when we found ourselves singing and laughing and calling out it meant we were doing what we were supposed to and he couldn't do anything about that. He would just have to stamp his foot on the ground and disappear.

'Bedtime!' my mum said from the door.

'Can I go up and say my prayers, too?' I said, because if my dad was wrong about the devil ... I didn't want to be on the wrong side.

Nana was in her nightdress with dark stockings on over the bottoms of her legs. I was lying down in the bed next to Busola with my eyes shut and our hands up by our noses praying. Nana was kneeling on the floor with her elbows on the bed praying over us. She had a hairnet and wispy, grey-black curls that straggled down over her ears. There were brown blotches on her hands and on her face where she was old and the skin ran down in creases from her neck to the middle of her chest where there was a cross. I wasn't sure I should be there because the threads of blood and bare skin and freckles on her arms made me feel she was undressed and I shouldn't be looking. I tried to keep my eyes shut, but she was looking back at me like she knew I wasn't praying properly.

I shut my eyes really tight and listened to her and Busola saying the prayer for going to bed, *Now I lay me down to sleep, I pray the Lord my soul to keep, and if I die before I wake* – I peeked through one eye and she was still watching me, so I closed it – *I pray the Lord my soul to take, Amen.*

'God bless and keep you,' she said. But she didn't get up, she went on praying silently as I listened to her breathing, the speaking under her breath with her tongue moist in her lips, the feeling of Busola's arm getting heavy on top of me as though we were both dead.

I didn't want to die. I wanted to wake up with Nana and Busola and everyone back together. I felt God was someone who came in the night through the smoke on rushing wings and took you away. But instead of flying I felt heavy, as though I was falling asleep on the way to the devil. I was struggling to wake up and fight him off, but it was my dad lifting me up and taking me off downstairs in his arms. I gave in because I didn't feel it mattered if he was God or the devil, or both, he was carrying me and I had to go.

In the Dead of Night

I'd come down to the kitchen to get a drink of water, and drank it straight out the tap but it splashed my pyjamas and I switched the light on to see. She was sitting on her own in the corner watching me. It was the middle of the night and there was no one about. 'What's a matter, Mum?'

'Turn off the light.'

It was bright for me too, I switched it off. My eyes got used to the light from the window again, and I saw her sitting there, holding out her hand to me from the corner.

'I'm thinking,' she said.

I tried to see from her face what she was thinking, but it was a shadow with the bright frown from a moment before.

'I can go back to bed,' I said.

'No, that's fine, come and hold me.'

I bumped into chairs on my way over until I felt her lap and climbed up on it, 'You scared me.'

'*Sh*,' she said, 'do you know what I'm thinking?'

I shook my head.

'That I haven't been a good mother, away in that hospital. Look at you all wet.' She unbuttoned my top and wiped my chest with the dry part, then hugged me up close. I could feel her heart and a big sadness pouring into mine that I kept getting it wrong. She felt it was her fault I was wet, and I couldn't have a better mum.

'I couldn't see the cup,' I said.

'*Sh*, it's fine.'

I put my ear up against her shoulder and listened to the quiet in the house. It was the safest place in the whole world. I wasn't afraid of the shapes in the dark, the way the night was coming in through the window.

'I'm just saying, it hasn't turned out the way I wanted. I hoped this could be a better life for you.'

'This is the best,' I said.

She took my chin up to look at me, and looked silver like a ghost with soft eyes moving in the dark.

'It's going to be fine,' and she folded her arms round me tighter. 'God will tell us how we go from here.'

I didn't want her to go, I wanted to hold on. 'It was hard you were gone,' I said. There wasn't anywhere to go without her.

'Did you ask after me?'

I looked up to let her know that wasn't fair, I only knew what Daddy told me. 'I even miss you when I've got you,' I said.

She smiled, so I let myself fall back to sleep in her arms. '*Go on, go up. You won't need a top, it's warm enough.*' I woke up again and told her what it felt like, 'I couldn't sleep.'

'Your dreams are for you,' she said. 'Go on.'

'Does Daddy miss you?'

She put her finger against my lips, and I closed my eyes. '*Go to sleep.*' A cloud was coming down, I couldn't fight it. I felt her hand come down to hold my feet, and I reached up to hold a strand of her hair. '*He's not romantic.*'

Whitsun

'Let's start again,' my dad said.

The telly was off and the homework tables were out with their flaps up. I could feel chewing-gum stuck to the underside of the wood, round and smooth and hard, not even sticky, so it must have been there from the last time. Or maybe the time before, because it came off in my hand, and I was trying to get it back but it wouldn't stick. I would have tried licking it but he might see me, and I didn't know whose it was.

'Twelve nines?'

Manus and Connor had their heads down on the other table doing long division, and I was being tested with Busola on our times tables. It was her turn with number nine and she was getting it wrong.

'Nine times twelve?'

Times ten was going to be easy, she was times eleven, and I was going to be twelve. I didn't have twelve in my head and I knew it was coming. I could feel the knuckles coming to knock on my head already, but that just made it harder. It tumbled over in my mind around sixty, then twelve nines was a hundred and ... He didn't even ask the sums in order. It was at random.

'A hundred ...' Busola said, 'No, ninety ...' She was counting on her fingers, that was a bad sign. '... eight?'

'Let's start from the beginning.' It was all right, he wasn't angry, he just pushed up his glasses and went back. 'Two nines are ...?'

'Eighteen,' she started, and went on, 'three nines are twenty-seven. Four nines are thirty-six ...'

It was like a drum beat – *six dah-dah fifty-four, seven dah-dah did-dee dee, ah dah-dah did-dee do* ... She gave it a bounce, because she could dance and that's what she wanted to do, not numbers, and by doing it that way you don't fall and the steps keep coming ... *nah-nah dah-di dah* ... I'd drifted off because the next one was 'Twelve nines are a hundred and eight.' That was it – twelve nines, nine twelves – only now it was me going over the cliff because she'd stopped. I had a panic but I calmed it, there was still times ten and eleven to go.

My dad was patting her on the head and saying she must know it off by heart for next time, but he could see she was working hard. He looked back at the sums and I thought he couldn't see me, because I put the chewing-gum in my pocket and made a sign at Busola with my hands over my head that she was a big-head and a show-off. Only it was too quiet, I could hear Connor scratching his head and Manus counting numbers under his breath, but my dad wasn't moving and Busola was staring at me.

'What are you doing?' my dad said.

The window was reflecting in his glasses and I couldn't see until I leaned back that even though his head was bent over the sums he was looking at me.

'Be careful,' he said in a voice telling me to get ready.

Manus looked up, checked my dad had his back turned, and gave me a warning with his eyes not to get it wrong.

'Now, we won't bother with ten, eleven,' my dad said. 'Your turn, twelve.'

It wasn't like a headache. It was my head feeling thick and heavy so my neck had to bend down, and everything was slow. It was like I could see all the numbers swimming like flashes off the edge of my eyes but I couldn't catch them.

'Seven twelves?'

That's seventy and two sevens ... 'Eighty-four,' I said.

He looked at me like he saw me working it out and said, 'By heart.'

My head was hurting, like it was burning, but I couldn't be ill.

'Twelve twelves?'

'Hundred and forty-four.' It was the last number in black on the back of the red exercise books that had all twelve of the times tables on and I remembered because it was the biggest number and if I could learn that –

'Nine twelves?'

'A hundred and ...' What was it? It was gone. I couldn't work it out because Busola had just told me and I'd forgotten. It was blocked. It was her fault turning numbers into a song so I'd forget the words, *twelve dah-dah ... dah-dah ...* It wasn't my fault there were numbers that didn't want to be learnt, that jumped about and swapped and disappeared.

'Twelve nines?'

There wasn't time and I'd had to help Mummy do the shopping, and clean the stairs, other children could play out, they were shouting outside the window, I couldn't think when the telly was on, and I didn't know it. I hadn't made time, but I could have all this time that was empty to look round at Manus and Connor who were both looking at me with their mouths open, Manus trying to count out for me by nodding his head until I lost count how many times he'd done it. I had lots of time because I didn't know what twelve nines was, and even more to look back at Busola who was trying to blink at me, and time to get ready because I was the only one who knew my head was empty until my dad stepped in and said, 'You don't know?'

I shook my head.

He took off his glasses, 'The only thing you will inherit from me,' he said, 'is your education.' And he put his glasses back on.

Connor leaned back in his chair like he didn't think anything was going to happen. My dad turned round to them on the other table and said, '*Oya!* You can finish.'

They closed their books and we were out of trouble.

'Not you.'

I was getting ready to go, and stopped with my arm on the table.

'Two twelves?'

I didn't know. My head was blocked, I couldn't do it. I could a minute ago, but I couldn't any more. I looked at him.

'Two times twelve?'

I didn't even want to shake my head.

He took off his glasses again, and wiped his eyes with both hands and looked at me. He wasn't going to explode but no one moved. I could see a vein throbbing over his eye.

My mum looked in the door. 'We've to go,' she said.

He nodded, and she went away and closed the door.

'You have to know,' he said. 'You don't like numbers, still you have to know. And you can't fool with numbers. They will say *no*, it's not true, you're not counting them.'

'They're hard,' Manus said.

My dad turned round to look at him and put his glasses on, 'Hard and fast. They won't change. That's something you can build on.'

'They don't do this in school,' Connor said.

'So we have to do the building at home.'

'The top of the street's been knocked down,' said Busola.

It was like the houses had been eaten from the inside. They just had the wall of them facing the street with the sky through the windows. And then they knocked that down.

'Like a bomb hit it,' a man said, passing by in the street as my dad was locking the front door. My mum was beside me putting her coat on and looking up at the flattened houses – you could see through to the back of the school playground. Bits of brick wall were standing, but the houses just weren't there any more. And they'd knocked down the first two houses on the corner of our street next to the bomb site.

'The council,' my dad said over his shoulder.

'Why?' The man paused on his way and shook his head, 'Because they got outside loos?'

My dad shrugged, putting the keys in his pocket, 'They want the land. Big Ben is just there.'

'We're being slum cleared,' Manus said.

My mum looked embarrassed and tried to hide it by taking hold of Busola's hand to go. But you couldn't hide it, the houses were gone.

The man looked at us closer and I looked at him. He was sunburned but his face was smooth except for the bald lines in folds on his forehead, his ears were too big and he had sandy hair in wisps off the top of his head. He wasn't a tramp, he had old clothes on and they were dusty but he knew where he was, and his eyes were blue like the sky.

'They didn't put down foundations under these houses,' he said. 'They got put up like tents on top of Vauxhall Gardens. There was always a storm gonna blow 'em down.'

My dad put a finger up in the air, 'What wind?' My mum shifted on to the other foot and pulled Busola closer. 'I'm not going anywhere,' and he put his chin out like he didn't care what anyone thought.

The man nodded and a grin came over his face, 'I used to live here. Loved it.' He nodded at my mum and went on up the street towards the missing houses, only turning back over his shoulder to call out, 'Good luck.'

'OK, we can go,' my dad said, and my mum made us hold hands to go down to the main road.

I was holding on to Manus at the back and whispered, 'What's slum cleared? Did you know they were gonna knock down those houses?'

'Open your eyes,' he said.

I looked back and saw the man climb on to the mound of broken bricks and stumble down the other side holding on to a wall with part of the windowsill in it, like that was where he lived and he was going home.

'They gonna do that to us?' We turned the corner towards the train, the cars were louder on the main road, so I stopped and pulled Manus's hand when he didn't answer, 'Are they?'

He looked at me and pulled me close so he could say it loud in my ear, 'Nine twelves, a hundred and eight!' He ran dragging me by the sleeve to catch up the others, 'You have to learn it ... if you don't want the house to fall on you.'

I couldn't wake up. Everyone was telling me wake up. My dad was telling me and the man with blue eyes was looking at me from the bomb site. Manus was shaking me and everyone was saying he's asleep. I could see everything really clearly, the clouds in the sky through the empty windows, my mum's face in the window at Sainsbury's, the girl looking down at me through the net curtains, the black eyes of the man at the door of the off-licence, but it wasn't what people wanted me to see, and I didn't know the answer. *'Open your eyes,'* Manus was saying, and I thought if I could close them, I could get them open. I blinked and we were getting off the train into the open air. 'Time to go,' my mum said, and my dad lifted me off the seat and carried me on to the platform to find my feet. I was feeling everyone was talking at me and I didn't understand, but they were speaking about which way to go for the way out.

'That's the way we were here, weren't we, the last time?' my mum said.

'Follow me,' said Connor, and he led us off along the platform with my dad smiling to my mum at him taking over.

I grabbed hold of Manus not to get left behind and get the strength back in my legs, but he shook me off. Then I got a surge back in my legs because I felt the edge of the platform pulling me towards it and I had to keep to the wall to stop myself going over. I hurried up past him and Busola who was holding my mum's hand and took hold of my dad's. I could see he was wondering what I was doing as I looked up.

'Hundred and eight,' I said.

It took him a moment and then he burst out in surprise through his nose and his eyes, letting his mouth open wide. He reached down round my waist and swung me up under his arm and carried me down off the platform.

'*Jump!*'

She wouldn't, she was sulking because it was superstitious and she didn't want to.

'*Jump*, now, it's good for you,' my uncle said.

'*Arrah*, that's old hat,' my mum said, and crossed herself with a worried look on her face.

'And a cup of tea's idolatry – *jump!*' He grabbed her round the waist and jumped with her over the fire. They both scattered the smoke and I could see she had her eyes closed. Everybody burst out clapping and she got busy patting and smoothing down the long skirt she was wearing as though she didn't want any smoke there and it might catch fire. Uncle Eamon patted her on the back, 'Didn't hurt, and now that's done you'll have a drink.'

'I won't,' she said.

'Ah, you will. Tess, the invalid has a thirst on her.'

My aunt moved in and gave her a hug, and they spoke to each other but I didn't hear what they said.

Uncle Eamon and my dad started handing out drinks to everyone. Nana was there, and our cousin Sean, who was older than all of us, even Manus, and Paul who was Connor's age, and their sister Carmel, but there was lots to go round.

'Put the kettle on,' Tess said. The backyard had grass and a fire and no one wanted to go in, so we sat round with our drinks watching the fire crackle with smoke. It burned with long flames that settled down into a red and yellow glow before another log got put on and sparks flew up and the flames started catching hold again.

Nana was sat under the tree on a chair with her yellow drink and my mum was on a kitchen stool beside her with a glass of Guinness she wasn't drinking because she put it down and let it spill into the grass beside her. Tess was smoking on a blanket on the ground beside Carmel, with Busola across from them on a rolled-up carpet beside Sean who was teasing Nana about the colour of her drink. Nana was looking at him with her head on one side to hear what he'd say because he was wearing a yellow Beatles jacket from *Sgt. Pepper*. Busola and Carmel weren't playing, just sipping their Coca-Colas and looking at each other across the fire. The rest of us were sitting on the grass or running round for things to poke and throw in the flames. The dogs had been locked up in their kennel with a stick through the cage handles to stop them getting out. They were making loud snuffles and pants with their wet tongues out, lapping up water and letting their eyes join in. Uncle Eamon said they were guard dogs and he wouldn't let them in the house. They crouched low and wouldn't bark if he was around, but I didn't go near them just in case. He was standing up with my dad by the table with drinks at the back door, talking about what happened in Ireland.

'They knocked it down, Arthur's Quay,' he said, with a sweep of his arm, 'and you wouldn't mind, the houses were haunted!' He turned round, 'Isn't that right, Nana?'

She looked up. 'What?'

'You'd to leave that house?'

She looked round at everyone, and shook her head.

'Back home!' He was raising his voice like she couldn't hear him. 'You'd to lock up the door and go!'

'Is he deaf?' she said, and turned to Sean. 'Your father, tell him put in the hearing-aid.'

He looked round at Uncle Eamon and pointed to Nana's drink, 'She says put in the lemonade, Dad.'

'And a whisky while you're at it,' Tess said, holding up an empty glass.

'I'll lemonade you!' he said, getting off his elbow where he was leaning on the window ledge and bringing the bottle over to Tess. It made a loud *pop!* as he pulled out the top and it started glugging into the glass. '*Haunted!*' he said in a deep, breathy voice like he was trying to blow out the fire.

'*Stop!*' Tess pushed the glass up to clink on the bottle and stop it spilling on Carmel.

'And wasn't it the fright, Nana,' he said, '*turned your hair white!*'

I looked at Nana, her hair wasn't white. She had it back in a bun and it made her glasses look big reflecting the fire as she kept still and looked at him. 'I'll be dyeing again tomorrow,' she said.

'Give us a song, Nana,' said Tess, pushing Uncle Eamon away by the leg.

Nana shook her head and smoothed her dress down over her knees. She had on a white woolly cardigan, I couldn't remember her in light-coloured clothes before. I had my white Sunday shirt on, we all did, everyone was in white, except Sean who was in yellow and my dad who was wearing his white flowery Nigerian clothes spotted with round holes edged in red stitches with a silver-blue cloth hat folded over. Busola and Carmel were in the same white, flouncy dress with a round collar and short puffy arms, except Carmel had white shoes on. That's why they were looking at each other. I suddenly felt something was going on. I looked at my mum in her white blouse and black skirt, Tess barefoot in a cream miniskirt. All the lights were off in the house, and I could see everyone beginning to be bright by the fire as the light was going.

Sean jumped in, '*Picture yourself in a boat on a river with tangerine trees and marmalade skies ...*' He had a croaky voice, but Tess said, '*Tch!*' because it wasn't an old song. He carried on anyway, '*Somebody calls you, you answer quite slowly ... a girl with kaleidoscope eyes ...*' Manus had joined in and they both knew the words, '*Cellophane flowers of yellow and green ...*' By the time they got to the *duh-duh-duh* bit, Connor and Paul were standing up playing drums and the guitar with sticks and singing along, '*Lucy in the sky with diamonds, Lucy in the sky with diamonds ...*' Nana was roaring out laughing with her yellow drink held up away from her and her glasses bouncing. Only Busola and Carmel weren't moving, Tess had her hand up shielding her eyes and my mum was nodding her head along to it. I looked round at my dad, he was just watching. I couldn't see Uncle Eamon, he'd gone inside.

He came out wrestling two giant logs he threw on the fire so sparks flew up into the sky, and everyone settled in to the warm, with my dad bringing up two chairs for him and Uncle Eamon. I stopped listening to what people were saying and looked at the fire. Paul and Connor had their knees tucked up facing each other over by the dogs, swapping Arsenal football cards of Charlie George, Bob Wilson and Eddie Kelly. My mum was chanting '*Football crazy, football mad*' but they couldn't hear. Even the dogs looked bored, '*Charlie George, I'll give you a gob-stopper,*' Paul said. '*2-1,*' said Connor. It didn't even make sense. I stopped, and listened to the fire crackling.

It started to roar. My face was hot. It changed shape rushing out into the air, bright hot yellow and black, with hands, fingers, tongues, wings folding and flying off into smoke, then orange flames and ash as the logs collapsed back into black and red-hot rubble, and white flakes peeled off and flew up into the night. I shifted round to Busola on the carpet to get out the way of the smoke, but I had to wait to breathe so she shifted away from me and held on to Sean. Nana was singing and my mum was holding her hand. Manus was up on my dad's lap. It was old-fashioned, there wasn't a tune, but she made the droning sound of something you feel when you've lost your way and have to sit down on the ground. Everyone was listening. I looked back at the fire. The flames were alive, licking their tongues to speak to me. Somebody had to, they were going to knock the house down and no one was saying. They leapt up and flickered together, like they'd been telling me all the time *this is it, this. Is it*. I heard my mum and dad talking. Charlie said it, and Lottie. Susan with her cats – her name wasn't Susan. That was someone else. Was there a Susan? I looked at Busola leaning on the arm of Sean's yellow jacket with her thumb in her mouth. Perhaps she wasn't saying because Susan was someone who had nowhere to be, who only came if you talked about her. Manus said we were being slum cleared – they were coming to knock us down. And I didn't see it. My eyes were wide open, but it took for the houses up the top of the road to get knocked down. They didn't want us, and we didn't have anywhere to go. It was too bright, my face was burning and my back was cold. My eyes felt dry and hot from the smoke, like they were going to melt in the cold breeze that came across, and I could feel I was going to shiver.

'Come away out of the fire,' my mum said. I skirted round to get up on her lap with her arms folding me. The song had finished and everyone was looking into the flames. My mum felt warm. I looked across at Manus, leaning back safe on my dad's lap. The flames were going down, and my shirt smelt ironed. I was glad to be folded on my mum's lap because what I got from the fire was still shaking me. Busola was leaning in on Sean's arm, Carmel was watching her. There was just the afterglow and the feeling that everyone was together. I looked at my dad's face, glistening in the light, the blue hat threaded with silver, and up at the night sky, dark blue with stars in it. I wasn't worried the house was going to fall down. My dad was holding on to Manus and keeping the house safe. I could look up and breathe. A satellite moved out the stars into the blue.

'Will I tell this fella what's gone on?' Uncle Eamon said, and he leaned forward. They all called my dad Fela, because that was his name and they could say it like fella. No one spoke, so he leaned back towards my dad, 'Eviction's a dirty word.'

My dad nodded, he was listening to my mum shift with me on the stool. He smiled and said, 'They are calling this one compulsory purchase.'

'They'd put the blinkers on you. If it wasn't Irish fellas in the council we'd never got hold of this house.'

'Ah, that's enough of that now,' Tess said, 'there's children about.'

'The house wasn't haunted,' Nana said, 'that was the story when they wanted us out.'

'Ah, Nana, no, it was,' Tess said.

'Did you see a ghost?' Nana said.

'Carmel has school in the morning,' said Tess, and she started to get up. 'Eamon, they'll only be five in the back, run them home?'

'Now the banshee,' Nana said, 'I heard that. And so did your sister.'

I was sitting on my mum's lap in the back, the others were squashed up. My dad and Uncle Eamon were talking in the front as we drove into our road. The streetlamps were out and it was dark through to the lights by the school. The missing row of houses at the top was an empty gap that had stars pouring into it through a dark funnel of the rooftops narrowing towards each other along the street. I'd never seen so many stars.

'Holy Mother of God ... it's a ruin.' Uncle Eamon got out on the pavement to look and opened my mum's door. She put me out off her lap and let me stretch while my dad got the others out on the roadside and sent them round to the pavement. My mum wasn't moving for a bit so we waited for her. My uncle shook his head again, 'They'll speak no word and they'll curse you.'

My dad came round to the pavement and shoved his chin at them knocking down the houses, 'They can do their worst.' He leaned down over the car door to my mum.

We all stood up by the front door and I put my hands in my pockets because it was chilly and watched Uncle Eamon taking it in. He shook his head once more, and turned to look at my dad helping my mum, 'The stitch, is it?'

'I'll be all right,' my mum said.

'Terrible squeeze, the lot of you there in the back,' and he held open the car door while my dad lifted my mum out on to her feet. She stood for a moment holding on to the door to get her breath back.

'I'll be fine,' she said.

Manus went over and put his shoulder under for her to lean

on. She laughed but it hurt, so she took it and came towards us, telling my dad over her shoulder, 'The keys.'

He started to look for them in his pocket, and said to Uncle Eamon, 'Please, come inside.'

'No, there's work in the morning, a clear head or a brick'll split it.' He was looking at Busola and she stopped in the middle of a yawn and frowned. 'It's not any old ugly duckling gets to be a beautiful black swan, I've to sleep.'

No one moved as he got in the car, turned round in the road and drove off, waving out the window. I saw my mum look at my dad until he shook his head and said, 'School tomorrow.'

He opened the front door and took my mum over from Manus, letting her go in first and holding her arm, but she said she was all right and just let her go slowly. I hung back behind Connor and Busola, looking out at the stars in the dark. No one was saying anything, but I didn't know if Uncle Eamon thought I was ugly. And Busola didn't look like a swan. She looked like a girl in a white dress, and she was yawning. The light was off in the hall again and my mum said, 'Everyone to bed.' Manus was holding the door open, but I didn't want to follow in because I liked the feel of the dark, the way the sound of the street had changed and the stars were coming down. I could feel the chewing-gum in my pocket, the stars were so close I could almost reach up and stick it there. Manus frowned and started closing the door. I stuck my foot in to stop him, and flicked the gum up like an asteroid at the stars as far as it could go.

Part Two

Cowboys and Indians

There was a crowd following us, we were trying not to run. Busola held my hand all the way past the shops, along the crowded summer pavements, up past an ice-cream van, a red pillar box, parked cars, people.

'Just ignore them,' she said.

They were following us, stomping and shouting, as we would if we'd found something loud like that to do in the long, empty afternoons of the summer holidays that end with you turning to stare sunblind down on the ground at the length of your own shadow.

'Just keep walking.'

There's a gang of you spot something ludicrous, shameful, and you want everyone to know you're keeping watch – *Hark, hark, the dogs do bark!* That's what it sounded like, barking. *Woof! Woof! Woof!*

'Don't run.'

So we walked, hand in hand, past the old ladies in flowery dresses, old men with their sleeves rolled up, prams and babies, shop windows and awnings drawn down against the sun.

'*Nigger! Nigger!*' That's what they were chanting. They were wrong – we were on a church holiday to give poor children fresh air in their lungs – we were beggars. Two whole weeks away with each other, in the middle of nowhere, wondering why no one had asked us. '*Do you want to go on holiday?*' We never went anywhere on holiday so we thought *Butlins!* holiday camp. No one told us it was to get on a train and go into the Forest and get left on our own. That was sprung on us. We were beggars and orphans, and we felt like it. So we clung together.

There was the statue of Paddington Bear at the station, the crowds and the noise of the engines, and we thought that was far enough, could we go home now? There were church people who took our names, the labels pinned to our clothes, waving goodbye to our mum out the window, and the gasp of the train as it set off without her.

We sat in the railway carriage with the windows open, a dusty sickly smell coming off the upholstery, the seats joggling, the countryside rolling past, and a sick feeling in my stomach wondering who was going to meet us the other end. A man and a woman got on at Gloucester to take us off. We both said under our breaths we hoped it would be them, and it was. But there was a smell as we got down that wasn't London and made me not want to breathe. I couldn't open my mouth, I was going to faint.

'Was it a nice journey?'

'Yes, it was, thank you very much, I'm Katherine,' Busola said, using a voice I hadn't heard before. 'And he's Michael.' They both looked at me – my head spinning, taking a huge gulp of air – looked at each other, and led us along the platform past the whistles, the oily metal heat of the engine and clouds of smoke towards the smell I couldn't breathe.

'They think you can't talk,' Busola whispered as we followed them.

'You can pick strawberries in that field,' they said as we drove past a raised bank with gaps in the hedge. I looked up in the back seat – picking strawberries to eat, a strawberry field, growing wild, juicy and red – just the thought of it made me bite down without thinking on my ice lolly. The electric shock went straight through my teeth, up to the top of my head and down through my feet, out through my fingers, and slowly along my back in trickles of sweat. It locked my jaw so I couldn't speak, even to tell Busola. There were star bursts in front of my eyes, bright blurs of tears. All I could do was blink. I hadn't been away this far before ever.

Bang! went the pop-guns, *click! Bang!*

It was our first time alone in the town, and they trusted us to walk down and look for presents to take back. We'd already spent all the pocket money we'd earned from picking buckets of fruit – which wasn't much because we'd eaten them as we went along and I'd been sick and couldn't take the smell of fruit again without throwing up. So we agreed to pretend we were looking with money we'd brought from home which we didn't have. We were going to say we hadn't found anything to buy – it was just being polite.

'*Pull your trigger!*' They made a firing squad with their fingers and guns, '*Bang! Bang! Bang!*'

Some of them were older than us, but I wasn't worried because everyone was watching and Busola was a girl so it wasn't as though they were going to move in and beat us up. They were following behind.

We passed a shop window, at an angle to the street, and I could see me and Busola holding hands in silhouette under the awning. Behind us, in bright colours lit up on the street, was a tail of cowboys and Indians, a big posse of feather headdresses and cowboy hats and pop-guns. They were after us.

Caps were going off and some not exploding – *Click! Pop! Snap! Bang!* – and I expected to get an arrow in the back of my neck. But it never came.

'*Nigger! Nigger! Pull your trigger!*' Then the loud bit, '*Bang! Bang! Bang!*'

It was to show they were in charge and we weren't. We weren't from there, so they couldn't know anything about us. If they were anything like us, they wanted to kill something, and go home and have ice cream, and come back and do it again tomorrow.

'Just ignore them,' Busola said.

I gripped her hand tighter and tried not to take off. We weren't going to run, we weren't going to play.

Pop! went the guns. '*Bang! Bang! Bang!*' they shouted.

The baying for our blood fell away as we moved steadily out of the town – packs of children licking into their ice lollies, the bristle of feather and contorted faces, screams of '*Nigger! Nigger!*', the alarm of shrill, noisy laughter, voices shouting themselves hoarse – all falling away into a kind of deafness as we made our way steadily uphill, towards the endless summer of white clouds tumbling out the blue, up over the brow of the hill and round the corner to our turning on the right.

'How was that?' they asked when we got in.

'Fine, thank you very much,' Busola said. 'We didn't find anything to buy but we'll take our stilts home to show, if that's all right.'

Mr Brown had built us both wooden stilts and we'd spent most of the holiday practising on the steps of the back garden. We were quite good at it by the end because that's how long it took to introduce us to the headmaster's children across the road and until then we had to play by ourselves. We had outings – for me to swim and put my head under the brown water in the river, to pick strawberries, go for picnics in the Forest – but it didn't get started until we were wrestling Charles with his sister on the lawn to keep him pinned down.

'What's the matter?' he said, because I stopped suddenly.

His trouser leg got hitched up and I was staring straight at the skin above his sock. It was blank, a white I'd never seen before – it was wrong, it wasn't supposed to be like that, it was shocking.

'You sure?' he said when I said, 'Oh, nothing.' I suppose I meant there was no colour there – *none* – but I pulled the trouser leg down and went on wrestling. It was the party for us going and his sister was in a long party dress and he was in long trousers. They were the first middle-class children I'd met and they were very nice. We met over the fence the day before as we were on the stilts and they were trying to get a look at us from the footpath along the back. We became friends straight away and let them try our stilts and they asked if they could give us a party for our going away.

'Perhaps we should have introduced them sooner?' Mrs Brown said, but they were both teachers and Charles's dad was the headmaster and had a really big house so I understood that we had to be invited. And anyway before we could get to the party we had to deal with the lamp. Somebody had broken it and the pieces were lying smashed on the bedroom floor. One of us must have done it in our sleep, we didn't have table lamps by the bed at home, so that was what did it.

'Who broke the lamp?' Mrs Brown asked, and Busola said it was me. I didn't know it was so I wouldn't take the blame and shook my head. I'd already decided to leave the talking to Busola, but she wasn't being fair.

'You can both go up to the room and come out when someone owns up. Just tell us who did it and you can go to the party,' which was very fair, I thought, except when we got up there Busola turned on me.

'It's your fault, why don't you own up?'

'Because it's not! What if it's you? It's on your side!'

'You coward, you broke it!'

'You can tell them it's me all you want, you're not getting out!' I said, and that's how it stayed until they came up to check on us.

'You've got another ten minutes, the party's starting,' they said, and closed the door.

So what we did was toss a coin to see who was going to own up.

'Heads I win, tails you lose,' she said.

The coin was still in the air when I said, 'No.'

'All right,' she said, catching it, 'but if I lose, you're carrying the stilts, all the way home.'

That felt like the best deal I could get, so we did it again and I lost. I went down on my own and apologised to them saying it was probably in my sleep and I didn't remember doing it but we worked out what must have happened and it was my fault.

They looked at me like they'd never met me before.

'Thank you,' Mr Brown said.

It occurred to me the most I'd ever said to them was yes or no, and thank you.

'You speak well,' said Mrs Brown.

'Thank you,' I said.

'No problem, it's only a lamp,' and she sent me upstairs to get ready for the party as he was shaking his head.

It struck me going up the stairs that I really was in trouble. I'd stopped reading and I wasn't talking. The only person to talk to was Busola – whoever she was pretending to be – and I wasn't getting on with her.

'Let's make friends,' I said.

She looked up and said, 'What, with those people over there? We're leaving.'

'No,' I said, 'you and me.'

She let out a cackle like a witch, and doubled up laughing. Instead of being with me she was against me. She looked up from the bed and there were tears in her eyes so I thought about the strain it was on her as well.

'We've had that lynch mob after us, and you think you survived it without me?'

I could see her point.

When we got to the party there were four new children, two of them were dressed up as cowboys with those horses' manes going down the sides of their legs, sheriffs' badges, waistcoats and cowboy hats with stitching around the brim. So we were careful of them and stuck to Charles and his sister. Their dad had a beard and smoked a pipe, he stood off and watched us, but their mum was lovely with jellies and biscuits and party games. Charles was going to grammar school after the summer and was older and cleverer than us. That was the story, but to us he was kind and floppy and still just wanted to play and we were his excuse. We wrestled him down on the lawn because his sister said he was a big puppy dog and we had to stop him drowning in the pond.

'What pond?' I asked when we stopped wrestling to catch our breath. His eyes clouded and started to cry without him making a sound. We looked at his sister and she leant over to us and said Charles had jumped in and tried to kill himself in the river because he was unhappy, but their dad had jumped in and got him out.

'It wasn't like that,' Charles said.

'What was it like?' said Busola, and I would have told her because it was so kind and grown-up the way she asked it.

'I don't want to talk about it,' he said.

Their mum came out with the other children reaching round her for cakes and called us over to the wooden table, while Mr and Mrs Brown came out with their baby and the dad came out carrying a big glass jug of brown lemonade with leaves in it for the grown-ups. They were talking and laughing, with the other children hollering over the jug of clear lemonade the mum was pouring. Charles wiped his tears with his finger and thumb and buried them softly in the grass. He looked older and darker in his eyes, as though his childhood was over. His sister looked at us as he stood up and walked away, she plucked a blade of grass and sighed.

'He doesn't want to go to grammar school,' she said. 'They won't let him just play.' And she looked across at her mum and dad setting up the jellies and the cakes and the glasses of lemonade on the table, 'I'm going to be left on my own.'

'What shall we tell them when we get back?' We were lying in bed with our bags already packed on the floor.

'That you broke the lamp,' she said.

The pieces had been cleared up for us when we got back to the room. There was only one lamp left on my side of the bed, so I got my own back by switching it off and making her lie there in the dark until our eyes got used to the light from the window.

'Perhaps I should tell them you stopped speaking,' she said.

I didn't say anything, thinking she would laugh. But after a while I began to worry what would happen if she did tell them. I was rude to the people who looked after us. I wasn't, I just let her do the talking. What happened was I got on with their daughter who didn't speak. We played and just looked at each other. I went back to being a baby. But I was counting the days in my head, so I wasn't a baby. I was just trying to hold my breath. Was I trying to kill myself? Why wasn't I speaking?

'What about that voice you been using?' I said.

'I haven't the least idea what you're talking about,' she said. 'Could you explain?'

She put on that voice to keep people away, for it to be there instead of her. It was scary.

'You know what I mean,' I said.

'Goodnight. Don't forget to turn off the light,' and she turned away under the covers.

'Weren't you frightened?'

She didn't move.

'They could have beaten us up.'

'But they didn't.' It was her own voice. 'And we still have to get back. So let me sleep, before they come in the room and look at us.'

I didn't know they did that.

'Busola?' I said, but she didn't answer. 'Busola?'

I listened for footsteps on the landing. An owl called outside. I thought about the lamp broken on the floor. About who she'd become on the holiday. About what she knew and hadn't told me. The way she'd been with Charles, giving him a hug as we left. And when his sister asked where we came from, the way she'd cut in and said, '*The moon.*' About us being followed and called names, she said not to answer. About the way she looked after me. And I wouldn't speak. About wanting to be brave like her, and I wasn't.

Our dad was in the station, standing with his foot up at a stall smoking and looking down the platform. He saw us from a distance and came over and chatted to the people who were getting us off the train with our bags. We showed him our stilts which we'd lifted ourselves off the overhead racks. He let us carry them all the way to the car, saying we had to write and thank those people as soon as we got home, what was their name? Mr and Mrs Brown, we said, they were teachers. Did we like being away on holiday? Neither of us said anything, but Busola looked at me and nodded.

We were in the green car going back over Vauxhall Bridge. It was old-fashioned, and the running-board under the doors was a bit broken, but it had red leather seats and orange lights that flapped out like ears at the side, and it was our dad's car and made us feel better. I felt a pressure come off my chest as we got over the river, like a weight I didn't know was there but that made it hard to breathe, and as we came down the slope the other side I was back home.

We stopped suddenly and the whole of the back seat tumbled over on top of us. Our dad didn't seem to notice we were underneath as he slammed his door shut and opened the boot to get our bags out. Busola looked at me across the stilts which had been on our laps. It was awkward because our heads were bent under the overturned seat, so we didn't speak. The door opened and he pulled us out saying he'd soon get it fixed. Our mum was at the window waving to us as he walked off with the bags and we pulled our stilts free. She was in her nightgown and her hair was grey. Manus and Connor were still away on holiday, our dad said, and she'd been in hospital.

He stopped at the door to wait for us with the key in his hand, glancing up at the window. Busola and me looked at each other, and got up on our stilts to show our mum and dad how good we were. We walked towards them along the pavement, taking tall strides because we'd grown up and they hadn't been there to see it.

Tribal Scars

'Your dad's got scars on his face,' Wilf said, backing away from me at the door. I didn't know what he was talking about. We'd been playing out and I wanted to go in for a drink.

'What?'

'Your dad's got scars,' he said, 'all over his *raas claat* face!'

I looked at him funny because his mum and dad were West Indian and he dropped his voice deep sometimes to speak like them, but I never heard them say that.

'What scars?'

Both his mum and dad were nice to me, especially Mrs Aarons, who looked down at me seriously with a long-drawn-out face that had those Deputy Dawg marks going down from her nose to the corners of her mouth. When she smiled, the lines lifted up under her cheeks and her eyes sparkled with fun. She said she liked me because I was a clever boy and I should please teach Wilf how to be brighter than he is and better behaved, because even though he was good at sport you can't spend all your life running.

His dad was a carpenter for the council and always shook my hand using both of his which were huge and soft, with short stubby fingers. He looked at you and sized you up and made a note in his mind before moving back quietly behind his wife, from where he fiddled with bits of wood to be doing up their house with.

'No, no,' he said, 'leave the boys, they have things to do.'

We got water from the tap in the back kitchen where they always sat, and you could see as you passed the open door of their front room there were lots of frilly things in pink and blue with glass bowls and plastic yellow flowers.

'What's in that room?' I asked, and his mum looked at me like it was a secret I shouldn't be asking.

'Curious, eh?' she said. 'And you would like to find out?'

I still had the cup in my hand, it was empty and I didn't know where to put it, so I nodded.

'Still fixing up,' his dad said, 'but you could go in.'

'Always fixing, never finish,' she said, and took the cup from me with a wink. 'Wilf could a learn some a dat.' She was shaking her head at me with her face long, 'Always finish, never fix – dash and done.'

'You' mother nag so?' his dad asked, looking up at me. 'Soon done,' he said, and looked down again.

'And you don' think is time I have my feet up like you was promising me the moon to get me in the boat and come? Seasick tek me an' me neck dangling over the side so! Him fixing me a deck chair on the *Titanic*, eh?'

I looked at Wilf who rolled his eyes, and at his dad who shrugged and went on fiddling.

'We're going now, Mum,' Wilf said, edging me out the kitchen.

'Soon come,' she said and brushed him away and took me by the hand back down the corridor. She picked up a pink feather duster at the door and told me, as she closed it behind us, the front room was '*for special*'.

It was dark because the curtains were half drawn, but there was a radiogram with polished wood she dusted down, pointing at all the dials with the feather duster like she was a fairy with a magic wand, and there was a cloth on top of it with its corners hanging down to form triangles, as well as some small polished side tables in wood and glass with smaller cloths and frilly edges. There were glass cabinets on both sides of the fireplace with long, thin legs that were full of cups and saucers and glasses and ornaments in glass and plastic on glass shelves with glass doors that had yellow and black patterns engraved on them, and it was all mirrored on the inside.

She shook a see-through plastic dome off the mantelpiece that had a palm tree inside and a beach with the word *Jamaica* written on it so it made a snow storm, and showed me and said, 'For Christmas.'

She drew the curtains fully closed and put on the side lamps. They had pictures of dominoes in black and white on the shades. She turned round and told me this was where they'd put her when she was dead and it was for me to remind them to take her out of the house feet first because she didn't want to have to come back and do all the damn dusting and plumping herself like some people who never would lift a finger would like. 'But you have a nice thing about you,' she said. 'You must help your mummy.' I nodded. 'And where she from?'

'Ireland,' I said.

'And Daddy?'

'Africa.'

She put her head back, and peered at me for a moment. 'Never mind. And you?' she asked.

I didn't know what to say to that, so I said, 'From here.'

'Wilf is a English boy, too,' she nodded. 'Don't let none of that hold you back. You have good in you.'

'What's that for?' I asked. There was a metal plastic thing standing on the floor by the yellow sofa that came up into a bubble with a knob on top and looked like a spinning top on a long leg. She pressed it down and it span inside itself like a flying saucer.

'Ashtray,' she said, wrinkling her nose up. 'That's a dirty habit. I don't allow it in my house.'

'Oh,' I said, and looked round at all the knitted and nylon things, flowers and vases, the framed photos of everyone looking younger, untouched chairs wrapped in shop plastic, the plumped, patterned cushions looking spotless, and nothing needing to be fixed. I looked back at her to see what else wasn't allowed, but she spread out her hand and waved the duster round the room and said, 'Now you see, this is my living *and dying* room, and the man promising me we going back home before it could catch me getting old.'

I must have looked like I had my mouth open because she said, 'You have a sweet tooth? So have I,' and lifted the lid off a bowl with some blue and yellow birds on it and gave us both a pink boiled sweet wrapped in see-through cellophane twists. 'Just you and me,' she said with a wink, and pulled both ends of hers so it unravelled neatly and popped it in her mouth.

'You can keep yours,' she said. 'Just pop it in your mouth when you get homesick.'

I didn't get homesick, I kept it in my pocket, but Wilf wouldn't come in with me. I'd been to his house but he didn't want to come in mine.

'What d'you mean?'

'He's got scars. They're ugly,' he said.

'What?'

'Scary. I'm not going in.' He was still backing away from me, shaking his head and getting ready to run – his feet were clever in the turn, he dropped his knees low.

'Oi!' I shouted.

'Haven't you seen?' and he stopped to draw his fingers in a claw across his cheek. 'Like a tiger's scratched him. See ya!' And he ran off.

'Is that why he's afraid to come in? He thinks we keep tigers?'

'No, Mum,' I said, 'just saying, he *has* got scars, hasn't he? How'd he get 'em?'

'You've no sense sometimes. Go and ask him.'

He was watching the news on telly, so I had to wait. I hadn't seen them before. I'd *seen* them, but they hadn't made sense. Like writing before you can read, you know it's there but you look at the pictures. The telly was reflecting on to his glasses. He had eight scars on each cheek, broad slits going across, in two columns ... How couldn't I have seen sixteen scars? I was sitting beside him and he put his arm around me. Tanks were clanking on the telly into Biafra.

'Daddy?'

'*Sh,*' he said.

I saw a man standing up and firing a gun, and lots of dust coming up. Children were starving. That was his country. '*United we stand, divided we fall,*' that's what all his friends were saying.

'What are those scars?' I said when the weather came on. He looked at me and touched some of the craters in his face around his glasses. I hadn't seen those before either. They were like black spots pitted round his eyes.

'Smallpox,' he said.

'What's that?'

'It's when God comes and takes away your children.' I sat rigid, but he shook himself out of watching the telly and gave me a hug. 'No, there's no god of smallpox in this country,' he said. 'I'm going to keep you.' But there were shadows in his eyes that weren't there before.

I looked up at him as his head moved and his eyes blanked out with the light reflecting on his glasses. I saw windows surrounded by spots of smallpox. I couldn't see what he was thinking. He must have seen I wasn't sure because he kept hold of me.

'Is that like chickenpox?' I said.

'At home we say *Obaluaye* – which means "king of the world". But it's not this world. It's another one, and a long time ago.'

It sounded like a story, I felt better. 'What happened?'

'The children I had before you gave up the ghost,' he said.

I wasn't shocked, I was calm, but I was tumbling backwards. I didn't know about children he'd lost. I didn't know what this was. I wanted my dad again. I wanted the peace between us. It was shattered.

'Who?' I said. But as he tilted his head towards me I didn't know what that meant, so I said, 'What children?'

'You're my child now,' he said. 'No one will come and take you away from me.'

I had to get my dad back. I reached out to touch his face and drew my fingers across his scars. They were smooth.

'There's no smallpox in this country.'

'That's what these are?' I was seeing them properly for the first time.

'*No!*' and he started laughing. 'These are *tribal* marks.'

I touched them again and thought about it. It was a story, but it kept changing. He was laughing. What was I getting wrong? They weren't scars, they were tribal marks. But I could feel them, they were scars, they were real. What about the children?

'Did it hurt?' I said.

He shook his head, 'When you're a baby, either it doesn't hurt or you don't remember.'

'Of course they've all got scars. They're like *zebras*,' Busola snorted, hanging upside down off the edge of the bunk bed. 'You're stupid!'

She had me in her sights, swinging from her legs. I let it go until she had the bucket between her knees in the downstairs kitchen. I reached over and dropped my peelings in, 'I'm not stupid!'

She gave me a sneer, the way our dad did when we were being thick, turning up her nose with her nostrils flared. It was our turn to be peeling yams for the party. Visitors were already barging in through the door with their loud voices on, banging about in the kitchen with big pots to take over the serious cooking and making themselves at home, but still leaving it to us to do the peeling.

A big man we didn't know turned round and caught her mouthing '*Stupid*' back at me with her lips and let his mouth drop open. 'And you? What are you? Are you stupid?' he asked.

Busola didn't answer, she wiped her eyes with the back of her knife hand and opened one eye at me behind it to let me know she was having to put up with this because of me. 'Just rude!' he said, and gave up and turned away.

'*Very* stupid,' she said under her breath.

Our eyes had started crying from the onions going on to the cooker, and there was the acrid, burning smell of hot peppers that reached into the back of your throat and made you cough. We carried on and tried not to look up in case people noticed us – either they'd flick drops of water off the wooden spoons into your eyes or pick you up and throw you into the air. They took you over and kept you up and wouldn't let you go until your mum said it was time for bed.

Sometimes you didn't mind, when it was the nice ones who took you up somewhere you wanted to go and held you tight for you to get a good look. But the ones who caught your eye and gave you daggers of withering looks, or flicked you with water so you'd have to keep your eyes shut to stop it going in, those ones had it in for you and didn't mind you could see it coming.

But when it came to plucking and scorching chickens, Mr Adebisi, who we loved, sometimes distracted us from the smell by giving us the raw chicken legs to pull. You pulled the strings and the claws moved. You could chase people around with them and scratch their eyes out. Even the nasty ones would run, it was really satisfying.

But there we were in the kitchen, doing the peeling and playing our stupid game – one by one as people came in, carving the shapes of their heads and showing each other, before cutting them in half and dropping them into the bucket.

We were used to Irish people being called *Spud*, so we changed it and did yams instead of potatoes for the Nigerians after we saw a woman come in with a great big tangle of yam roots on her head. They still had earth on as though you could have turned her upside down and planted her. Some of the women plaited their hair like that in loops and folds, with spikes that stood out to make them look beautiful or scary. But yams were bigger and tougher than potatoes, and that felt right for the people who trooped in to please our dad on the days we had our big parties.

They were all his townspeople, and in London he was the leader of his town. They had ceremonies and meetings and discussed things and took notes and turned it into a big bash that went on late into the night so we could stay up. And the feeling was this was going to be a really big one. So we just kept our heads down and watched.

People were arriving done up in their best clothes. The way they walked in changed – proud, almost dancing, instead of trying to be cramped and invisible alongside English people which they were never good at. The men were wearing *agbadas*, stiff, patterned robes with matching trousers and long loopy armholes that folded back over their shoulders. Most of them wore cloth hats, flattened over to one side, or stand-up berets with a bobble on top, though some of them, the modern ones, wore English suits with razor-sharp creases and had side partings in their hair. The women were all in high-waisted, wraparound skirts folded over blouses in different patterns, with hairdos or the *gele* headwraps tied up at all angles off their heads. It was instead of the normal blouses, cardigans and stockings they wore with dark skirts and thick glasses to blend in when we saw them outside.

They would come to us first on the ground floor to say hello because we were working and then go upstairs. Up there the ladies would kneel to my dad and the men would drop down and lie on the floor in front of him. Usually, when the men went down on one knee with a leg stretched out behind and their heads bent, he'd stop and lift them up and hug them, but sometimes he'd let them go the whole way down and touch their heads to the ground and stay there. Then you knew they were in trouble and he wouldn't look at them as they greeted him, he'd turn up his nose, pick his ear and just ignore them. That's when everyone would start talking at once and the trial was on.

It could go on as long as they wanted with voices for and against, pleading the case or accusing them of even more. Sometimes he wouldn't decide it then and there but put everything off until after people had eaten and had time to digest. When they felt a bit better, they'd go at it again – this time, though, they were reasoning and my dad's voice was urging and consoling, so I could see he had to work hard at it.

Once, when a woman came in and went to lie all the way down on the floor in front of him, her starched clothes ballooning out everywhere, there was the biggest explosion of shouts I ever heard. Her wig fell off along with the tangled up headwrap she was wearing. It was like her head had been cut off and was rolling on the floor, and her scalp was grey and grisly. People were screaming and shouting, pulling her up off the floor with the lampshade swinging from the ceiling, and my dad jumped up and went out the room. The whole house was shaking and it spilled out on to the street. From the window, I saw people pulling each other on the pavement and passers-by being startled. A man crossed over to walk past on the other side but then started running, and a car went into reverse and backed all the way up to the top of the road.

I ran to find out what was happening. In the downstairs kitchen, Mr Adebisi was busy restraining his wife who wanted to go up and slap the woman with her wooden spoon, so I didn't ask him. Mr Lawal was smoking in the backyard, he was the only one not bothering about what went on and it suddenly occurred to me he was the cause of it, so I went out and asked him.

He looked down his cigarette at me, screwed up his nostrils and spat out a bit of tobacco. 'She's an insult. To go down on the floor – as a woman – never! Unless it's the dirty whore you will wipe your penis on.'

I wasn't sure what he meant but I knew it wasn't good. The trouble went on for the rest of the evening, and because no one was bothering about us we heard a lot and we saw a lot – there was a struggle between the men and the women – and it was one of the best parties ever. The whole town was in uproar and my dad was working hard to calm it, even though it was the women who did most of the shouting and Mr Lawal had to go when they started flinging wooden spoons at him. The house only stopped shaking later when people stopped to catch their breath and there was dancing that slowed to a rhythm like the sobbing before sleep.

Anyway, there we were in the kitchen, peeling and playing our game. Manus and Connor were off somewhere because it wasn't their turn, and my feeling was it was something to do with them that people were coming and they were being kept out the way. Busola started giggling as a woman we didn't know came in adjusting her wrapper and rolling up her sleeves. She had a baby on her back who turned and looked at us. She was the spitting image of her mum, with the same four lines of scars going back across her cheek towards her ears then turning sharply up towards her temples. There were also another three little scars standing upright on the lap of those bigger ones, over her cheekbones. We laughed because they looked like mummy scar and baby scar, except the baby winced at us and turned away, burying her face in her mummy's back.

'*Oya!* Don't sleep!' her mum said, and gave a shake with her shoulders.

We let that one go, but we made up for it by really laying into the other people coming and going. We peeled the rough shape of the head, leaving a patch of skin and tendrils on for someone going bald and letting some be monsters. But then we got down to the real work – tracing the different scars that walked into the room. If we didn't like someone, we'd do a big cross over the face and drop them – *plop! bang!* – into the metal bucket. A beautiful person would take time, and you'd want to hold them in your hand longer than you should. No one noticed us until Busola nudged me finishing off a nice smiley man's five scars on each cheek with a flat, squat head and big, bulbous nose. I showed her.

'You're so *stupid*,' she said.

My dad was looking at me from the door. He didn't say anything, he came over and looked in the bucket. He picked up one of the chunks, took my knife and cut it again in two. The pieces fell down – *slap! thud!* – into the bucket with the other yams.

'That size,' he said, and walked off.

'You're *adopted*,' Busola said, and I couldn't say anything.

'Why so miserable?' Mr Adebisi asked.

I was hanging about on the stairs. I wanted my dad, but I

didn't want him to see me. So I just shrugged.

Mr Adebisi picked me up and gave me a big kiss on the cheek. His bristles scratched into my skin which was the only thing I didn't like about him. I turned in his arms and looked at him. Under his beard he had tribal marks going everywhere.

'Why have you got that beard?' I said.

'For professional reasons.'

'To hide your scars?'

He laughed, and swung me. 'You're sharp! You can be a lawyer.' Then he dared me, 'Go on, touch them.'

I put my finger in under the beard and traced a scar with it.

'How does it feel?' he asked.

I just nodded.

'Do you want some for yourself?'

I tried to shake my head but it wouldn't move. My neck was stiff. So I said, 'You have to be a baby.' And then, because he didn't say anything, 'Is that when they did it to you?'

He was looking at me. That's what Mr Adebisi was like. When he used his eyes you knew he could see anything you were feeling. 'So now you're grown-up. And you're upset you haven't got?' he said.

I didn't know why I nodded, I didn't want to. But I didn't know why I didn't belong.

'Look around,' he said, moving me into the front room. 'Lots of people – that man over there, he doesn't have marks, and he's the king.'

I twisted in his arms to look. The man in my dad's chair was leaning forward, looking at everyone. He hadn't been to the kitchen so we didn't draw him. He came later with lots of people shouting and calling after the party had already started. My dad had gone down on the ground in front of him, which startled me because I hadn't seen that happen before. Now it was like Mr Adebisi was turning me in his arms to see the world upside down and blood was rushing to my head.

'He's everybody's teacher,' Mr Adebisi whispered.

I shifted and put my arms round his neck and stared at the man. He had a big face and a broad smile, he turned his head to look across the room at me. I hadn't seen anyone that colour before. His skin was smooth like a blackboard, the whites of his eyes shone out as though he was open and curious about everyone. A tooth rested against his lip like a piece of chalk and made him look like he was amused at me staring.

'What do you think?' said Mr Adebisi.

I kept looking as the man turned away and looked back again. He was listening and watching with a calmness that made everyone feel comfortable, so he could be the centre of everything going on, without saying anything. It was like when my dad was with people who liked and wanted to be with him, but really he was alone with himself and detached so he could listen to everyone and everything at the same time.

I blinked and still he was looking at me, people were talking and laughing all around but we were meeting in silence. I questioned him with my eyes and he let me, tilting his head slightly to be the face of all the people I'd been meeting since I was born. I liked him, and I let Mr Adebisi see it. I looked again to make sure – there was a slight scar on his forehead, his eyes were waiting for me to speak.

'Are you the king?' I said.

Everyone stopped talking and turned to look. They looked at me and they looked at him. He put his head on one side, like he hadn't heard me, so I said it again, 'Are you the king?'

He nodded, and everyone burst out laughing, slapping my dad on the back and cheering. My dad was grinning, so he couldn't tell me off after that, and he gave a thumbs-up to Mr Adebisi who joggled me in his arms.

Connor came in first with a face like thunder, Manus was dragged in by my mum, he'd been crying. It wasn't I hadn't noticed they were gone, but I'd got caught up and forgotten about them. I felt something bad had happened while I'd been enjoying myself, so I kept quiet.

We'd just finished eating out the shared bowls, pounded yam and stews which were delicious and left your mouth on fire. I'd been allowed to eat with the grown-ups in the front room, and Busola had been in the kitchen which she said had all the best bits of beef and stock fish while we had all the tripe and knuckle. But I'd had the *ewedu* which was made by pounding and grating green leaves with the end of the witches' broom Mrs Adenle said was a grater until it ran thin and sticky off the end. You couldn't get enough of that, it made the hinges on your jaw ache just to smell it. Busola kept drawing air into her mouth to cool down and tell me how much pepper I'd missed out on, but we were both having fun telling Mr Adebisi we *shouldn't* only be eating with our right hand because that *was* the hand we used to wipe our bums. The door banged downstairs, and Manus and Connor came in furious from the hospital.

'What's the matter?' my dad said.

'The anaesthetic wearing off,' my mum said. 'They'll be all right.'

Mr Adebisi was the first to start heaping money on to their heads, sticking it to their foreheads, dancing and praising them for being brave. People joined in with money and turned the music up on the radiogram to drown out the sounds of Connor fighting people off and Manus not trusting anyone. My dad picked them up and did a dance with both of them in his arms, Manus sulking and Connor pushing my dad's face away. He pushed out his chest and stomped with his legs, going lower and lower with his back bent until their feet nearly touched the floor and the boards shook from him about to leap. People cheered and sprayed money – *pound notes!* – all over them. And when he put them down, people pressed forward to stick even more money on their foreheads. Everyone was up on their feet, dancing and calling, and you could see as Manus and Connor filled their pockets, the money spilling out their hands, that what they were feeling was starting to change. I bent down to pick up a note but my dad pulled my hand away and told me to go and sit down. A big hole opened up and it was only my mum bending down in her coat to pick me up that stopped me bursting into tears.

She took me up to her bedroom on the top floor, where we could hear it still going on, and sat me on the bed as she took off her coat and gave me a hug.

'Are you enjoying the party?' she said.

I looked at her, fighting back the feeling of being pushed away by my dad. She looked worn out, there were wrinkles under her eyes and in the corners. 'Where have you been?' I said.

'With your brothers to the hospital. I'm back now. Have you eaten?'

I nodded, and clung on to her.

'So what's the matter?' she said.

'Why do they all get the money? Why's it always about them?'

'Hasn't Daddy told you?'

I stopped to think about it, and shook my head against her arm.

'Look at me.' She put her tongue up on her top lip which she did when it was going to be difficult. 'They've – it's their big day. It's an operation, they've had. Down there –' and she pointed to my willy.

'Why only them?' I asked when really I didn't like the sound of that and wasn't sure it was worth the money.

'Because God already blessed yours, and he hadn't blessed theirs.'

I wondered for a moment if she was fobbing me off. How could God bless your willy? Wouldn't an operation leave a scar? I must have looked like I didn't believe it because she said, 'You were a baby, you wouldn't remember.'

I had a feeling something had happened to me and I didn't know what it was. I didn't know if other people could see. I didn't know what it meant.

'Am I scarred?' I said.

'You are,' she said, 'and blessed. Something has been taken away.'

That was too much. No one had told me. It was loss and anger and sadness at the same time, and I couldn't handle it.

'Do you know about Daddy's other children?' I said.

'I'll know when he tells me.' And she stood up from the bed with her face turned away.

Busola looked in the door, 'Daddy wants you to come, the *Oba* wants to see you.'

'I'm coming,' my mum said. 'Close the door.'

Busola just stood there and looked at me.

'What d'you want?' I said.

And she waved a pound note at me.

Wilf had his finger in his ear with his shoulders crooked, he was moving his jaw from side to side and knocking his knees together. Connor was saying he wasn't coming out for football because they'd chopped his willy off and he couldn't run.

'Why d'you tell him that?' I said.

'Why not?'

'Sorry about the other day,' Wilf said, patting me on the back. 'But look what goes on in your house,' and he burst out laughing.

'What d'you mean?' said Connor. 'What goes on in our house?'

Wilf looked down at the pavement in case he was gonna have to make a run for it, and shrugged.

'He didn't want to come in because of Daddy's scars,' I said.

'What scars?' said Connor.

'On his face,' Wilf said, trying not giggle.

I could see Connor weighing it up, could he catch him? But he decided against it, and used his mouth. 'Yeah, I suppose he has, but your mum's off with the fairies, and you're a wanker.'

I didn't know how he knew about Wilf's mum. I still had her sweet in my pocket. 'She's not,' I said, 'she's nice.'

Connor looked at me like what was the point?

'My mum likes you, though, more than me,' Wilf said, and I had a pang of feeling sorry for him and then guilty. But he smirked, and it changed around to mean he didn't really like me even though she did.

He took his finger out his ear and flicked his willy under his trousers. 'Mine still works,' he said. 'How d'you go for a pee?'

'Come here, I'll show ya,' said Connor, but Wilf backed away shaking his head.

'I'll tell everyone,' he said.

'Tell who you want,' said Connor, 'but you better keep running.'

Wilf flashed a smile and ran off up the road waving back at us.

'Do you know his mum?' I said.

'What of it?'

'I think she wants to go back home,' I said, as Wilf jumped up around the corner by the corrugated iron, laughing his head off.

'Mum?'

'Yes?'

'Does it really leave scars when you get your willy chopped off?' I said.

'Have you got scars?' she said.

I shrugged because I didn't know, I couldn't tell.

'Well, then.' And she walked out the room.

I went to find Manus.

'Manus, does it still hurt? Can you show me?'

He was drinking a cup of water out the sink and nearly choked. He looked round at me severely, took a sip and blew a splash of water into my face so it dripped over my shirt.

'There you go,' he said.

'Daddy?'

My dad looked at me and wasn't cross even though the news was on. I didn't say anything, I got in the door and curled up under his arm and watched the war going on. A skeleton boy with a big belly was holding on to the arm of his baby sister to get up a step and go for help, but she couldn't do it, she was too weak to lift her head, she fell over on the step and curled up, and he just stood holding her bony arm because he couldn't let go. I felt for the scars on my dad's face and found a place for my fingers where I could touch him. It was wet, but I held on to let him know he was my dad and I was still there, I wasn't gone.

China Walk

The halfway house was on Glasshouse Walk, that's where Emily stayed, she was in my class and they were calling her a fleabag. All her brothers and sisters had white hair and grubby faces. There were lots of them. They came in the summer and someone said they were gypsies. I couldn't go near because she wasn't one of us and they stuck together. In class she spoke in a mumble and didn't really have a voice. No one spoke to her, just about her to say they weren't sitting next to her or on a chair she'd sat on. She didn't say anything and it stung me she didn't feel it was wrong, or didn't say it was. I wasn't sure what it was you were catching, if it was only fleas. She wasn't dirty, only her clothes were, they were old, and to me she just looked sleepy. I could see she was different from us, the way her face was covered in a white cloud and her eyes were far off, but I couldn't see why people didn't like her. She wasn't saying she was better than us, she just wasn't joining in saying she was worse.

Sonia grabbed her hair in the playground and swung her round by it, trying to make her hair come out. A circle of people crowded round to watch and they were on Sonia's side. It was mostly girls, but some boys too, shouting 'Fleabag' and I could see there were tears in Emily's eyes. Her younger brother and her sisters were watching. She wasn't fighting back, she was being dragged and trying to get her hair back from where she was bent forward and being swung. She had one hand on Sonia's wrist and the other trying to keep her balance on the ground and stop Sonia pulling her over. It was a girls' fight so I couldn't get in and get Sonia's hands off even though I could feel them hurt. I had to go in close and use my voice to put her off, 'If she's a fleabag, why you touching her?' There was a moment when it was Sonia or me who was gonna come off worse, but she let go the clumps of hair and looked at her own hands like they were greasy and people laughed at her and moved away so she couldn't touch them, so she was *it*. I could feel people looking at me so I didn't get away with it completely, but I didn't care who found out I was on Emily's side. I was only worried she heard me call her a fleabag.

The reason was when we had to take our clothes off in PE, Emily was allowed to keep her vest on and the shiny, scaly skin on her neck went down both sides of her shoulders. It swirled in flows of pinks and whites down her arms and sides into the back of her knickers. It was a burn she got from an iron pot of water when she was little. She had to be careful to keep it covered up, so I only ever saw glimpses of it moving and changing under her vest. It was like watching splashes of paint turn into skin. She didn't mind me looking, it was her skin, she lived in it. She said it didn't hurt. It was her quick body, the way she threw herself around, I liked. The way she drew her legs up under her chin and looked around at what we were doing and enjoyed being her. It was the way we got on. She knew I was there and let me see where the burn went down the back of her vest, but she never said anything.

It was only when her older sister came up and took her away with her lip cut and bleeding and her hair pulled out of place she looked at me. I was standing there like I'd called her a fleabag, and people were looking like they weren't sure what I'd caught.

I told my mum about it, the way I felt about stopping the fight. She looked at me sideways and shook her head, 'Ah, no,' she said, 'you're barking up the wrong tree. Those people will take from you, but they won't owe you a kindness.'

I didn't care. I showed Emily how to do the sums and carry the numbers across with 77 and 99 ... 9 and 7, 16. Put down 6 and carry across 1. 7 and 9, 16, add the 1 you carried across, 17 ... 176.

I wasn't sure that was a clear example. People were looking at me, I was sat next to her, helping her with her sums, but they were the sums my dad was showing me and we hadn't done them in class yet. I was giving her everything I could think of. Maybe she thought I was showing off because she blinked, like that wasn't what she was thinking about and she wasn't getting it. I put my hand up to scratch the back of my head and the girls on my table started giggling. I looked at Emily, she was going back to being blank in her eyes, like she wasn't there and I was calling her fleabag. The teacher looked up from her desk and frowned.

'What are you doing?'

The whole class turned round to look because it was quiet time and you were supposed to be getting on with work. Yakubu was looking, and Patrick, and Shelley, Sky, Bobby, Sonia, everyone. My face started to burn, I put my pencil down on the table and the click sounded too loud because everyone was listening.

'Sums, miss.'

The teacher told everyone to get on with their work and came over to me and moved my chair to another table. She spoke quietly to me and said, 'Leave Emily alone. Go on with your work.'

I looked at everyone on the new table after the teacher was gone. No one was looking at me. My ears were hot and I had to cool them down with my hands and pretend I was leaning my elbows on the table to read. Nothing was going in because Yakubu reached over and turned my book round the right way. He had his head down and wasn't looking at me, no one was.

'Can I come home with you?'

'No,' she said.

'But if I help you with your sums?'

She shook her head and wiped her nose with her sleeve because she had a cold. 'Don't.'

I went up the halfway house on my own. There was a dark courtyard inside with pipes going up the walls and washing hanging down out the windows. Water was dripping down the pipes and making puddles. It smelt of the drains and there were some boys and a girl playing out with their dogs. They saw me come in and stopped, and the dogs started growling. A dog with a stiff tail and scabs on its back started barking at me. I couldn't move, so I stood there looking up at the windows, thinking I didn't know which one was Emily's.

'What do you want?' one of the boys said to me. He had dark hair and was older so I didn't know who he was.

'Does Emily live here?'

'What do yous want with her?' one of the younger ones said. He had ginger hair and I'd seen him in school, but I didn't know him.

'She's in my class,' I said.

That gave me the right to stand there against the dogs who'd stopped growling and started moving up and down in front of me like they were excited and waiting for someone to say *bite*. Emily came out one of the stairwells. She must have seen me from the window. She leaned out by the brick wall covering the bins and shook her head.

'Go away,' she said. 'Go home!'

The big boy growled at the dogs and got them to come to him. I didn't know why they called it the halfway house except from the outside there weren't any doors. There was a narrow passageway with a tall iron gate to go in and that's the way I came out with the sound of the dogs panting and scuffling their feet behind me. It closed up again like it was somewhere I shouldn't be.

Rows of houses were standing empty all the way back, with broken windows and dirty curtains left up. I couldn't see why the halfway house was any different from the other houses they were going to knock down. I started to run, past the shut-up doors and windows and the ones lit up with people still living inside. There was a damp smell of charred wood like there'd been a fire. The sound of thunder, it was going to rain. Emily told me in school they were moving on, but when I reached out to touch her elbow she shook me off. She said they were going near the sea to pick hops and everyone would get drunk. I didn't want her to go and she shrugged and said she had to. Everyone was going, I didn't know where. I ran my hand along the bumps of the corrugated iron. I didn't know why people were trying to stop me being with her, and I didn't care. I was going to follow Emily. And I wasn't going to tell my mum.

My mum was in the front room telling this story that in the old house they lived in down by the quay in Limerick there was a hook in the ceiling which they couldn't take down because it held the roof up.

'And let the rain in,' Busola said. 'Why don't we just move?'

Buckets were out upstairs again in the big bedroom because it was starting to rain, but we couldn't repair it because the council were knocking us down and it would be a waste of money.

Busola wanted to move, we all did, but my dad was holding out and Manus shouted her down so we could get on with the story. And the story was that a Spanish sailor had hanged himself off that hook and sometimes you could hear it creaking in the night and it would stop you sleeping.

'Boring!' Busola said, pretending she wasn't listening.

'Why you telling us this?' I said because when I got in my mum asked if I'd been with Emily, and when I shook my head said, '*Don't be sad.*' I could see she thought that was why I wasn't sleeping. I didn't want her to bring it up again but Manus shouted me down as well because we were in the middle of the story.

Anyway, my mum said, when she was a girl they lived at the top of the house and there were times coming home in the dark they'd find strange people on the stairs. My uncle said goodnight to an old lady on the step as he was going up, but when there wasn't an answer he looked back, and she wasn't there.

Other families moved out, the house emptied and they were alone at the top. No one would come and visit them. My mum had to wait for her brother to come home before she could get the courage to go up. Then one night she'd woken up to see a woman in old-fashioned clothes leaning over her sister's cot. She couldn't speak and wasn't able to call out when the woman turned and looked at her with dark eyes and the white face of a ghost. All she could do was go under the bedclothes and not move till the morning.

When she told that story no one could breathe. Our dad wasn't home, the house was dark and it sent shivers down our spines.

'What about the hook?' said Busola. Manus told her it was all part of the story and if she didn't believe it she should go on her own to bed, see if she liked that. There was a squabble and I didn't get involved and didn't listen because it was stopping me thinking. Then Busola said, 'Wait till Daddy gets home!'

It stopped for a moment.

'And then what?' he said.

But our mum told us all to get ready for bed, there were plenty of stories to be getting on with before the ones that wouldn't help. But no one wanted to leave the room.

I thought about it feeling like the story our dad told when he had to leave for school in the morning in the dark because it was far. He met a man on the road who worked for his dad, who looked at him strangely and wouldn't answer when he said hello. He was so upset he complained to his mum when he got home, but she took him to see his dad who told him he was lying because that man had died in the night and he shouldn't be telling lies like that. It was only when they saw the look on his face they realised he wasn't, and they all got a fright at the same time.

It was the same story that they'd both grown up with ghosts. The stories they told about the countries they grew up in were ghost stories. And the story was you couldn't go back there because everyone would be dead, and you wouldn't be – 'Let's turn on the telly,' Connor said.

'Can dead people cross water over to this country?' Busola asked, which was what I was worried about.

Manus said there were dead people everywhere and we shouldn't think we wouldn't meet one, so we better be ready.

'Can they come over from there?' I said.

And my mum said *yes* – that a man had followed her over and called up at the window. She'd looked out and told him *no*, to go away, she wasn't coming back. So though she never saw him again she was haunted by him, not knowing was he alive or dead, and only the dark tinker's eyes to remember him and the sadness on his face that it wasn't going to be possible.

'Who was he?' Connor asked, and she said he was a tinker because there were lots of those people in Ireland and though they didn't live long they had beautiful eyes and they could steal your heart.

I was going to ask more but Connor put on the telly and while it was warming up my mum said we could stay up as a special treat until my dad got home. She put a blanket on over our laps and the crackle of the television turned into a roaring noise. It was King Kong banging on the doors of the jungle. I didn't want to be in the same room, 'Turn it off,' I said. '*Turn off the telly!*'

They couldn't hear me because Busola was snuggling up with my mum who was looking at her not me, Connor's lips were looking at the telly saying '*Shh*' ... and Manus was hiding part of his face under the blanket.

'I don't want it!' I said, and jumped up to the door.

Manus looked up at me from far away and said if I didn't like it I should leave the room.

'Go to bed,' said Busola.

I couldn't sleep, so I sat up on the stairs. I tried to keep pressing in the button for the light to stay on but it wouldn't. It was dark upstairs with the buckets for the rain and downstairs to the front door. I didn't want to be on my own, so I sat outside on the landing with the front-room door between me and King Kong where I could be close to the others. I couldn't think about running away, my heart was pounding and the telly was screaming. It went quiet, there was a sound of water. But then they switched the light off in the front room and I froze, watching the blue flicker of the telly under the door. I could feel the draught coming up the stairs and started to shiver and sweat at the same time.

I had bad dreams going on from when I saw it before that King Kong had me in his fist on the edge of a cliff and was waving me about. Down the bottom, the devil was standing over a boiling hot cauldron of fire, shaking his horns and roaring to have me. I couldn't go anywhere. That's how I was until downstairs the front door banged open and my dad came home.

'What are you doing?' he said.

I looked up at him, standing in his work clothes with pieces of solder on the sleeve, mud on his boots and rain on his face.

'Hiding,' I said.

'What happened?' My mum was looking up at my dad with a hand over one eye. The light went on and the telly went off, so I could go in with everyone blinking and frozen by the film. He got a blue airmail letter crumpled out his pocket and showed it to her. He looked like he'd seen a ghost because his dad was dead. He opened it on the bus on the way home and didn't know what happened next until the conductor told him it was the last stop and the bus had to go into the garage. He walked home knowing his dad was already in the ground.

'Oh, God!' she said, and put her arms round him because he looked like he was going to fall. He shook his head and sat down by himself on the edge of the armchair and looked at the floor.

'Sorry, Daddy,' Busola said.

He looked up like he didn't know we were there and had to think about why everyone was still hiding under the blanket. Then he nodded and said, 'Everybody, get ready to write home.'

'*Tch, shh ...*' my mum said, even though my dad was upstairs and couldn't hear. We were brushing our teeth out in the bathroom and Busola was saying she didn't even know what his dad looked like or what his name was.

'How can we write if he's dead and we don't know who anyone is?' Connor said. 'Who we writing to?'

'Your grandmother.'

Connor gave her a look, and she said, 'Don't use his name, it's Ajagbe. Just say you're sorry to hear the news, and do it before the pain goes away and you bring it back. Do it tomorrow.'

'Daddy says she doesn't speak English,' Busola said with the toothpaste in her mouth.

'Oh for God's sake, someone'll read it to her, just write, I'm going upstairs.'

'Did you ever meet him?' Manus asked.

'No,' she said, 'but look at your father and he'd not be far off that.'

I wasn't sure, we didn't look anything like our dad, but Manus didn't say anything and neither did I. But when she'd gone back indoors and left the lights on for us to come back he did say, 'That's the end of that.'

'What?' Connor said.

'Him taking us back to show off,' he said.

'The sun's so hot it burns you as you get off the plane,' Busola said, and spat out.

'What makes you say that?' I said, but she ignored me. I felt wobbly at the thought of getting on a plane.

'I don't want to go to his hot country and get burned,' Manus said. 'I want to stay here.'

Connor pulled the string of the bathroom light off and ran into the rain in the backyard leaving us in the dark. We all made a rush to the door not to be the last left out and I hadn't finished brushing my teeth. I kept hold of Manus and didn't let him get me off in case a ghost got me. The door banged my shoulder and Busola trod on my foot but that just made me go faster. Our dad was by the stairs coming out to the toilet and watched us piling in through the back door and pulling each other back. He could see everything and Connor looked like he'd been caught.

'Don't be frightened,' he said. 'Go to bed.'

He moved back and we filed past with our heads down. I glanced up at him from the bottom of the stairs as he stepped out in the rain and pulled the back door shut.

'At least we're alive,' Busola said.

The next day I told Emily my granddad was dead.

'How did he die?' she said, and I didn't know and I'd forgotten what his name was. We were hiding on the back steps at playtime where no one could see us.

'He's from Nigeria,' I said. 'I don't know how they die.'

'My dad's dead.'

I didn't know that. I couldn't imagine what her dad was like, if he had white hair like her. Her cold made her nose raw and her top lip red. I couldn't let her go shivering like that, but I felt I couldn't leave my dad in case he died as well. I wasn't going to be able to love her enough.

'What about your mum?' I said.

She looked at me with her hands squashed up against her cheeks and her elbows on her knees, 'She drinks.'

The pub her mum went to was over by the China Walk. You could sit out on the steps or go in the cubicle where they sold you crisps through the hatch. You could see people inside there when the side doors opened into the bars. And Emily's family sat in the rough part, which meant I could go in and look and they couldn't send me away, and dogs weren't allowed.

'I'm coming to talk to her,' I said.

'She'll only tell what I'm telling you,' Emily said. 'You can't come with me.'

I put my foot in the side door as it was closing and looked into the pub. Her mum was sitting there, smiling and laughing with her head back on the wall, surrounded by people with drinks on the table. Some of the men had their caps on, they were all dressed in clothes that were different from other people's. Their clothes looked dusty like they came from a long time ago and got worn out with working. The women had big earrings, Emily's mum didn't, like her smile was all she had on. She was looking at me over people's shoulders and they all began to turn round and notice me. 'Shut the door, I'll be out,' she said, like she knew who I was. I'd seen her before when she came into school after the fight, and I saw her through the pub window when I was standing on the ledge and holding on to the sill to see who was in there. But then Emily came out the pub carrying her little brother and looked at me. I got down and looked at her sandals on her feet where the straps were broken and couldn't say anything, or even lift my head up.

'What you doing?' she said.

I couldn't say, so I said, 'Can you play with me?'

She lifted her brother higher up on to her side because he was wriggling to go, and shook her head, 'I'm going a different way from you.'

She was sending me away but looking over her shoulder at the boys who were playing football in the road in between the cars, and shouting for them to be careful, '*Car coming!*'

'Just stay with me,' I said.

She turned back and shook her head with her hair going everywhere so I couldn't see her eyes and said, 'I've got my family.'

'What's your mum say?'

She pulled the hair back off her face and shrugged, 'She says there's no one for you to fight.'

Some of the boys were watching from their game in the road, her brother struggled free and ran over to them, so she didn't stay with me and I went in on my own.

I didn't move at first because I wasn't sure what Emily's mum was saying, she was telling me go outside, but then people were whispering and I wanted to know what they were saying. I didn't know how to tell my foot to move back, I had my face wedged in the door and people were looking at me. I felt stupid and said, 'I'm Emily's friend.'

Her mum said again, 'I'm coming,' and a man took off his cap and shook his head, but he smiled like he wasn't sure and that gave me the feeling I could step back and not let the door bang on my face, my ears were stinging and hot already.

'So you're the fella with Emily to carry numbers in your head and wants to teach her, is it?' Her mum was sitting down on the steps of the pub with me one side and Emily on the other, handing us crisps from a packet. I nodded and she said, 'Do you love her more than me?'

That stopped me chewing.

'Learning's a fine thing,' she said, 'if you've love in your heart.'

I couldn't follow the different ghosts that swooped down and went different ways through me. Emily's mum had straggly silver hair, I didn't know what my granddad looked like but my dad's hair was black, Emily's was white, so her dad's must have been like hers and that's where it was leading – I couldn't love her like her dad did. Any more than my dad could go back and change anything now his dad was dead. The ways were cut off and the ghosts were guarding them.

'What was Emily's dad like?' I said.

Her mum looked at Emily, and then back to me. 'I see,' she said.

Emily's eyes were darting around the cars as though she could see an accident coming, or she could see her dad and I couldn't. Her eyes were always moving, going somewhere I couldn't follow or coming in close so there wasn't any room between us.

'I'll tell you he was a dreamer. Are you that?'

I looked back at her mum, leaning down towards me with her silver hair, her face full of lines and hairs round the bottom of her chin. I could smell the drink on her breath. She blinked and I looked at her eyes, grey flecked with yellow and dark eyelashes.

'Are you?'

I nodded a little bit because I was still getting woken up by King Kong.

'Who are your people?' she said.

I didn't have an answer, but I didn't want to be rude, so I looked around – there were people passing in the street, going up the Cut for the market with their shopping trolleys now Lambeth Walk was closed. 'The people here,' I said.

'Which ones?'

I shrugged. 'All of them.'

She put her head back, and then she nodded. Emily was looking at me and listening.

'It's a big world out there,' her mum said. 'Are you ready?'

I wasn't because I shrugged my shoulders, and then I shook my head. I felt myself getting smaller, and felt ashamed that Emily could see it. There was a lump in my throat and my chin creased up. Emily looked down so I could only see the side of her face, covered in cloud. I didn't have anything else to say, so I told her mum, 'I don't pick people who want me.'

Some of Emily's sisters came jumping round the corner of the pub, chasing marbles past us along the pavement with the other girls. Her older sister stopped when she saw me, her mum nodded her to go on.

'Go over there and play with them,' her mum said to Emily, getting her to jump off the steps and run over. Then she turned to me and gave me the packet of crisps, 'That's all for you.'

I didn't want them, so I shook my head to give them back, but she took a crisp and put it in my mouth.

'There's love gone into the making of you, and it's not everyone can pick and choose,' she said. 'Emily's told you we're away?'

I nodded, and so did she.

'She asked if I'd put it to you.'

I knew she was sending me away but I couldn't move.

'We only moved here for the hospital and that's – no more.' She stopped for a moment, and swallowed, lifting her eyes up to catch back the tears and look across at the girls. Emily flicked a marble and ran after it, throwing herself into the chase like a white cloud in a grey dress with one of her sandals flying off. She told me this would happen. She didn't tell me when she said her dad was dead that it was still going on.

'I'm sorry,' I said.

Her mum tried to smile and shook her head, 'A dreamer. And you could drink the stories would come out of him, to Emily and all of them sitting here as you are now. Where we are there with the drains, in that halfway house, he told them there'd been a garden with a palace out of China was good for work on the way down to the coast and he wanted to see the sea. He put me in that palace and he put the gold in my eye, do you see?'

I nodded at her eyes and let her see me looking.

'I'm not the one now to let his name go out of the community.'

I frowned because I couldn't follow everything – was there a palace? There weren't any gardens left round the halfway house, just the green across by the flats. There were factories along the railway, and there was Glasshouse Walk, was it a glass palace? We were by the China Walk, but that was a dark old estate, it was a long walk back to the halfway house, over Black Prince Road. 'What garden?' I said. 'Do you mean Vauxhall Park?'

She laughed and shook her head, 'It's not to be found. This garden's a dream not a memory. But Emily knows now there'll always be dreamers.' She leaned in towards me and went serious,

'We're going down to the sea. I'm telling you this not because your skin is different from ours – you've a fine pelt on you,' and she rubbed the side of my arm with the back of her hand, 'but because he'd want me to be careful of you. You've tried to help Emily but she doesn't need it. You've your own people and Emily has hers. Take those crisps, now, and go on.'

I turned the corner of the pub towards Bedlam Park, not because it was the way home but because I didn't want to see Emily watch me being turned away.

'Mum?'

She looked at me as I got out my wet clothes from school and she was searching for some trousers for me to put on.

'Emily didn't come to school today. None of them did. They've gone.'

'What makes you say that?'

'Emily's dad died,' I said, 'in the hospital. They were going away.'

I couldn't undo the button on my shirt because it was wet down the front and if I pulled too hard it might tear. I looked up at her for help and she was looking at me like I'd already said too much. I looked down at my button.

'I'm sorry to hear that,' she said, 'but I've something to ask you.'

I thought of Emily playing marbles up by the China Walk, their swirls of colour as she flew to pick them up, and there being no one to fight. Maybe someone saw me on the steps of the pub with her mum. What was I doing there? My mum lifted up my chin so I had to meet her eyes, and I could see I'd done something wrong.

'Have you written your letter?'

Tired of Fighting

Ian Barrett was going to kill me. Everyone was saying so. He was the best fighter in the school and I was dead.

Even Kat came to say goodbye.

'Ian Barrett's gonna kill you. Can I have your pocket money?'

'When he kills you, can I have yours?'

'We'll see about that,' she said, and skipped off back to her gang to watch. They were all watching. I was on my own.

I saw Ian Barrett in assembly, but he didn't look at me, he smiled at someone behind me. I looked round to see who it was, but no one looked back. Everyone was avoiding me, they all knew I was in trouble. He was smiling because I couldn't stop him killing me.

My brothers beat me up, but they could see in my eyes they couldn't beat me up badly enough for the way I was going to get my own back. I was going to stamp on my glasses, I could make my nose bleed look really messy. They had to bear that in mind for when it was time to go home.

There was a new teacher in assembly. She put on some cowboy music. A creepy, gravelly voice crawled out, *I was born under a wandering star* ... But there was nowhere to run. She was swaying to the music. Everyone looked bored. They were waiting for Ian Barrett to kill me.

Right now, I thought, *I don't like anyone*. I listened to the gravelly voice. I could feel the grit in my teeth as he punched me. I could see stars.

The bell rang. It was breaktime.

'Aren't you going outside?' the teacher asked. I thought of telling her there was this boy with hard fists who was going to break my nose and bang the tears out my eyes – but she was new.

'I've got a cold,' I said.

Round one to Ian Barrett. Only I didn't go out lunchtime. I wasn't ready. I wasn't feeling well.

'Let him be the best fighter in the school,' I said out loud to the shafts of light falling from the tall windows on to the empty classroom, screams of laughter echoing up from the playground, 'I don't have to get beaten up.'

It wasn't true. Ian Barrett had to beat me up. Manus and Connor were the best fighters in the school, but they'd left. The only person who ever stood up to my big brother was my other brother. No one else got a look-in. They'd knock you out so they could get on with it. One wanted to be Cassius Clay, the other was a bulldozer. When they couldn't find each other, they found me. I couldn't always see it coming, it would just spill over. But they never expected me to take it personally, even the time I got my tooth knocked out. '*What you crying for?*' '*Stop snivelling!*' It wasn't about me, it was about them. It was about fighting, and being the best fighter in the school.

'*Cat and dog!*' my dad said, when I got my mouth home, crumpled and bleeding. '*Chinese, Japanese, Congolese, Cat-and-Geese!*'

I started complaining they were out of control but I couldn't get used to the new way my mouth felt, the feeling of being sore and sorry at the same time with my tongue in the way, I couldn't get the words out. I was annoyed and ashamed – it hurt – and started blubbing, which made it worse, especially the way my mum was shaking her head, so I had to use the tight, angry look in my eyes until I found a way of spitting blood out through the gaps in my teeth to tell them I'd had enough.

Not even them getting beaten by my dad could stop it. Manus and Connor weren't only the best fighters in the school, they were the only ones. There wasn't room for anyone else. No one else got beaten up, and no one had to worry about being beaten up but me.

Manus left, but that left Connor, and people knew not to cross him. He tried to be fair and control his temper. When he had me on my back with my arms pinned down under his knees and he was going to punch me in the face, one of his mates said, *'Mind his glasses!'* He stopped, and snorted up the snot from his nose instead and gobbed it on me the way Manus used to. He was saying he was the only fighter in the school and I shouldn't challenge him. People were standing round in a big circle and even they went, *'Urgh!'* He looked up and shook his head like *What you looking at?* and they all moved back. It was Kat who stepped in and said, *'Get off him.'*

When Connor left everyone said I was the best fighter in the school. Until Ian Barrett said he was gonna kill me. Lots of people didn't come back after the holidays, and more were leaving as their houses got knocked down, it felt in the playground anything could happen now to anyone.

'What you gonna do?' said Patrick.

It was the afternoon and the new teacher was letting us muck about while she did something out the room. It was only Patrick with his sticky-out ears who came up and said anything. He was a loner and everyone knew he didn't speak much. If he hadn't asked me, I wouldn't have had to come up with an answer. I would have gone on avoiding it. But the way he asked didn't let me – pulling on his ear which made it look bigger when he was so little.

'I'm on your side,' he said.

All the loners were on my side, that's what it made me think. That's what I was now and I knew how it felt. I was on my own and my brothers were at bigger schools.

'What am I gonna do? What *you* gonna do?' I said. 'After me he's gonna be beating up everybody.'

He looked worried and a bit lost.

'You on my side?'

'Yeah,' he said.

I suppose that's all it needed, Patrick with his big ears coming up to say he didn't want Ian Barrett to be the best fighter in the school. I had to do something.

I couldn't have got home anyway.

'Tell everyone it's after school in the playground. I'm gonna deal with Ian Barrett.'

It went round like wildfire. People started coming up to me, 'What you gonna do?'

'You scared of Ian Barrett?'

I could see they weren't sure what to do.

'He's gonna kill you, so do what I tell you.'

When I came out in the playground, he was there with his gang. They were making out they'd already won, climbing up on the roof of the shelter with their sticks like he was king of the castle. People were running around the playground like they were going home, but they weren't, they were waiting to see what happened.

'You gonna come down?'

'No,' he said, and looked down his nose at me. That was a mistake, people getting ready to run saw he was strong but he was stuck, so they stayed. A crowd built up by the chain-link fence on the rough ground separating the infants from the juniors. Some of them started climbing up to get a better view. It was like they were getting up high to show we were strong too. I told them to get down. They did and that put me in control. I told everyone to start picking up stones.

'You coming down?'

'Why should I?' and he looked at me trying to see what I'd do. I threw a stone and hit one of his mates who gave a look like it stung him on the leg – he looked stupid. They all did, they hadn't seen it coming. It stopped them jumping up and down. I threw another one and missed – they flinched – another one hit Gilbert from my class on the knuckle. He dropped his stick and it fell backwards off the roof. Everyone joined in stoning Ian Barrett and his gang. There was nothing they could do, it was raining stones. A whistle went off from a teacher on the steps but we ignored it. What could they do up on the roof with their sticks? The ones only in his gang because they were scared started climbing down off the roof. We let them off with a kick. One by one, they were skimming down the drainpipe but the stones got thicker and even the girls joined in. A stone caught Ian Barrett on the lip. The ones who were with him because they were gonna win got lots of people kicking them. The bell started ringing. I told people let them go, and they ran off. The last ones, his mates, looked at him, climbed down and got pushed about. They ran off, leaving Ian Barrett alone on the roof, holding his stick.

'What you gonna do?' said Patrick.

'Leave him,' I said.

'We won the war, in 1944!

  Guess what we done?

  We kicked 'em up the bum!'

Lots of people didn't want to go home because we'd won, but teachers started coming out and made them stop stomping round the playground and go home. They called Ian Barrett down off the roof.

I waited for him outside school. I had Patrick sticking to me, so we sat up on a car bonnet together and waited.

He came out without his stick. He had a welt bruising up on his lip, and stopped when he saw us like he was thinking of running.

'All right?' I said.

He nodded.

Patrick slid off the bonnet and shrank back along the side of the car as Ian Barrett walked over. I didn't move, but I got ready to kick out with my feet. He stopped in front of me. I hadn't seen him this close up before. He was in the year above and Kat said he was bigger than me. She was wrong, he was the same size, older, more bony. And he had green eyes. I could see flecks of brown and yellow in them. It was his hair made him look bigger, brushed out and frizzy. But his face looked tough like rubber, with brown skin that was paler than me, I could see freckles on his nose and his cheeks. His fists were clenched, and his lip quivered like he was trying to stop himself from crying, I couldn't tell if he was hurt or angry.

'Let's be mates,' I said.

'Yeah,' and he nodded, but his voice came out twisted up with what he was feeling.

'All right,' I said.

I watched him walk away with a limp like a stone must have got him on the leg.

It was all right until Errol Clark stood up to me the next day and said he'd enjoyed that. He didn't have any supporters, he was dangerous. His older brother was in prison for killing someone. He looked skinny and tough, and wore a black Crombie coat with the buttons missing that he held closed with his hands in the playground because he didn't have a lot of clothes. He had scars on his face and bony knuckles, and I didn't feel I should fight him.

'Fuck off,' I said, and he smiled and walked off.

One of the dinner ladies on playground duty came up and said to me, 'Were you involved in the stone throwing yesterday?'

She had Theresa and Kat on her arms like they were steering her, then making out they didn't know me. I looked up at her and didn't say anything.

'They're watching you,' she said.

'How's school?' my mum asked.

My uncle Gerry was there who'd been away fighting in the army when we were growing up.

'It's all right,' I said. 'I had a fight.'

They both looked at me, and looked at each other.

'What you fighting for?' he said.

'Not to get beaten up.'

He looked at my mum and shook his head, 'A rough school is it?'

'It's who's doing the fighting,' she said, turning on me. 'You're not to be fighting with your fists and you must never hit anyone with glasses, do you hear?'

'They hit me,' I said, and touched my glasses to make the point.

'Who hit you?' she said, looking suspicious.

I didn't answer because Manus and Connor flashed into my mind and I didn't want my uncle Gerry to know.

'Can you teach me to fight?' I asked him.

He put up his big fist in front of me and said, 'Here, catch that!' I tried to grab it as it moved about prodding me in the face and the stomach, but he pulled it away as strongly as he prodded it. 'Have you no strength?' he said, and caught my hand in his and crushed it.

'*Ow!*' I said. 'That's cheating!'

'You've got to know your own strength,' he said, and let go. My hand ached and I couldn't use it. I felt tricked, he'd damaged me, I felt mean.

'Did you kill anyone?' I said.

'That's enough now,' my mum said, pushing me away. 'Go on with you.'

I wouldn't budge and stared back at him as he lifted up his cup, I could smell it was whisky.

'I'll tell you one thing,' he said, putting it down and making his eyes larger than saucers. 'If you start fighting, you've already lost.'

The new teacher was telling me my work wasn't neat and I wasn't concentrating. That was because Errol Clark was waiting to get me. He didn't have anything to lose. He didn't have socks, there were holes in his shoes – in the toes and under the sole. He watched me in the playground and he hung about after school to see where I went. I had to go out the other gate and take the long way round.

At first I ignored it, but Patrick came to school and he'd got beaten up – he had a black eye and a bit of his ear missing. He said it was an accident, but everyone soon knew it was Errol Clark.

'What d'you say to him?'

'Nothing,' and he looked away from me, 'he just came up and bashed me.'

'What you gonna do about it?'

He looked back at me like I'd let him down, like I was a coward, like he'd learnt his lesson, like he'd trusted me. 'Nothing,' he said.

'Was it because of me?'

He shrugged and pulled away, 'Why should everything be about you?'

I didn't have anything to say.

'When I leave school, I'm gonna join the army,' he said. And he stopped talking to me.

I was gonna have to think about it. What did Errol Clark want? He was a loner, his brother was in prison. No one wanted to play with him. He did everything on the sly, but he wanted people to notice him, make way and be afraid of him. He was pulling pieces off me and I was pretending he wasn't, picking on my friends and showing everyone I was a coward. He hadn't touched me, but he made me feel weak. He'd taken a bit out of Patrick's ear, and it wasn't even about him, it was about me.

Or was it? I saw Patrick walking off with the flap of yellow skin loose on top of his ear, everyone did. It was about fear. Fear stops you feeling properly. He was making everyone feel he was there. It wasn't about me, or Patrick. It was about him, Errol Clark. He didn't have a feeling for people. He was fighting because fighting stops you feeling afraid. It stops you feeling –

'*That's enough!*'

We were in assembly and the headmaster gave a warning about fighting, they were going to come down hard on it.

'*I believe in every one of you!*'

The school nurse found a penknife on Errol Clark but he wasn't going to be expelled. He was gone, but then he was back in his black Crombie smiling at me. He had the same shoes on but different trousers, too short that showed above his ankles even though they were let down at the bottom. There was a strange smell as he kept pushing past me in the corridor. I didn't know what it was, it stuck in my nose. He got too close and I grabbed his sleeve to push him off. His coat came open, his T-shirt was torn and dirty, and where his sleeve came up there was a bandage round his wrist with brown stains on it. That was the smell. He pulled away fast and walked off. I could feel the violence like a shock from his arm. It wasn't like anything I'd felt before.

I walked out the gate from school and he was standing on the corner with a metal pipe hanging under his Crombie, he saw me and pulled it out. He was in the way between me and home so I didn't slow down, I kept walking towards him. He turned out the way with a swagger, folding the pipe back into the coat flap.

I was trying to keep my walk steady until I got round the next corner. My shoes had holes in the bottom and my socks were wet on the puddles I wasn't avoiding, the pavement felt cracked and uneven, every step was heavy and clumsy, I felt I was going to trip.

'You want my help?'

He wasn't sure he'd got me right, and gave me this puzzled smile like he couldn't believe I was going to take on Errol Clark. I needed Ian Barratt on my side. I looked at him, there was still a red mark on his lip, his face was puffy and he had rings under his eyes like he couldn't sleep. It was like looking into a mirror.

'He's not like us,' I said. 'We have to talk to him.'

'Why don't you just beat him up?'

We stood there looking at each other, and it took a while to sink in. I shrugged and said, 'I'm tired of fighting.'

He blinked his green eyes and brown lashes at me. A look of being hurt welled up in them. He could have shook his head or thumped me, I wouldn't have blamed him. He pulled his lips shut and looked away.

'You gonna help?' I said.

He was thinking, but there was a shy look in his eyes I hadn't seen before that made me like him. Like he recognised what I was saying, I wasn't trying it on but where did that leave us?

'I like you,' I said. 'And I don't wanna fight any more.'

'You don't like Errol Clark,' he said.

'Do you?'

He stopped for a moment, looked away and back again, 'You know he's mad, don't ya?'

Errol Clark did up his zip as we came in the boys' loos, it was too quick, he got stuck and spilt a bit on his pants. He made both his hands into fists and faced us. It felt like we shouldn't have cornered him. He was looking both of us up and down, trying to find a way through, his face stony and hard. I thought he was going to charge at me, but Ian Barrett shook his head, 'You can't beat both of us.'

'We want to talk to you,' I said. But we'd gone about it wrong from the way he was breathing. He was squeezed into his chest, ready to ram his way through. His shoulders were back, his chin up and his mouth was pressed shut so he breathed through his nose. His nostrils twitched and his eyes were glassy and bloodshot. 'But not if you don't want to,' I said.

He said if we wanted to, come and try. He had big people could come and he wasn't gonna talk to us. We should get out his way and not vex him, he could look after himself so we should mind out.

I looked at his trousers and the holes in his shoes, 'Who looks after you?' But I already knew he didn't have anyone looking after him, he was getting himself to school on his own.

'No one,' he said.

'Leave us alone,' Ian Barrett said, 'and we'll leave you.'

We turned to go but he started shouting we were scared of him, cussing like he wanted us to fight him. We looked at each other but Ian Barrett shook his head.

So we left him there, screaming at us to come back, on his own in the toilets with the pee dripping down his pants.

I didn't have a lot of time to think about Errol Clark going home with no one to look after him or being frightened, or what was happening when he came to school. I punched him in the face as he tried to whack me with the metal pipe. The clatter as it hit the pavement set off a reaction – my arm was bruised and the blood moved from my head into my chest. I could still use the arm and tried to grab him but he slipped out backwards and found a milk bottle he brought down on the side of my face. I was distracted by the glass smashing on the pavement, I didn't realise it cut my cheek and tore open my ear lobe and there was blood streaming out. I'd gone down on one knee on top of him but he picked himself up and ran. I jumped up over broken glass to go after him, but a grown-up grabbed me from behind under my arms and pressed my head down so I couldn't move. I thought it was one of his big people and lashed out backwards with my foot against his shin. It hurt him but all he did was tighten the pressure down on my neck so I had to go limp. Errol Clark came back to give me a kick but the man swung me round away from him and shouted, '*Oi!*' It turned out to be a man from the Lord Clyde pub who could fight because he let go one arm and grabbed Errol Clark by the collar, knocking the legs out from under him and pushing us both down on the ground. I saw my blood dripping on to the pavement and there was a look on Errol Clark's face like he'd won and I'd got the worst of it. I struggled to get him but it was over, the man pushed my face down into the blood and I ended up in hospital.

I had stitches in my ear and a padded plaster over my cheek. I felt I could face Patrick again, but he didn't say anything and he wasn't going to. I felt like a walking bandage and I wasn't going to talk about it to anyone, either.

When the plaster came off I couldn't smile properly. It looked ugly from the stitches and lopsided in the mirror, so I tried to smile only on one side of my face, but that didn't work, it made me look sorry for myself. I didn't feel like smiling anyway. There was a mood in the school like that's what you get for fighting. No one looked at me like I had stitches hanging out my ear or a big patch on my cheek, they looked at me like I had it coming and Errol Clark had done it. But no one went over to him – there wasn't a best fighter in the school any more, only a bad smell hanging over it and nobody was going to get involved.

The new teacher, Miss Lollard, wasn't new any more. She said, 'Concentrate on getting your sums right. The cut will heal.'

Shelley told me they were going to expel Errol Clark, but it wasn't about me, it was Patrick's mum complaining. Then I heard they were going to send Errol Clark to another school, but he went missing. The fight was over and I'd lost. There was no way of getting my own back and I had to face people knowing I couldn't make it add up. Fighting wasn't worth it, I was proof you couldn't beat people up to make them like you. You ended up losing friends, and you looked like me.

'How is it?' my mum said, peeling back the plaster they put on once they'd taken the stitches out.

'It's all right,' I said, looking in the mirror, 'it doesn't hurt.'

It did, it throbbed. And there was the purple-brown smell of the ointment they put on – and something else, that smell again my mum had when she wasn't well that was like stale soap.

'You'll end up looking like Al Capone if you're not careful,' she said, and I couldn't stop my smile making the crack of the scar look longer. I changed it quickly to the other side of my face. She watched it happen and held me in the mirror. 'You're still handsome,' she said. 'Come on, let's dance.'

There was music coming from her radio in the bathroom, with us swaying from side to side in her old-fashioned way that there wasn't a care in the world and I was the best dancer she'd ever met, and it was just the two of us *dancing cheek to cheek* ... My dad came to the hospital and told me, as well as my cheek and my ear, my eye was bloodshot. I'd nearly knocked it out and they'd put a stitch in the corner. If I wasn't so badly injured, he'd have beaten me himself, but for now I should recover and he'd be watching me. It made me feel safe to be in hospital, out of reach but looked after. And that was how it felt in the bathroom with my mum holding me up. I was all right, I was going to get better. But as we danced I had a flashback to Errol Clark in the loos with no buttons on his Crombie and his pants wet, crying out he could look after himself. I went stiff and couldn't dance any more. My mum felt my arms go heavy, I couldn't disguise what I felt because I didn't know until then I was still carrying him, that I was on his side.

'What is it?'

She looked at me seriously, so I told her about him wolfing down dinners at school and waiting for seconds, the look of still being hungry, about the holes in his shoes, not having socks or anyone to go home to, about not knowing how to be with people and being scared on his own. She frowned and pushed me away.

'You're too sympathetic,' she said.

The news went round Errol Clark had been stabbed and was dead. He'd been found in a boarded-up house you could climb in by pulling back the corrugated iron over the front window. They'd found him there and taken his body away. He'd got into trouble with big people and that was what happened. He hadn't been to school, but being dead brought him back and people looked to me to see what to feel about it.

I could still feel my scar when it itched, and see it the wrong way round in the mirror, but I couldn't always remember what side it was on when I wasn't looking. I was told it was going to fade, so I waited.

When the police had gone and boarded up the house again, I climbed in the toilet window you could reach by going through the bomb site at the back and getting over the wall. The top flap fell back and I was standing on dust and floorboards in the loo until my eyes got used to the gloom. It was dank-smelling out in the backyard with overgrown weeds and the stink of cat pee, but inside there was a smell of old people. I listened but I couldn't hear anyone. The toilet bowl was cracked and stained, there was poo but no water in it. I started to go through the rooms. They were full of rubbish. Furniture was left but it was broken. There was a Crombie in a pile of dirty clothes and blankets pushed up against a wall in the back room. That was his bed. Empty bottles and chip packets were scattered about on the floor. In the front room there was a toothbrush with the bristles flattened and a dirty bit of soap stuck to a plate. He was living there. I didn't go upstairs, the banisters were broken and there were some steps missing, it was too dark. I panicked and got out, scratching my stomach on a nail where the flap hooked shut from the inside. My legs were shaking and I couldn't get over the wall, so I stood for a while in the backyard looking up at the house. I was afraid Errol Clark would look down from a window. A tree was growing up out the brickwork just under the roof. It was still. The sky was high up and clouds were moving slowly over as though the wall of the house was going to fall back on top of me. The house was dead and the windows were dark, and I was down underneath in the earth. I don't know how I got out of there.

'What's the matter?' Connor found me on the street, squeezing back out the bomb site under the corrugated iron.

'Nothing,' I said.

'What you gonna say about that?' He pointed at the cut in my shirt where it was torn across my stomach, there was a patch of dried blood along the edge of it.

'Nothing,' I said as I put my finger in it. 'It got caught on a nail.'

He stood back to look up over the fence at the backs of the houses like he didn't believe me, then turned and shoved his chin out, 'What did Errol Clark say?'

I punched him hard on the face. He got me, banging my head up against the corrugated iron with his hand under my chin, holding my arm and kneeing me on the inside of my thigh. 'You're fucking mad!' he said.

'I hate you!' I shouted.

He pushed me off and made a big bang kicking up against the metal fence. People came out the shops along the street to see what was happening. They saw us and shook their heads – Connor with his bloody nose, me with my cuts – and Mr Edwards the greengrocer shouted, 'Get outta there! Go on, bugger off!'

I followed Connor down the road, keeping my distance, waiting for it to start up again.

We got home and went straight out the backyard. He got a dirty shirt out the washing and a towel to clean up in the bathroom, and put some of the brown ointment from the medicine cupboard on the scratch across my stomach telling me to let it dry before I put the shirt on. It stung the tears out my eyes but he told me not to make a noise. He had dried blood round his nose and washed it off with a bit of water.

'What you gonna do?' he said.

I shrugged.

'You'll get yourself killed. You have to stop.'

'You fight.'

'Not like you. You fight to lose.'

I wanted to hit him again, but I stopped myself. Because that would make it true. He wasn't fighting me, he was talking. I was the one punching out with no one there. I was losing because I couldn't stop. I was always going to be losing to Errol Clark, I was fighting for breath.

He tapped his forehead. 'They wanna drive you bonkers,' he said. 'You're stupid if you let 'em.'

'Who?'

'Because you're black,' he said.

'No, I'm not.'

'You are to them. You stand up for yourself and they say you're aggressive, and push you into fights. What you gonna do about that?'

I wasn't sure what he was on about, so I shrugged.

'What you gonna do?'

'Stop fighting?' I said, but I was guessing.

'They can't treat you like that, it's wrong!'

He looked angry, so I got ready. 'I don't want to win, I just don't want to get beaten up.'

'You've got to! Or you'll always get beaten up!' He was

waving his arms with his fists clenched to stop all the punches, 'But there's more of them than you ...'

'More of who?'

He looked at me like who was he talking to? 'I'm telling you. Are you listening? You have to pick your fights. They want to see the black boys fight each other. You can't give in.'

Everything turned round in my head. It wasn't about me, it was about him in school having to fight. He was in his big school, and Manus was in a different one. I was getting beaten up by Errol Clark but I hadn't thought about him coming home with holes in his knees, my dad complaining about his jacket being torn. He was black there and they were making him fight. He was stopping all the punches in the air, talking about going mad. But you can't pick your fights if you can't think –

'Can yer?' he said.

I looked at him. It sounded clear but he felt confused, like he was looking at me but talking to himself. It wasn't going to get better when we had to move school, it was going to get worse. He was out there having to fight and everyone was against him.

'You got any friends?' he said.

He was looking down his nose at me like I didn't. I thought he was gonna bash me because I was on my own and a loser. But he shrugged and didn't bother, I wasn't worth it.

'All the black boys are on my side,' he said. 'We're picking off the ringleaders.'

Ian Barrett was avoiding me. I got him outside school on the swings behind the pub on Vauxhall Street. He was on his own smoking with a cloud round his face but threw it away on the ground when he saw me. He shifted on his swing, then changed his mind and picked it up again. As I came over he was sucking it to come alight and coughing. Then he chucked it away. I sat down on the swing beside him and rocked it with my feet on the ground.

'Are you black?' I said.

He'd been holding it in and let it cough and stream out in grey smoke between his lips. 'You smoke?' he said.

I shook my head.

'Go on, have one.'

He held a fag out from his top pocket and got a box of matches out his shorts. I could smell his fingers and shook my head again. He lit up and made a big cloud of smoke blowing the match out. It looked like it was coming out his nose and ears as well as his mouth and I had to dodge it coming my way. He shook his head to clear it and turned the fag round for me.

I only took one drag but it burnt my mouth and came out my nose and made my eyes water. I felt sick and there was a taste that made me feel poisoned. He took it back while I tried to stop coughing and went on smoking.

'My dad's black,' he said, 'but I don't know him, he doesn't come round.'

I tried to imagine what not knowing your dad was. I couldn't, it was just blank.

'My mum's white.'

It was me who asked him, but I couldn't get used to black and white like it was television when it was my mum and dad. I hadn't thought of my mum being white. Only being my mum. It made me feel sick. It was the cigarette smoking. I rocked my swing back to stand up straight and sort my head out.

'So what are you then?' I said.

He chuckled and spat tobacco out on the ground. 'Same as you,' and he looked at me with his green eyes. If that was true, his face was looking yellow from smoking. 'But I'm not on your side any more.'

I sat back down on the swing and took it in. No one was on my side.

'Do you blame me for Errol Clark?'

He took a deep drag like he was drawing in all the different things that happened and breathing them out slowly between his fingers like it was all just smoke now anyway.

'Didn't help, did it?' he said.

Everyone thought it was me, but it was him too. I'd dragged him into it. He was never gonna be on my side.

'So what do you want?' and he flicked the cigarette into a puddle.

I didn't have a side for me to be on.

'Why did he want to fight me?' I said.

The rain was drying up, but it was still chilly and windy enough to make everyone go home. We were both in shorts, I could see goose pimples going up both our legs. It looked like chicken skin, but I was shivering and he wasn't.

'He was scared of you,' he said, and stood off his swing to go. 'You scare people.'

I didn't know what to say to that. I watched Ian Barrett walk away across the playground, jumping over puddles with gusts of wind rippling the surfaces. He turned at the gate and shouted out, 'You know he was my dad's cousin?' He swung the gate closed between us. 'That's why he came, but no one looked after him and his brother went to prison.' He went round by the pub and left me there.

I watched the sky pass in the puddles. When I got up and leaned over one to look in at myself I was standing under grey-white clouds with blue patches. I put my foot into the dirty water and let it seep in through the hole in my shoe. It was cold. I felt my toes go numb. There were cigarette butts and metal bottle tops all round the swings. Brown glass smashed over by the fence, and clear glass scattered everywhere. I thought what would happen if I got my feet cut or fell over on to my palms.

I couldn't see a way through. I looked down in the puddle and told myself to stop fighting, and kicked my reflection away.

Cat and Mouse

Tom was pretending to be a baby because the dog was looking for him. He had a milk bottle to suck on, but Jerry had a safety-pin for the nappy, and when he stuck it in you could see Tom's tonsils. The dog caught Tom coming down and rubbed his back to burp him, but it was still a dog looking up and down for a cat and checking the nappy to see if that was the cat in there. It didn't smell right. Jerry put a clothes peg on the dog's nose and passed him a new nappy. The dog nodded to thank him and stuck in a safety-pin. He had to hold on to the nappy until the baby came back from hitting the roof while keeping an eye out for the cat and thanking the mouse for his help. Then he stuck the milk bottle back in the baby's mouth. Because cats like milk, Tom kept sucking. Jerry tossed him a fish out the fridge, and Tom snapped it up, and gulped, and swallowed. Which was fishy. The dog was holding the milk bottle with a look on his face about the baby, seeing himself sat in a wet nappy, holding a smelly cat dripping off the end of a fishing rod. So Tom stuck the milk bottle in the dog's mouth, and went after Jerry, and the dog dropped the milk bottle and nappy and went after Tom. Only this time Jerry got caught, bumping into a bottle of baby powder and a white cloud of it fell on top of him, followed by a wobbling pile of nappies. All you could see was the white sheet of a nappy staggering about like a lost ghost. Tom stopped, and put out his hand to stop the traffic. The dog stopped, and a tear dropped from Tom's eye. Tom pointed, and the dog looked as the nappy sneezed and the powdery white ghost of the baby he'd dropped stepped out from under the sheet. Wings appeared and a halo as Jerry flew up, and the body of the white mouse baby fell down flat. Busola started making the sound of the funeral march, and the dog's face crumpled up. But something else went wrong with the projector, as well as no sound, the film stuck and burned brown and black into blinding white.

'What's going on?' my dad said, switching on the light. We heard him come up the stairs from work while the film was running but my mum had Busola on her lap and didn't move. He came in and stood by the door. So we went on watching what happened with the two social workers. They didn't know who he was so they just nodded and turned back to watch the film. Only they weren't really watching it, they couldn't make the sound work or even operate the projector properly. They were watching us. 'It's burning?'

'No problem,' the man said, jumping up to the projector and switching it off. We sat there blinking at the white of the screen with the film rattling, 'I'll have it fixed in a minute.'

The woman was sitting with her legs crossed in a long woollen skirt and cowboy boots. She had both hands over her knees with rings on her fingers and bangles on her wrist, and was wearing big glasses with her hair pinned up at the sides. She was looking at us like we couldn't see her. She saw me looking out the corner of my eye and smiled, but it made her lips look thin. I fixed on the man's trouser leg, it was caught on the back of his short boot and bell-bottomed out. He had on a brown corduroy jacket and had long reddish hair and a dark moustache that made him look like a detective off the telly. He was fiddling at the projector like he was in charge, but she was.

'I think, Johnny, that's all we need to show them just now. Would you like to come to the youth club? We'll be showing films Mondays and Wednesdays after school? Would you like that?'

'Yeah,' Johnny nodded, 'it was a cliffhanger.'

He was pretending to be stupid. What was interesting was it was in colour, *Tom and Jerry* was black and white on the telly. We looked at our dad.

'Which youth club is this?' my dad said.

'For the young people in the area,' Johnny said. 'We're opening one.'

'This area?' my dad said.

'Yeah.'

'That's being knocked down?'

'This is a priority area for us,' the woman said. 'We can see the need.' And as Johnny nodded and started disconnecting the projector, 'Are you the father?'

My dad looked at my mum. She let him see she wasn't going to say anything, and moved Busola about on her lap.

'Yes, and they must go to bed, I won't offer you tea,' he said.

'Our concern is the children,' the woman said, uncrossing her legs and standing up to go. 'This gives them something to do. It must be a difficult time,' and she gave her thin smile.

My dad gave her his charming smile back and said, 'All of you, thank them and go.'

We all stood up and said thank you on our way out. But we couldn't go quickly because when they knocked on the door it was us who bullied our mum into letting them in. We didn't think he'd be back till later and she knew we were bored.

'*It's your own fault,*' she said, but there was nowhere to go and only four houses left between us and where they were knocking down. Most of the rest of the street was boarded up. So we mobbed her, saying it wasn't fair not letting us see a film in our own house, and got her to let them set up the screen and projector in the front room. It was only when they started asking questions and he couldn't get the sound to work that we said we'd watch the *Tom and Jerry* anyway, and hoped it would finish and they'd go away. They didn't speak like real people, he was pretending to be one of us and she talked down like she was being nice but had other ways of thinking about us than the ones she was saying. So it was a shock for my dad when he heard it.

'I can see you keep them under control,' she said. His smile stopped being charming.

'Thank you for coming,' my mum said. 'My husband will see you out. Children, let's go and brush our teeth.' She came down the stairs with us to the backyard, and put a finger to her lips at the back door so we could listen to them going.

My dad was asking on the stairs how they heard of us and the woman was saying lots of agencies were involved to help people with the move and that we were well known to them. Johnny was telling my dad where the youth club was in the old Beaufoy Institute on Black Prince Road, and would we be coming? We could hear him getting open the front door and them lugging the equipment out. She was asking if he'd like to set up a meeting to discuss it. As the door closed we heard him saying, '*Please, thank you, and don't come back.*'

He couldn't wait till we'd gone to bed, he came straight out the backyard, 'What are you doing letting them in?'

She had us around her and said, 'The children need something to do.'

'You can't see they are targeting the children?'

Busola had her arms wrapped round my mum's waist and I took hold of my dad's hand, and we let Manus tell him it was our fault wanting to see cartoons in colour and first we thought they came through school because they knew our names. Connor wasn't getting involved, he was kicking loose bits of brick off the wall. Mrs Banacka had moved out next door and stopped mending it, but he was making it worse because he wanted to go more than anyone and was saying we lived in a house that was falling down.

'How do you expect me to protect them?' my mum said, 'They can see themselves what's going on. Those people won't stop till they bring the roof down on top of us.'

'What can I do? We have to hold on. They won't pay, I won't move.'

'It's hard on the children, that's all I'm saying. We have to do something to stop him kicking bricks, otherwise they're the ones paying the price.'

We all looked at Connor. He stopped like he'd been caught and couldn't see why he had to be dragged into it. My dad let go my hand and went to pick him up until they were looking into each other's faces. Connor dropped his eyes but you could see the anger, and my dad lifted him up more so he could look up at what Connor was feeling. He shook him gently and said, 'Look up.'

Connor did, but he was telling my dad off. They were like each other losing their temper, but it was hard to see how they could meet up. Connor was letting himself go limp and hard to carry.

'Tomorrow is the weekend,' my dad said, putting him down. 'We can go in the car and drive round.' My dad had just got a car again, which was all right for making him feel good but Manus and Connor were calling it a pile of junk because it was old and worn-out and kept breaking down. 'All of us can go,' he said, 'and do the day out.'

Even Busola let her mouth drop open that he wasn't getting it, but my mum said, 'That would be lovely,' and moved us all into the bathroom to brush our teeth. I could see Manus was laughing and trying to hide it in case Connor found out. But my dad was looking at us with his face crumpled.

'Thank you, Daddy,' I said.

'What you thanking him for?'

I didn't answer because that would be dangerous and Manus wasn't there, he'd already moved in to the room upstairs next to my mum and dad, and it was only Connor and us alone in the bedroom. I got in under the covers on the top bunk and shrugged.

'Shut up, then,' he said.

'What's that there?' said Busola.

'*What?*' Connor wasn't nice about it because she was just trying to put him off blaming someone else for having to spend all day in the car with our dad instead of being free to go off. It served him right for kicking bricks. He was the one who put us all in it. He was just trying to be a bully now Manus was gone.

'That, there,' she said.

There was scrabbling on the lino so it was mice. The light was off but there was still light coming in through the curtains.

'*Lots of them.*' She sounded like she wasn't making it up. '*They're coming on to the bed!*'

I looked down at the floor. There wasn't a carpet but it looked like there was, a dark one coming from one corner of the room and spreading. I looked down at Busola, she was kicking her legs in the bottom bunk and the whole bed was shaking.

'Jesus! Jesus! Jesus! *Jesus! Jesus!*' Connor was trying to tuck the blankets into his mattress to stop them climbing up. He shook the covers and some went flying into the air.

'Get them off! Get them off!' Swarms of them were spreading across the floor and climbing up to Busola like a dusty grey blanket pulling itself over her head. She pulled the sheet over and started screaming from underneath, '*Daddy! Daddy! Daddy!*'

Connor was standing up in the bed with his back to the wall doing a dance with his feet moving. My dad burst in and put the light on. The mice were scattering everywhere and my dad froze. My mum came in behind him and screamed, '*Oh my Jesus!*'

My dad leapt over and pulled the sheet off Busola and started beating them away. Connor was clinging on to my mum with his arms and legs, sobbing with his face pressed up against hers and his eyes wide. I was holding on to the top bunk in case I fell off.

The room emptied and I watched everyone standing there, Busola in my dad's arms with her bottom lip going and her chin wobbling and Connor with his face wide open against my mum's. I saw stray mice scurry into a hole in the corner and I was worried everyone would go out the room and forget about me.

'Daddy?' I said.

He looked at me kneeling on the top bunk and started to laugh. He shook and Busola held his cheek to steady him. My mum bit her lip and frowned, 'Oh, for God's sake, Fela! What's there to laugh at?'

'At least one of you is safe up there,' he said.

'Thank you, Daddy.'

I said it to annoy Connor as they were tucking us up into their bed. Busola got in the middle between us and wouldn't move, my mum and dad were gonna sleep in the front room because there wasn't space at the sides. Manus hadn't come out his room and wasn't making a sound.

'Don't put the light out,' Busola said.

'It's over now, it's over,' my mum said, but it wasn't like a dream and I'd woken up, and I didn't see anybody else look like they were going to sleep to get over it.

'Was it real?' I said.

My dad smiled like I was asking for a bedtime story and sat on the bed. 'They are just passing through,' and he reached over and put his hand through Connor's hair. 'They are mice on the move from the other houses.' He pinched Busola's toes through the blankets, 'At least they're not rats.'

My mum slapped his hand away and sat down next to Connor, 'I'll not have you worsen the plague, settle them down.'

She leaned over and started whispering *Our Father, who art in heaven* to Connor who was nodding his head. Busola made a big sigh and burst into tears. My dad looked at me and winked, 'It's time now we need that Tom.'

But my dad didn't think it was doing its job and said it was lazy. He got really good when he came home and sat down in front of the telly at suddenly throwing his work boot and knocking out a mouse. The mouse would be stunned and he'd have to heave himself up out the chair again and go and finish it off, '*Where's that bloody cat?*' But we thought it was frightened. There was a big mouse with a long tail sitting up one night watching the television with us. My mum and dad were out and we had to run out the room but the cat didn't want to go in, even though Manus tried to throw it in and close the door. It scratched his hand with its bottom feet and then bit him, its body wriggling out from under his arm, and I felt sorry for it. 'Let him go,' I said.

'It's a she,' he said, sucking his finger as it pelted down the stairs.

That cat didn't stay, so we adopted another one, Bluey, which was wild and browny-yellow and scrawny so I didn't know why it got that name. We left saucers of milk out for it and propped open the bathroom door so it would have somewhere to go in out the rain. My dad said milk would attract visitors we didn't want and my mum shivered and told him to stop, we didn't want any more social workers. But Bluey knew it was a bargain and started to leave mice out by the back doorstep and I saw him once by the back wall shaking a big one by the back of the neck. So my dad had to be quiet and let us have Bluey as our pet.

He had bluey eyes as you started to look. He wasn't for stroking but he followed you with his eyes down from the wall like what you were doing was going to be a spell to turn him back into being a prince. But he wouldn't come into the house. He was wild and wet and walked alone along the walls of the backyards, smelling the drizzle on his nose and stalking the rain for small birds to be holding their wings in his teeth.

Missus got brought home by Manus in his jumper to be a cat for inside and he kept it locked up in his room for days to get it used to being there. I first saw it peering out his V-neck like it wasn't ready to be born even though it was older than a kitten and had a deep cut by its nose just under its eye.

'How'd it get that?'

'She got in a fight,' he said. 'I'm rescuing her.'

'She's not really a mouser, is she?' my mum said, but she changed when Missus reached out a paw to touch Manus's nose and mewed at him like she was asking her mum what to do next. 'We'll have to let your father decide.'

She had soft white markings that made her look like a girl, and browny-red and black fur in swirls up to her tail which waved and twitched like a flag in the breeze, my dad said.

They didn't say anything for days while Manus kept her up in his room except to ask where he was going with the white bits of his fish fingers. When she came out to us she was his cat, and you didn't want to do anything in front of her because she'd tell him. She must have been deaf, though, because she didn't hear any scrabbling and thought all she was supposed to do was play a bit with us while she waited for him to come home so she could sit on his lap.

'How you going to feed her?' my mum said because she was keeping the fridge closed. He bought tins of cat food out his own pocket money and my dad said it wasn't fair but she had to start catching the mouse because money was short.

We all joined in training her to chase balls of wool, or when my mum complained about her knitting, to go after pieces of string and people's shoelaces. She was a natural, curving her paw to catch at things, but we didn't see her claws come out and everyone looked at Manus like we could see it was gonna end badly. 'Get Bluey to teach her,' Busola said. We weren't sure how they were gonna get on, Missus was a luxury cat and Bluey was a smelly old tramp. He got in a bad temper, hissing down at her from the wall. So Manus kept her inside and used toilet paper to pick up Bluey's mice by the tail and take them in to her on a plate to have a sniff and wrinkle her nose up. She'd got used to fish fingers and tinned food, and it smelt like Bluey was telling her to get lost.

'What you gonna do?' we said.

Manus arranged it like there'd been a murder and it was Missus who did it. There were body parts all over the hall when my mum and dad came in, he'd rubbed her nose in it to look red. They looked at him, and my dad shook his head. How could they tell, when you could see Missus licking her paw and wiping it off?

'Clear up this mess and come, we want to talk to you.'

We all squeezed in the front room with Missus looking up at Manus like she was on trial and he had to save her. 'First,' my dad said, 'no one is on trial here for the murder. The wild cat has done this.' He looked around to make sure we could all see he had the evidence and was going to bring it out the bag. 'In the first case, if you don't know, the difference between rat and mouse, it's not just big and small. And ... *what's her name?*'

'Missus,' Manus said.

'Eh-heh, she has no chance. Before she can sneeze the rat will bite her nose.' We all sat there absorbing it. It was a rat, and Manus had smeared it, and he had to clean it up. And Missus was licking rat blood with her tongue. And there was a problem with rats and only Bluey was keeping them back. 'In the second case,' my dad went on, 'I won't mind when we can afford. But for now ...' A mood came down over us that Missus was innocent, and guilty at the same time. And it wasn't fair, but that was what happened if you were a cat. She half closed her eyes and sniffed at the teardrops running down Manus's nose, got ready in his lap and licked them off.

'Ah, no,' my mum said, 'we'll find a good home for her, don't worry. It's just we can't afford it right now.'

My mum put on her coat and was going out with a shopping bag while Manus was out with my dad. We didn't let her get out the front door. The bag was moving and she was holding it closed tight in her hand.

'What you got?' Busola said.

'Never you mind!'

'You gonna drown it?' I said, like what if she'd done that to us.

'Out of my way!'

'Let it stay, Mum,' Connor said, but he sounded like he was helping her run the taps when he should have been pulling the plug out. 'We'll look after it.' He wasn't getting on with Manus and left it late to do anything. 'I'll take it to school, they've cages for pets on the roof.'

'It's decided,' my mum said, 'she can't stay. Don't make it hard, she'll be better off where she's going.'

There was a lump in my throat and a look of distrust in Busola's eyes, and even Connor was shaking his head at how cruel she was being.

'For the love of God, I'm just going over the park, it'll have to learn to climb trees!' and she pulled the front door shut behind her so we were left in the hall with light flooding in from the glass above the door, and the feeling that we couldn't even blame Connor who had his head hung down for failing to stop it.

'Don't tell Manus,' Busola said, and we both looked at her. She had a glint in her eye like Bluey getting ready to pounce, but scarier, 'I bet she drowns it.'

Manus didn't say anything after his day out and no one else did. But after three days Missus was back. She was changed in that she looked draggled and used to being outside and a bit thinner. We saw her on the back wall and called Manus out to look. She was lying down on her front paws with her back to Bluey who was sitting the same way further along, looking like they were married.

'It's a fairy-tale ending, Mum,' Busola said, changing her tune. 'Bet you didn't think of that!'

'Oh no, it'll take a cat to get from A to Z,' my mum said, shaking her fist like she told it to stay in the park. She put her hand on Manus's shoulder, 'Tell your father we've two cats and that's as much as I'm having to do with it.'

She went in and we watched Manus get a scratch on his hand before Missus let him lift her down off the wall. But that's all she did to tell him off, and Bluey watched like he didn't mind she went in sometimes so long as she came out. So we had a cat for outside and a cat for inside we could feed on scraps, who went outside for the night and had kittens in the downstairs kitchen, which Mr Ajani didn't like until they all disappeared except for a ginger one we called Ginger. And Mr Ajani said that was the one that was going to catch the rat.

Mr Ajani was staying on in his room on the ground floor, the big downstairs room was empty except for junk. It struck me I didn't know what he was doing there.

'Is he studying?' I said, because that's what lots of Nigerians who came to stay were doing, and my dad liked that and helped them.

'Life-long learning,' my dad said.

'Why's he down in that room?'

'It's on the ground.' That was all I could get out my dad until he looked at me like I shouldn't be asking and kept his eyes wide, 'He keeps the house safe.'

'Fuckin' ridiculous!'

One of the neighbours opposite was in the front room when I got home with my mum from shopping. He hadn't been in our house before, except when he came in and got Busola out the fire – it was Mrs Ralf's son.

'Cut yer lights off! Throw rats at yer! Just to get yer out?'

The council wouldn't do anything about the rats, he was saying, and they were the cause of it, knocking the street down before we moved out. My dad was getting him to talk, and nodding.

'Cat and mouse game, ain' it? To them. My mum's old, don't do that. They won't spend no money, they're knocking it down. Well, they broke open the sewer. No, you move out or you'll get condemned – you won't get rehoused, you'll get evicted. We pay our rent. Don't matter, non-compliant, you'll get moved round all the dumps, at her age, door's closing, think about it –'

My dad interrupted, 'Who's saying that?'

'Council bloke – private like, tells me, that new estate up the Oval, get two more wanna move we can fit you in, what about a garden? Fuckin' ridiculous!' He looked round at my mum leaning up on the door handles, 'Ooh, sorry!'

Busola laughed, she'd been sitting next to my dad watching. My dad shushed her and let him go on, and my mum listened because she wanted a garden.

'Think we're stupid? I work bins for the council, that's not stupid to you got no one collecting 'em! I won't take no rubbish where I live!'

'What do you want to do?' my dad said.

He had a piece of cloth bunched up in his fist and was shaking it like he wanted a fight, but then he slowed down. 'Got my guv'nor get the lights back on, we don't pick up bins in the dark. Had to get police on 'em! *Oh*, they say, like no one's reported it. Take yer energy, dunnay?'

He rubbed the back of his neck, his hands were thick, with big fat fingers and broken fingernails. He frowned and there was a low line across his forehead where his short, curly brown hair came down and made him look even more bulky than he was. He was big, but his face looked soft and upset.

'Like for like they're saying, two-bed, fourth floor. How long we lived that ground floor? Dug our heels in, no estates, we won't move for that. She can't do stuck up a tower block. That new estate's maisonettes, modern – wallpaper walls, ceiling on yer head, but inside loos and it'll last her out.'

He shook his head and blew his cheeks out into dark red and purple knots that made him look like the wind had gone out his sails and he couldn't blow any more. 'We're giving up,' he said. 'We have to, it's not far. If you wanna go and have a look, she says,' and he looked round at my mum again, 'let yer know, it's up to you. It's on offer.'

They were asking us to come with them. My mum and dad looked at each other. I didn't think his mum liked us, there weren't any children, it was just them. But then I didn't know why I thought that, we didn't have anything to do with them.

'My mum says she'll miss this lot,' and he looked at me, 'watching 'em get up to no good.'

I suddenly felt everyone had been watching me. I didn't know what I'd done but they'd seen me do it and my mum and dad were gonna find out. I felt like something was coming to get me.

'She don't want you kept out – she don't want 'em closing the door on you cos yer coloured.'

Busola looked up at my dad, I couldn't see what he was thinking, she leaned forward again to Mrs Ralf's son with her plastic sandals dangling off her feet on the edge of the sofa.

'How is your mother?' my mum asked from the door.

He smiled for the first time and put the piece of cloth he had in his hand on his head and straightened it out – it was his cap. 'Sorry she couldn't get out more. But she's kept that window open, says your lot are smashing. Sorry they've had to see all this trouble, been a great street to live in,' and he stood up, bigger than I remembered.

My dad stood up to see him off and shook his hand. 'Thank you, you have been a good neighbour to us,' my dad said, and my mum stepped out the way of the door.

'Oh, and she sent this over,' he said, stopping to drop a gold chain out his pocket into Busola's hand where she was sitting. 'For you.'

She had her head bent over it. My mum and dad looked up and said thank you to him, but he just shrugged.

'It's been good,' he said. 'They wouldn't understand, chucking rats at us. Wouldn't want 'em to.'

My dad shrugged, 'Don't mind them. We are not stupid, they are corrupt. And they won't see we can see them coming.'

They went downstairs and I looked at Busola's chain with my mum to see what Ralf's mum sent her, but there was a hand hanging off it with an eye in the middle of the palm.

'What's that?' I said.

'It's to ward off the evil eye,' my mum said.

'What's that?' Busola said, looking like she couldn't work out whether she liked it.

'It's for you to go on and have children,' she said, 'that's what it is.'

Busola shook it off her hand on to the floor like she was having kittens.

My mum gave her a look and said, 'Who'd be your guardian angel watching over you?'

And Busola gave her a scowl.

My dad came back upstairs and asked my mum to come to the kitchen with him.

'Are you going to help me put away the shopping?' and he laughed like she was dreaming. She looked at him and nodded, 'A garden would be nice.'

In the Ruins

The windows had blown out and smoke and flames were gushing up from the first floor. A big boy went past with a sweaty face and his eyes glazed over, grinning at the fire. Firemen burst out the front door in clouds of smoke with breathing masks on. They'd bashed the door down and gone in on top of it, but now the hoses were on and another fire engine was coming round by the main road. Policemen were moving people back from where the hoses and puddles of water were spreading on the road. An old lady stopped beside us on our side of the pavement, looking up with the light on her chin and her glasses – the flashing blue lights of the engine coming up the street which made a squawk as it switched its siren off and the blue lights of the ambulance as it turned in from the top of the street. No one was in, the house was empty. People had been lighting fires in the buildings because they were knocking them down anyway. But this was the closest it had come to us. It was Danny's old house over the road. More firemen jumped down in yellow helmets with dark baggy clothes on, and one of them that had gone in was bent over coughing with his mask off and shaking his head at what they were asking him, so he got patted on the back and left to get his breath back. His hair was plastered on his forehead and he looked greasy and sweaty and dirty from his neck up. There were gusts of air coming along the road you could breathe, and then you got mouthfuls of smoke and bits of ash and soot that were blowing. That boy came back, but there were two of them, they were trying to get as near as they could. The other one was swaggering with his shoulders back like he knew all about being a fireman with his feet in the puddles and his hair blowing about in the fire. There was a gang of them going round the policemen and the fire engines and running in and out the crowd to get a good look at the fire. The crowd was growing and more policemen came in cars to keep everyone back – the fire was swirling up black and orange on to the street with hoses pouring water in through the windows.

'*Get back!*' the policeman shouted as he came up the pavement towards us. The old lady shook her head and walked away. Behind her a tramp was leaning back on the corrugated iron fence, smoking a cigarette and talking to himself. I watched him put the fag in his mouth like he was trying to whistle, raise his eyebrows, and pull on it till it glowed like that was the fire going on in his face and he was talking to it. It burnt his fingers and he let go, shaking his hand as he walked off and shrugging like it wasn't him who dropped it, and he knew he'd get the blame. A woman went past holding a bloke's arm, shivering and looking worried. She saw us and her face went blank. People were moving back because the fire was spreading and they thought something might explode after the top windows burst open and smoke started to come out from there. We were already out the way up the top of the street by the corner when we put the telly down, so we stayed where we were. Busola said it was too heavy to carry and she wanted to see what was going on. I couldn't lift it without her so we were sitting on the television watching the fire when the policeman came up. Busola ignored him. There was a look in his eye that he wasn't sure what we were doing, maybe we'd nicked the television out one of the houses, but the street was all empty except us and the students squatting the first house next to the factory on that side of the road. He couldn't work it out so he looked away and shouted at the boys hanging round the ambulance and let us get on with it. But then he came back and said, 'You watching it on television?' We didn't answer, another fire engine came round the corner by the main road so he shrugged and went off to help clear the way.

'Look at them,' Busola said. She was nodding her head at some of the men knocking everything down who'd come out the Lord Clyde where they drank. They were pointing up at the clouds of smoke coming out the top windows now the first floor was damping down. 'Bet they did it.'

I didn't have time to see what they were doing because then she said, 'Don't look, there's Daddy!'

He was coming out the house with the big wheelbarrow he got for the move because he didn't have a car no more. The barrow was loaded up with a blanket over the top to keep it in. My mum followed him out, putting down lots of bags of clothes and buttoning up her coat. They didn't see us, she was looking up at the fire and my dad was locking up.

'*Don't look*,' Busola said, 'they're going down that way.'

My mum stayed by the door as my dad went over to speak to two policemen keeping people back towards the main road. I could see he was telling them to change where they were blocking off so we could get in and out. He was taking his time and showing them the other house that was lived in, and getting them to nod and laugh and pat him on the back. He put his hand on a policeman's shoulder, pointing up at the fire like it was their job to keep that away, and pointing at our house like they could come in there for a cup of tea once he got back with the wheelbarrow. But it was my mum who was getting all the looks from people, with the bags and the big wheelbarrow by the front door. She pulled her coat tight and her lips and waited.

I could tell she wasn't feeling right. We'd been moving our furniture through the streets with two smaller wheelbarrows for Manus and Connor, but no one was looking until the fire broke out. Now we had to do it with everyone watching. She was looking at my dad and the fire, and ignoring the crowd. My dad had found somewhere to rent up by the Oval and said it would do for now, and he was going to borrow a van from work to move the beds and the cooker but we had to carry everything else ourselves. He was still saying it was daylight robbery and he wasn't moving unless they paid him properly for our house. But the damp had started coming in the walls, and we couldn't stop it spreading from the front room down the stairs into the hallway and the kitchen. My mum was coughing, and all the wallpaper on that side of the house was mouldy and running with water. We weren't even saying we were moving, but we stopped bringing anyone home. I was there at the window when Connor came home from football, it was raining and they were dropping everyone off. Instead of stopping by the house the minibus passed us and stopped on the corner. Connor got out with all his mates from school pressing their faces up to the back of the bus so you could see their mouths open looking up at the empty ruins of the houses. He jumped down and didn't look back. He didn't come in out the rain, he turned and ran away down Tyers Street. I went and told Manus who said, 'Serves him right, let him stand in a doorway and get wet.'

They weren't getting on, there was trouble with the two of

them having to carry things together on their shoulders until my dad got the wheelbarrows and they could have one each. Me and Busola were getting off with just carrying bags. I didn't mind the walk, but Manus and Connor were going up Vauxhall Street round the back of the Oval because they didn't want anyone to see them. The shortest way was down the main road where my dad was going. He made the cars and even the buses stop and go round him pushing the wheelbarrow on the road, with my mum and me and Busola walking behind on the pavement to make sure nothing fell off. But then Busola and me had to carry the colour telly in our arms because of bumps on the wheelbarrows going over the pavements. 'Don't drop it,' Connor said, 'I'm watching the Big Match.' Busola said he should carry it if it belonged to him. 'Don't make me come after it,' he said. Manus wrapped the lead round into a knot and said, 'Take it steady, don't trip.'

It was heavy and we were trying to work out how to carry it. But by then Manus and Connor had gone on with the wheelbarrows up the back way and the fire had started, so we put it down. Over the road was burning, and I was watching my mum pretend there was nothing going on as though the fire brigade wasn't flooding the street and crowds of people weren't coming. She put her hands in her coat and wrapped it round her, and made her shoulders stiff like she was gonna stand up by the door in spite of anyone looking. I hadn't seen it before but she looked skinny in the big coat. The fire was making it hot, but her face looked pale and white like she was freezing. I wanted my dad to stop joking with the police and go and get her. I looked at him, nodding and smiling to them as he moved back to the wheelbarrow, making a big fuss about the fire being too close like he didn't want them to see what we were doing.

My mum couldn't see us and didn't look round because she was trying to go on like we weren't moving, and so was he.

They turned to go, my dad lifting the wheelbarrow and my mum grabbing hold of the bags, when a chunk of stone fell down off the edge of the roof and broke into pieces on the ground, sending sparks up and exposing the roof on fire with flames reaching out to the sky. The crash of rubble sent the firemen running back while a roar went up from the crowd that was scared and excited. It felt like everyone was watching us being burned out and the building coming down, and they wanted more. Busola jumped up, I looked for my mum and my dad. They were walking away with their heads down, past the growing crowd, pushing the wheelbarrow and pulling the bags out on to the main road. 'I'm not going,' Busola said, and sat back on the telly. 'Let them go first, we'll go up this way after. I'm not running.' She was making me stay and watch what happened. The hoses moved up to the top floor and it took the firemen leaning back to hold them. Water splashed off the walls making a spray that blew over towards us so I could feel it on my face, then the jets broke into the top windows and on to the roof. A cheer went up when two of the firemen slipped over, jerking the hose so a cloud of water fell over our way on to the crowd. People ducked and fell back, but the workmen out the pub stayed there with their chests out telling it come on and shouting when they got drenched. I turned my face away as the rain whipped across me, trying to sit my legs in front of the telly to keep it dry. It was like being slapped. I wiped my face off with my sleeve, feeling exposed and shaky, and saw a boy bouncing along behind his mum at the edge of the crowd on Tyers Street. He was holding her hand while she pushed a pram, and it looked like his feet were twisted out, or one leg was shorter than the other. He was hungry and happy all at once, with scraggy, orange hair on top of his head and red marks round his mouth with some teeth a bit crooked or missing. His mum was trudging along with her shoulders slumped like she was worn out. The boy was lurching after her, looking all around as if his head wasn't connected to his body. He saw me looking and his head went on one side to see what I was doing. I was watching him, so I waved my wet arm. His face lit up, and his chin tipped up into a smile so his neck went back into his shoulders. Then he was off to the next thing he could see. I felt he was on my side, and I was on his.

Busola was trying to lift the wet bits of her dress off her legs, and just nodded when I said, 'Let's go.' We picked up the television and turned down Tyers Street trying not to bump into people.

'Hold it.'

'You hold it!'

'There.'

'Don't drop it!'

'Stop.'

'Put it down!'

It felt like they'd given us something we couldn't carry and we weren't supposed to get there. Busola walked backwards and then I did, but we could feel it slipping and had to put it down again. We got up as far as the Marmite factory on the main road and stopped in a covered doorway, and sat on top of the telly watching the cars go past.

'What we gonna do?'

'Run away,' she said.

I wasn't sure she wouldn't run off and leave me, I wasn't

being nice to her. It was her fault we got wet, I was angry and upset she wouldn't hold it properly and my arms were aching. But the strength was gone out my fingers so if she got up to run I couldn't grab hold of her. I could see me waiting on my own in the doorway with the telly for Connor to come and look for it, all the cars going past and the light going, so I changed what I was feeling and said, 'You carry that side and I carry this side and we both walk forward.'

'It stinks!' she said, wrinkling her nose up. The smell of Marmite from the factory was stale beer but inside the doorway there were pee marks up against the wall and dribbled in the dirt. It smelt like a toilet, and drink.

It was her fault we were there, so I said it wasn't me smelt like a tramp. She looked like she was gonna do something horrible to me so I stood up. 'You're the tramp,' she said. 'You've got snot in your nose and your face is dirty, and you never clean your knees, they're black. Not even with a scrubbing brush.'

I looked down and it was a bit dark under my knees, but I didn't have to get my own back because her face was dirty too, she had white bits stuck in her hair from the fire and she didn't know. 'Look at you,' I said. Her dress was drying, but there were dirty black marks across her front where we were lifting the television.

She looked down at her stomach and her face wobbled. 'I don't care,' she said, 'what anyone thinks.' We stopped talking and picked up the telly with the screen in front and walked forward sideways up on to Harleyford Road.

People were streaming down both sides of the pavement from the Oval to the trains at Vauxhall, spilling on to the road so cars were slowing down to go past. Everyone was pouring out of a cricket match which meant we couldn't get along the pavement because more and more of them were coming. They tried to step out the way, but then there wasn't room, and some blokes stopped and looked into the screen of the telly, shaking their heads and saying, 'Nah, can't see it, mate,' in Australian, 'it's all over,' before they went round us. We moved off the pavement on to the road but we were still blocking the way and a car beeped us as it went past because we were blocking there, too. We crossed over in a gap in the traffic and tried walking in the road on that side where we could see the cars coming, but the people were taking over everywhere and we were going the wrong way. It was crowds of cricket people with white hats, some green underneath, carrying bags and hampers, the older ones wearing jackets and ties, and mostly men but lots of children. I didn't know about cricket except they all wore white, and I didn't know these people. They were smart and made me feel scruffy. I started sweating and it got into my hands and started making the telly slip, but we couldn't put it down because we'd get trampled. I shifted the weight to get a grip and Busola looked panicked but took it until I got hold again and frowned at me to keep going. '*Look at them, Daddy,*' a boy said, holding his dad's hand, but the man just shook his head and marched them on. It was the sound of feet, thumping and clicking and marching on the pavement. '*Leg stump.*' '*Away through the mid-wicket.*' '*A really bad short ball.*' Everyone walking against us. '*Terribly good.*' '*Only day three.*' I couldn't understand it. But I could feel them. '*Off how many overs?*' '*Watch out!*' A teenager wasn't looking and bumped into us. He stepped back and frowned, looking at everyone like what were we doing, and went round us. '*Locals?*' It was a blur of people and we couldn't fight our way through. We looked at each other, and pushed back on to the pavement, up against the gate by the big school, and put the television down. We didn't sit in case they trod all over us. We stood leaning back on the gate and let the television get in the way to keep us safe. They kept flooding past and I couldn't look at them any more, it hurt my eyes and pulled away at me. I clung on to the gate with my fingers. A faded sign painted on the wall of the cricket ground opposite said STOP THE KOREAN WAR NOW. I held on to Busola's hand, and she let me. It was like standing on a ledge with white water rushing past. '*We keep the ashes.*' We could only do it if they didn't see us. '*Is that a television?*' So we crouched down to let them go over our heads.

It was late when we got back home. My dad said if there was anything we wanted to do in the house, to do it now because tomorrow we weren't coming back. I was on my own in Mr Ajani's old room at the back on the ground floor, Connor stayed behind in the new place to watch the Big Match and was coming home later, Manus went up to his room at the top. Missus got in and stayed on the stairs, but she was a wild cat now. She sat up like she knew we were leaving and was waiting for us to go, the house wasn't ours any more. The lights were on everywhere, with brown speckles from the flies on the bare bulbs, but there was an echo with most of the furniture gone that felt like the house was already going dark. I followed my mum into the big room on the ground floor where she was standing on a chair to clear out the last of the cupboards. Busola looked up from lifting the edge of the lino off the floorboards, 'Look, it's all yellow,' she said, showing newspaper underneath with stories and pictures and adverts from the '20s for soaps and bicycles. There were people living in the house before us and we didn't know anything about them. The paper had turned yellow and I didn't want to get too close to people being there before, so I told my mum I was going to have a bath. She steadied herself on the chair because I was pulling on her skirt and said, 'Your father's in there, have one tomorrow.' I let go and didn't say anything, but didn't know what to do, so I just stood there. She glanced round at me, 'What have you been up to?' Busola let the lino flap back and went over to the other cupboard to see what was in it. My mum glanced at her and turned back to what she was doing. 'Cat got your tongue?' I couldn't speak for a moment because I had to jump over everything to what I'd been doing since we got back. I'd sat in my room making up a list of all the things I should do before we left, but I couldn't think of anything.

'I've been making a list,' I said.

'What's on your list?' My mum dropped a pile of dusty curtains behind her on to the floor with a thump and a cloud of dust.

'I made a list of all the things I could hear,' I said, because that's what I did saying goodbye to the house.

'Oh? What?'

'Aeroplanes, cars, trains echoing on the railway, the sound of trees and their leaves rustling – I made that up – people calling out on the street, Daddy coughing, the kettle boiling, accident emergency police sirens, lorries going hush and turning the corner, creaks on the stairs, wind outside shaking the windowpanes, doors banging, and birds.'

She looked down at me, wiping her face on her arm, and got down off the chair. She put her hands on my shoulders and then round the back of my neck, they were cold and clammy.

'And whose fault is that if you're bored?' she said.

'I'm not bored. I'm home. Are we really going?'

She nodded, 'It's time.'

'Look, Mum,' Busola said, 'it's that wig.'

We turned round and she was putting on the wig she'd found out the cupboard, black and straggly over her hair. My mum screamed and ran over and started slapping her. Slapping and slapping her head and her face and her shoulders. It was too much, there was a look on Busola's face that it wasn't happening, until she started doing it herself. Then my mum started stroking Busola's face and laughing and stroking down her shoulders.

'Get it off!' Busola said. '*Get it off!*'

It was already off, my mum was stamping on it and kicking it across the floor, 'That's *filthy!*'

I thought it might still be alive and got ready to jump on the chair. But it wasn't, it stayed where it was in the corner. I looked at Busola and saw black things crawling out her hair as she scratched at it with her fingers. My mum was helping her scratch and laughing her head off. That's when my dad burst in from the bathroom with the towel round him and shampoo in his hair.

'What's going on?'

My mum pointed at the wig on the floor, trying to get the words out and the laughing under control, 'Who – let that cat in? It's *riddled!*' He looked down at the wig crawling over in the corner by the torn lino, and looked at my mum and Busola, still shaking out her hair. He shook his head and turned to go back. 'She's next after you,' my mum said, scratching her own hair.

'Please, that's enough,' he said. And he looked at me, 'What are you doing? Go to bed.'

I sat up in bed in my underpants and vest with the light off, listening to people coming and going out the backyard to the bathroom. My mum came down the stairs to get Busola out the bath, so I got up to do a cross on the window in case the door went on banging in the backyard when no one was out there – but doing it in my mind where no one could see, through the net curtain on to the glass, without moving my hand, *In the name of the Father, and of the Son, and of ...* I saw my dad come out the toilet. My mum stepped into the backyard and took his hand as he went past.

'*It's been good,*' she said.

He nodded, but didn't really agree because his face creased up as he pulled away from her like he was about to sob. I moved back not to look.

Lying back in the bed I heard Busola complaining she didn't want her hair cut, she wanted her own room when we moved. She didn't want people looking at her. My mum was taking her upstairs after her bath and saying there was good and bad in everyone, so to take people as she finds them. The front door clicked and that was Connor tiptoeing up the stairs. Manus came down and spoke to Missus on my windowsill out in the backyard. He wasn't allowed to take her. And she knew it. He came back out from brushing his teeth and called for her, and again softly, but she didn't come. '*See you,*' he said, and went in. It was the same feeling when we weren't allowed to keep the toys. They opened the door of the factory at the bottom of the road, and it turned out it was full of toys. We didn't know. We just saw lorries coming in and going out. But because it was closing down they opened the hatch in the big door and put boxes of toys out on the street, ripping open the cardboard to show what was inside. There were only a few houses left, so there weren't many of us playing out and we went wild, pulling the toys out on the road, winding them up and setting them off. There were metal spinning tops and aeroplanes with rubber wheels in bright metallic colours. I got a toy robot with a metal body and lights flashing in its head that moved automatically by itself when you wound it. It was like the door opened and all the toys came out, boggle-eyed and crazy, as though the street was taken over by an invasion of robots and UFOs spinning to a halt, and everyone's toys together made a whirring army of metal that flickered and stopped. 'Not one toy in the house,' my dad said. 'They are not ours, we don't want.' It was the end of the world. No one was playing out any more. We were being knocked down, and the silence in the street was man-made. Not even the toy factory closing down could change that. 'They are not coming with us,' my dad said, it was charity, they were treating us like children. I took in my robot and hid it under the bed. At night, I wound it up under the covers and let it blink red and whirr at me in the dark. In the morning, when I woke up, it was gone. Someone took those toys, and the tramps folded up the cardboard to use as beds and sleep in the doorways, huddled up in their red skin and blackened clothes. 'They live rough lives,' my mum said. 'And every one of them someone's child.'

Connor had come back too late and my dad lost his temper, shouting at him for wanting to stay out all night. I stopped listening as my mum tried to settle it down. After a while I heard her come down and cry by the stairs, trying to keep it quiet. She went out to the bathroom, but I could hear her still sobbing. She didn't come out for a long time, so I got up and sat out at the bottom of the stairs to wait for her. The lights were off and there wasn't any noise in the house as though everyone had gone to be alone. I didn't think I was cold, but I was shivering. There was a sound I thought was mice scrabbling down the stairs, and I froze. It wasn't. It was behind the wallpaper, coming down the wall – the sound of plaster crumbling. The house was falling down, and it was only me who didn't know how to move. My mum found me alone on the step, because she leaned over in the dark and whispered in my ear, 'Just remember, this isn't your life, this house. It's mine. You've your whole life ahead of you,' and walked on past me up the stairs.

I waited until everything was still again, and got up and opened the front door and stood looking out at the empty street in my bare feet. The fire was out, and there was new corrugated iron nailed up over the door and ground-floor window of the house over the road. The ripples of metal looked shiny against the blackened windows and burnt-out roof above. The street had been cleared of rubble but the road was still wet, so the light reflecting off it made it brighter than the black and orange sky. At the far end of the street that was already knocked down they'd left the telegraph pole, all its wires gone. It was a tree trunk again with no branches, in the place where that girl had fallen. I tried to remember her face, closing again at the window, but I couldn't bring her back any more than I could bring back the sparks and embers of the fire blowing about in the air. It was gone, and the houses were gone, but I remembered everything that happened. I put the latch on and stepped out on to the pavement to say goodbye, to show everyone I wasn't sad, I was ready to go.

'You'll catch your death,' my mum said. I turned round – my mum and my dad were leaning up out the top window sharing a cigarette, and wondering at me. 'Or what do you think?'